Chapter One

As Angie skidded along the Amtrak platform, wind-whipped mini-icicles assaulted her face like pin pricks. "Damn," she said, rubbing her face to ease the stinging.

Curls poking from beneath her hood trapped clusters of snowflakes, dropping like icy beads onto her cheeks. God, what wicked weather.

At the end of the mini-platform, her fellow passengers spun out, landing on their butts and bouncing like North Face-jacketed beach balls down a half flight of ice-glazed steps. Disheveled and dazed by their rapid, bumpy descent, they picked themselves up, collected their belongings and vanished into a cloud of snow.

Angie remained on the platform, peering into the late afternoon darkness searching for the trolley bus that was supposed to transport her to the town of Whispering Pines in upstate New

York. The lady from her hotel had e-mailed it'd be waiting near the parking lot steps. 'You can't miss it.' Yeah. Right.

Not sure what to do, Angie stood alone on the platform clutching her hood around her face like a medieval monk. If she hung around waiting, the trolley would never come. If she went inside the one-man station to ask, it'd show up while she was gone and leave her. "Damn."

"Miss!" a man's muffled voice called. "Are you looking for the *Sleigh Bells Express*?"

She yelled back at full throttle. "Yes. Where is it?"

"Stay put. I'll come get you."

Peeping through a gap in her hood, she looked for her rescuer. When the man's dark silhouette emerged in near-whiteout conditions, Angie stifled a dumbfounded gasp. He stood close to seven feet tall with a large, rectangular head atop a body with arms and legs proportioned for a man a foot shorter.

"Here, let me take your bag," he said, wrestling it from her. "You must be Angie. I got everybody else. Sorry you had to stand out here in the cold. The Mount Pearl Ski Lodge bus took my usual spot, and I had to park at the back of the lot. My passengers wandered off like cattle finding a hole in the fence. Froze my ass off rounding them up. Glad you waited on the platform near the steps. Right where you're supposed to be."

Stumbling Through

An Unlocked Door

Stumbling into Murder Mystery Series

Book 2

The second novel in a mystery series

for women of all ages

Pat Meece Davis

Falling Waters Publishing

Copyright

This novel is a work of fiction. Names, characters, incidents and places are products of the writer's imagination or have been used fictitiously. Any similarity to actual people, living or deceased, or actual events is entirely coincidental and not intended by the author.

Copyright © 2016 Pat Meece Davis
Falling Waters Publishing 2016

ISBN 978-0-9909059-5-0 Paperback edition

Edited by Carol Crawford
(www.carolcrawfordediting.com)
Cover Design by Natasha Brown
(www.fostering-success.com)
Formatted by Rachelle Ayala
http://rachelleayala.me

Thank goodness the woman at the hotel included her name on his passenger list. Although rattled by his appearance, she was grateful he rescued her. "Thanks for finding me."

"No problem. Watch the steps," he said, pointing at her high heel boots. "This blizzard hit fast. Everything's slick as hell." Yeah, she believed it after watching her fellow travelers wipe out. A quick learner, Angie held onto the rail with both hands. Her feet skied ahead of her body, but she landed semi-upright.

Hunching over to keep the snow and sleet out of her face, Angie followed the man, keeping her eyes fixed on his stooped, elongated figure. Plodding against the storm, he rocked her snow-crusted suitcase over the parking lot's icy ruts.

Without warning, the trolley driver came to a halt, putting down her suitcase. Angie tripped over the parked suitcase, head-butting the man in the back. "Sorry," she said.

"It's okay. I'm sure-footed. Comes in handy in weather like this. Here's the trolley. You hop inside where it's warm." She obeyed, hustling toward the trolley bus door.

The soft glow cast by the trolley's decorative lighting provided Angie a look at the driver. Dressed in vintage coachman's black garb, complete with a topcoat and tails, he swooped off his stovepipe hat and bowed as part of his opening-the-door ritual. Minus the hat, the trolley driver shrunk a foot, and his enormous head resized itself to match the rest of him. Angie smiled at his goofy garb and stovetop hat. However, she couldn't shake a time-travel feeling that she was trapped inside a Norman Rockwell snow globe gone amok.

She flopped into the first empty seat, grateful to be plucked from the blustery storm even if it was by an odd-looking man dressed in silly-looking clothes. To his credit, he had persistence, a kind manner, good balance and a warm trolley bus.

Safe from the elements and buoyed by the good-humored chatter of her fellow travelers, Angie's spirits soared. She couldn't wait to begin her assignment as a newly hired magazine journalist.

***

While attending an autumn carnival a few months earlier, Angie had stumbled over a murder victim lying on the ground. After finding herself on the suspect list and responding to a tearful plea for help from the victim's former fiancée, she and her college-aged daughter, Caroline, got involved in the police investigation. Angie seized a long overdue chance to pursue a journalism career by writing a riveting first-hand account of their sleuthing experience and submitting it to Ted Merrell, her close friend from college days and current editor of *American Scene* magazine. Ted published her article, which was a hit with readers. He began finding other assignments for her, including the current one, Whispering Pines' winter festival.

Having postponed her dream of being a journalist while she raised two children by herself, Angie declared that nothing and nobody were going to interrupt her research and writing this time.

***

The trolley stopped at Angie's hotel in the center of town. Housed in a beautiful Victorian home, the Lantern Inn was the quintessential country inn. Painted soft yellow, hidden spotlights accentuated its architectural detail and ornate white trim. The inn's most charming feature was old gas lanterns, now electrified, welcoming guests as they approached on the walkway.

The driver opened the door for Angie and set her luggage down beside the reception desk. Acting like a kid, he banged the bell on the desk, followed by a yell. "Hey, Clarice, I got Angie Stephens out here."

A woman, the personification of elegance, emerged from an office off the reception area. "Welcome to the Lantern Inn. I'm Clarice Winston, your innkeeper. Exquisitely outfitted, coiffed and jeweled, she looked like *Vogue* stylists had dressed her for a cover shoot.

Clarice turned off her charm for a second, aiming a chilly glare and cold dismissal at the driver. Although Angie wasn't the target, she still flinched. The man ignored Clarice's hostility, and with stovepipe hat in hand, gave a sweeping bow to her and Angie. His comic departure earned a not-amused eyeball roll from Clarice.

"Your inn is lovely. I'm delighted to be staying here." Angie's eyes roamed the reception area furnished in period antiques, resembling the foyer of a stately home rather than a hotel.

Angie handed Clarice the obligatory credit card. "Oh, no need for that. *American Scene* has arranged everything. Are you free to tell me why you're here, or is it confidential?"

"Nothing secret about it." Angie reveled in her new status as a journalist. "I'm researching and writing an article about your winter carnival for *American Scene*. I'm not acquainted with the town or carnival, so I hope the local folks don't mind my questions."

"Oh, my goodness, when word gets out that the town is going to be featured in such a popular magazine, everybody will be begging to help you. This kind of publicity is a miracle. Our town's economy depends on the carnival."

"In that case, I hope my article helps. What I saw of the town from the trolley looks charming. The story will be fun to write and fun for the readers. Plus, the magazine's going to include some photos with the article."

"That's wonderful. Please call on me for any assistance. I'd love to help." From their brief conversation, Angie concluded Clarice would be a good resource and a pleasant acquaintance. She welcomed her offer.

Scott, a handsomely dressed young bellman, with an infectious grin and thick blond hair falling in curly wisps on his forehead, picked up Angie's bag and led her to the elevator. "If I can help with your article, let me know. It sounds like fun."

"Thanks. I'll keep you in mind," she said, returning his smile.

"Just say when."

Learning the town's economy depended on the carnival added momentum to Angie's determination to write the most enticing story imaginable about snowmen and ski races and whatever else people did at winter festivals.

***

Angie scurried around her room getting dressed. To add the finishing touch to her outfit, she wiggled her toes into brand new strappy black heels, the perfect shoes for stepping into her new life. She glanced at her watch. Show time.

When the elevator opened into the hotel reception area, Angie hit a non-weather related snag. The Lantern Inn's schedule of events, posted in plain sight, announced *Dessert in the Library* would begin at eight-thirty, not eight o'clock as she misread when she checked in. Rats. Half an hour early. She needed something to occupy thirty minutes. For sure, going back to her room wasn't an option. She could've stayed in North Carolina if she wanted to sit home by herself, the all too frequent plight of a forty-something single female in her small town.

Going outside wouldn't cut it either. She could do without being battered by those ice missiles and tripped by parked suitcases. Not to even think what the nasty weather would do to her fantastic new shoes. She lifted one foot slightly off the floor and twisted it back and forth. She was in love with these shoes.

Picking up a brochure with a diagram of the inn's layout, Angie got her bearings to set off exploring the beautiful Victorian building.

Calling to her from the reception desk, Clarice waved a slender, bejeweled hand at her. "Don't forget dessert at eight-thirty, dear." Angie acknowledged the reminder with a wave. Not much chance of forgetting since she was already a half hour early.

Angie passed an empty Billiards Room, which held no interest for her. Moving on, she poked her head into the Media Room, full of teens gathered around a big screen TV. She withdrew unnoticed and crossed the hall to the next room. Its door sported a small plaque labeled *Private*. Clearly off limits to guests, Angie turned away.

Taking only a few steps, she stopped. Angry voices came from behind the private door. To be accurate, one angry male voice did all the talking.

Angie knew better than to eavesdrop, but her nosiness, or *journalistic inquiry* as she preferred to call it, won out. She eased close to the door. The man's measured words sounded like he pushed each one through clenched teeth. Angie couldn't make out everything he said, but his rage sliced through the door like a buzz saw. His intensity made Angie cringe. "Don't you get it? I don't care- -you stupid bitch--if you know what's good for you--"

A woman, the apparent target of his fury, cried, her frantic sobs obscuring her tortured reply. Thinking quickly, Angie slipped an audio recorder out of her purse. She couldn't pass up this chance to test the touted capabilities of her new high-tech digital recorder. The hallway was clear so she held the device close to the door and switched it on.

Angie's heart beat faster. Although it disturbed her to hear the woman so cruelly berated, the confrontation piqued her curiosity in a perverse way. She'd give anything to know why the couple quarreled, why the man ranted, why the woman collapsed in despair, why she didn't stand up to the man and fight back.

The man delivered an ultimatum in a tone so hateful that Angie almost dropped the recorder. "Don't ever call me again! Stay the hell away from me! And keep your mouth shut! Understand?"

The woman responded in sobbing, fretful spurts. Caught up in the drama, Angie squashed her ear against the door until it turned numb, but she couldn't understand any of the woman's words. Did she agree to his demands? Or did she tell him she wouldn't stay away? Not shut her mouth?

Sounds of movement came from the room, but no one spoke. Had the clash ended? Just in case, she needed to vamoose before the man and woman emerged from the room and found her ear and recorder glued to the door. She didn't want him to turn his fury on her.

Angie scurried down the carpeted hallway, impressed how fast she could sprint in high heels. Double wooden doors stood open at the room next door. She ducked through them and found herself in the unoccupied library, all gussied up for the evening dessert festivity.

Unnerved by the thought of almost getting caught eavesdropping, Angie slipped behind one of the library's carved doors. Almost as quickly as she disappeared, she popped out of her hiding place. What was wrong with her? Journalists didn't hide behind doors.

Besides, she wanted to catch a glimpse of the man and woman when they left the room. She wanted to attach faces to the man's acrimonious ranting and the woman's pitiful weeping. Maybe she'd spot the couple at the inn or around town and, on the sly, figure out what was going on between them. Latch onto an opportunity to polish her investigative skills by doing some harmless snooping. Sneak in a little journalism practice without anybody knowing.

"Let it Snow," sung by Dean Martin and appropriate for a snowy evening, drifted into the library through speakers concealed in the antique tin ceiling. Angie inched her head around the doorway for a peek at her dueling couple. What happened to them? Did she miss seeing them come out of the room during the time she was behind the door? That didn't seem possible. Did they make their way back to the busy reception area? Oh, please, no. She wouldn't be able to pick them out if they mingled with the other guests. Maybe they changed their minds and stayed in the room. Instead of leaving, maybe they started a new round. Angie could find out only by going back for another listen.

Just as she readied herself to bolt into the hallway, a voice from within the empty library brought her to a standstill, almost stopping her heart as well.

"Angie?" She spun around. A man about her age, forty-ish, stood casually, propped against a bookcase, at the side of the room.

Puzzled that he knew her name, she regained her composure and asked, "Have we met?"

"Sure. This afternoon. Remember?"

"No. Must've been someone else." She'd met Clarice and Scott. That was all.

"You don't remember me. Bummer," he said, amusement dancing in his brown eyes. "I'm

George, the driver of the *Sleigh Bells Express*. I picked you up at the train station. I thought I made an impression on you." He flashed a disappointed pout, which broke into an easy smile.

"You're the trolley driver?" Angie's question came out like a barnyard chicken squawking. "Uh--nice to see you again." Granted, because of the blinding blizzard, she hadn't gotten a good look at his face, but she had the impression he was an old man. Maybe the coachman's black frock coat and black patent knee boots did it. Not to mention a thick wooly red scarf wound around half his face, distorting his voice. To an already fantastical image, the stovepipe hat added a foot to the height of his head, making him look like a monster out of a low-budget horror film.

This man was a third incarnation. With dark hair cut short, but not short enough to conceal a mass of curls, and wearing a stylish suit and tie, he looked a whole lot more like an Armani model than a creature that would send kids running for the safety of home. Angie's eyes traveled cautiously down to his feet. Thank goodness. Black leather dress shoes replaced those shiny patent knee boots.

He walked toward her. The closer he got, the better he looked. To put it plain and simple, he was the best-looking man she'd seen in many a day. Friendly eyes met hers. The corners of his mouth curved into an easy smile.

Angie replayed his transformations from bigheaded monster to antiquated trolley driver to trendy hunk with admiring approval. He returned her appreciative onceover with a regard of friendly amusement. Was it life in general or this situation in particular that he found entertaining? Certainly if he witnessed her storming into the library like a runaway truck wearing designer high heels, he was bound to be fascinated as well as baffled.

"May I get you a cup of coffee?" he asked. Sounding genuinely concerned, he added, "You look a little--out of sorts. The festivities won't start for a bit, but I could snag something for you."

"Sure. Coffee's great." Good-looking or not, the sooner she got rid of him, the sooner she could go look for her couple. Time was running out to find them. Letting his gaze linger on Angie, he walked past her and disappeared down the hall toward the back of the inn.

Angie ran to the door to look for her sparring man and woman. She didn't see them or anybody else in the hallway. Taking advantage of the moment, she dashed to the door of the private room and listened. Not a sound came from inside. Angie turned the knob slowly, but the door was locked. Mustering up her nerve, she timidly knocked. Nothing. Crap. She'd blown her chance to see what they looked like. She hustled back to the library, puzzled how the quarreling couple disappeared from beneath her watchful nose.

George returned with steaming cups of coffee. He borrowed a small tray with sugar and cream from a dessert table. Angie helped herself to a couple of sweeteners and took her first sips in silence while stealing glances at her companion. One thing about this contemporary hunk version that resembled the trolley driver was his kindness.

Kind or not, he probably wondered what the hell kind of fool she was. But he didn't ask, and she didn't volunteer. She had an active imagination, but, on short notice, she couldn't think of any story that would explain her skidding entrance into the library or her keen interest in the hallway.

Still puzzled about George's sudden appearance in the library, she asked, "Where were you right before you spoke to me?"

"There." He pointed to the spot between two bookshelves where she first saw him.

"No. I didn't see you when I first came in. How did you get in here?"

"I was already here," George said, dismissing her questions.

Angie opened her mouth to question him further, but waiters streamed into the library carrying trays of luscious-looking desserts. A staff member started a fire in the massive stone fireplace and lit candles nestled among an extravagance of evergreen boughs and flower arrangements. Guests filtered into the library, waiting expectantly as the staff continued to parade into the room with delicacies.

"Uh-oh, here comes trouble," George mumbled, looking around as if searching for a hidey-hole. The lovely Clarice squinted at George and leveled a no-nonsense gaze at him. "I better get out of here in a hurry." He took Angie's empty cup and headed for the door, but Clarice, dropping her innkeeper's gracious facade, intercepted him and dumped a load of fast-talking on him.

While Clarice monopolized the conversation, George studied the floor with a frown burrowing ever deeper into his forehead and hurried out of the room without looking at Angie. Did the trolley driver crash dessert? Maybe that's why he was skulking at the side of the room when Angie first saw him. Did Clarice just now kick him out?

Like a flashlight being turned on, Clarice's cordial innkeeper's face lit up, and she summoned her guests to indulge themselves. "Chef Henri and his staff outdid themselves tonight. Please help yourselves and enjoy." Responding to her invitation in a subdued ramble-scramble, the guests didn't need coaxing.

The long table, covered with white linens and lace, received oohs and ahs as the guests drew close. A mixture of patterned platters, gold trays and glass tiered stands displayed desserts. An aficionado of entertaining and table settings, Angie studied the eclectic but artful mix of serving pieces. Well done, Clarice. No wonder this event was so popular. Who could blame that poor tongue-lashed, handsome trolley driver for trying to sneak in?

Angie wiggled into a little space for a turn at the table. "Doesn't this look delicious?" she said to the woman in front of her.

"Just wait 'til you try them. They're addictive." From the size of the woman's bum, she spoke from personal experience.

Angie piled bite-size confections on her plate. Every sweet she ever imagined, and a multitude she hadn't, lay before her. Dipped in glistening chocolate, topped with sugary rosettes, or rolled in crushed nuts, the choices were irresistible. Angie felt piggish until she noted other guests digging in too. Loaded plate in hand, Angie threaded her way through the crowd away from the table to an empty standing spot.

Before she could pop a bonbon in her mouth, Clarice swept across the library toward her. "Angie, this is Whispering Pines' mayor, Cliff Schouten, and his wife, Polly," she said, introducing the man and woman trailing behind her. Angie shook hands with a pleasant-faced, expensively dressed couple in their fifties. Angie assumed Clarice clued in the mayor about her magazine assignment, and his first sentence verified it. "Ms. Stephens, welcome to Whispering Pines. The town is so grateful for the publicity your article will generate for the winter carnival.

It'll help us attract visitors from all over the country."

"I certainly hope so. Of course, keep in mind, the article won't be published until *American Scene's* winter activities' edition comes out next fall."

"I don't think I can wait that long," Polly complained jokingly. "I can't believe we're going to be featured in such a prestigious magazine. It's so exciting." She bubbled with anticipation at the town's reputation spreading across the country.

Angie liked Polly's vivaciousness. The town should've elected her mayor instead of the more reserved Cliff. Polly was born to be head cheerleader.

A couple across the room summoned the mayor. He and his wife excused themselves and moved on.

As soon as Cliff and Polly departed, a plain-looking man wearing a plain suit approached Clarice and Angie. "Sorry to interrupt, Clarice, but have you seen Jenny? I lose her everywhere we go."

"Not since a glimpse when you arrived for dinner. Sorry I can't help."

Clarice introduced Angie to the newcomer, Adam Harden. "Adam owns the town's hardware store. His window display of antique horse-drawn sleighs and old sleds is a must-see. Plus, he loans some to the carnival for sleigh rides around town. Such a lovely and romantic experience."

"I'm planning to look at town tomorrow. I'll stop by your store."

"Anytime. Glad to give you the tour." Open invitation issued, Adam forged into the crowd looking for the missing Jenny.

"Be sure to take a sleigh ride while you're here," Clarice said to Angie before she excused herself to attend to her guests.

Angie envisioned Adam loudly summoning one of his drivers. "Sleigh for party of one." How humiliating. She'd look worse than pathetic. Cancel the sleigh for party of one.

Being alone for the moment had its advantages though. With no one to observe or judge, she could pig out on her feast of sweets. And a feast it was. Each sinful bite was better than the last. Nothing like a sugar fest to set her right with the world.

Angie wandered around the library looking at its holdings. As she worked her way from one book case to another, she found herself positioned in the same spot where George was standing when she first saw him, when he announced his presence in the library by scaring the crap out of her.

"What's this?" she said in a whisper, facing a cleverly designed door, almost camouflaged by surrounding bookshelves. Wondering where the side door led, she ran the layout of the inn's rooms through her head. Was it possible? Yes. It led to the private room where the scathing argument between the man and woman took place. Not only that, but the door was only a few steps from where George was standing when she first saw him. Was the gorgeous trolley driver the man yelling at that poor woman?

The door would explain George's sudden appearance in the library. When he'd finished his tirade, he slipped through it while Angie was watching the hallway for the man and woman to come out of the room.

George seemed so nice and thoughtful. He couldn't be the yelling man, could he?

Of course, he could. This was so-o-o her luck. If she found a good-looking man who seemed to be patient and understanding, why wouldn't he turn out to be the most verbally abusive male on the planet?

Speaking of whom... George was back in the library and standing at one of the dessert tables. What was he doing? Helping himself to dessert? No, he wasn't eating. As she watched, he stacked plates and cups on a tray and carried them from the room. George was a bus boy? He worked on the kitchen staff? So when Clarice blasted him, she was giving him orders, not throwing him out. He worked here at the Lantern Inn as well as drove the trolley bus?

Determined to resolve her curiosity and standing with her back to the half-hidden door, Angie reached behind her body with one hand and fumbled until she got a grasp on the doorknob and turned it. Unlike the locked hallway door, this side door was not locked.

Putting on a bright *Hi Y'all* face for the benefit of anyone glancing her way, she pushed the door open a few inches. Out of the corner of her eye, she was overjoyed to see the lights on. She'd take a quick peek in the room, close the door and mosey away. No one the wiser.

As she pushed the door farther, she took a step, caught her toe on an uneven floorboard and stumbled into the private room. To keep from falling, she held onto the doorknob to steady herself.

A head-splitting scream filled the library. Angie heard it louder than anybody. She was doing the screaming. Lying on the floor, a woman in a pink dress stared at the ceiling with wide-open, lifeless eyes.

Chapter Two

The buzz of amiable conversation halted in mid-sentence as Angie's screams ricocheted off the walls of the library. By the time the echo wound down, the room was silent, its occupants stunned, their mouths frozen in the shape of their last syllable.

Two men, followed by a blonde woman, emerged from the immobile crowd and started toward Angie. Shifting their gaze to the woman lying on the floor, the men attempted to squeeze past Angie, but she unwittingly blocked the doorway. The blonde pushed the men aside, urging, "Please, let me through." Deftly brushing her slim body past Angie, she promptly knelt and examined the motionless woman.

When she finished, she rose to her feet, surveying the scene for a moment. Angie followed her eyes, noting a room outfitted with rows of open shelves laden with folded tablecloths and various dining necessities. Exiting the room, the woman stepped past Angie again and toward a man with salt and pepper hair, military posture and a striking air of self-confidence. "I've got bad news, Nev," she said. "A woman's dead. Call the police." She spoke in a whisper, but Angie was close enough to hear.

"Dead? You can't--mean it." Nev's voice quivered, but he maintained an untroubled composure.

"Oh, she's dead all right. Do you want me to alert Clarice?"

"Please do, Kate. I'll call the police."

Nev reached in his pocket for a cell phone.

A few people standing nearby overheard bits of the woman's remark to Nev and started passing the word. News rippled through the library that a woman lay dead on the floor in the next room. The dinner guests talked among themselves, their voices becoming high-pitched with emotion as speculation accelerated about what could've happened.

A man spoke up. "Probably a heart attack."

"I don't think Clarice had any employees old enough to have a heart attack," added a woman who was obviously a local.

"Oh, my God, it's probably somebody we know," said her friend with a tear trickling down her cheek.

"Nah. I bet it's a guest. Drug overdose or something," a nearby man said with conviction.

Angie didn't buy the heart attack or drug theory. Considering the vicious argument that took place in the room a short time ago, Angie suspected the yelling man killed her.

Waving his hands to hush the crowd so he could place the 911 call, Nev spoke to the police. "Yes, this is Nev Winston at the Lantern Inn. We need the police here right away. A woman--uh-- lying on the floor of our linen storage room appears to be deceased." Nev's polished British accent bolstered his commanding manner. Even in the midst of increasing pandemonium around him, he sounded intelligent and in charge. He struck Angie as a man who could handle about anything. She wished him luck because he had a bad scene to deal with in the next room.

Kate, as Nev called the blonde, tapped her fingers on a tabletop while he summoned the police. Angie, paralyzed in the doorway, strained to hear above the developing clamor. "There's more to this, Nev. I don't think the guests should know yet, but the woman was strangled with her own scarf. You've got a murder on your hands."

"Murder? Do you know who she is? Local or guest?"

Kate leaned close to Nev and whispered. Angie couldn't hear the name, but Nev did, and he recognized it. His forehead creased into a deep frown before recovering his authoritative demeanor.

Angie already knew the woman had been murdered, but she didn't feel any satisfaction in being a step ahead of the others. The poor woman died feeling helpless and heart broken.

"While you were talking to the police, I dashed to Reception and gave Clarice the basics so she can deal with guests," Kate said.

"How did she take it?" Nev asked.

"Your wife's a master at handling difficult situations."

Nev's manner belied the tragic news of the murder of a woman in his wife's hotel. Acting like a British Army officer preparing to mobilize his troops for battle, he took charge of the crowd and admonished the dessert guests not to leave the inn. "Scott," he ordered Angie's personable young bellman, "direct the staff to secure all the entrances and exits of the building." He added emphatically, "No one is to leave or be admitted until the police arrive."

As word of their imprisonment spread, the guests began to grumble. Their protests reached a point of erupting into a brawl.

"Who does Nev think he is anyway?"

"He's got a lot of nerve."

"Yeah. That poor woman's death's got nothing to do with us."

"Nev can't keep us here."

"Well, whether he can or can't, he is. So, you might as well pipe down." A ninety-pound, feisty, white-haired woman shut up the bellyachers.

Angie, who hadn't moved from her spot since she opened the door and spotted the body, felt someone trying to force her fingers loose from the doorknob, the only thing holding her up. If she let go, she'd collapse. The realization that she'd overheard a murder in the making was too horrifying to absorb.

George wedged himself into the open doorway beside her. "Angie," he said in a firm tone, "let go of the doorknob." Responding to his command, she released her clenched fingers. "Good girl, let's get out of the way. We need to close the door until the police arrive." He pulled the door shut and, with his arm around her waist, led her to a sofa where she plopped down in a heavy and unladylike fashion. "Would you like a drink?" he asked.

She shook her head.

"I've got a couple of things to do. Keep your eye on this door while I'm gone. Yell, if anybody attempts to open it. Okay?"

"Sure." She needed to get her wits together. Here she was practicing to be a serious journalist, but when faced with a big story, instead of pouncing on top of it, she screamed like a banshee, squeezed a doorknob to mush and went fuzzy in the head.

She had to get herself together and in record time. This was a chance to do some real investigative journalism. Not only that, she had a head start. She knew about the quarrel that took place in the room next door. It was time to start asking some questions.

***

George and Nev stood off to the side of the room alone. George did most of the talking, gesturing frequently with his hands. Nev, arms crossed against his chest, expression thoughtful, leaned in close to George so as not to miss a word.

When George finished his conversation with Nev, he returned to sit beside Angie.

"George, I heard Kate whispering to Nev about the deceased woman. Do you know her?"

"Yeah. She lives in town. Usually comes here for Saturday night dinner." She studied George's face carefully, but he showed no emotion at the mention of the woman or her death. Angie hadn't forgotten George's unexplained proximity to the side door from the library to the linen room right after the fight. He was in the perfect spot to have been the enraged man who strangled the woman.

"So not all the people who ate dinner here tonight were inn guests?"

"No. Usually about half and half. It's the best place in town for a nice evening out, so Clarice gets a lot of locals. Typical Saturday night. Packed dining room."

If the woman was local, her killer was likely local too. Somebody she knew well. Very well. That kind of bad blood between two people didn't develop without a stormy history to spawn it.

Angie asked George. "Who's Kate?"

"Kate Mahoney, town doctor. She came back home after medical school and took over her dad's practice." No surprise the woman was a doctor. She acted like she knew what she was doing.

"And Nev is Clarice's husband?"

"Yeah."

Angie watched as Nev moved around the room, talking to guests, trying to soothe their anxiety. He was smooth and polished and soothing, but the crowd was losing patience.

A man grouched. "I feel bad that woman died, but there's no reason for us to be locked in here. This blizzard's not letting up. I got to get home while I still can. I got to be there to feed my animals in the morning. They can't feed themselves."

George glanced in the direction of the man who spoke. "I better talk to Nev. The natives may mutiny," he said, excusing himself.

Angie was glad for the solitude. Being around George made her uncomfortable. As appealing as he was, his sudden appearance in the library, a few steps from the murder, rattled her.

"Hey, Angie. You doing okay?" She jumped at the sound of a voice behind her. It was Scott, the cute bellman. "Sorry about your bad luck. Finding somebody dead right after you got here sucks." He paused and added, "Actually I guess it'd suck anytime."

"It definitely sucks. No good time to make that kind of discovery," Angie said. "I thought Nev had you blocking the doors."

"I conscripted the kitchen staff and posted them at the exits. They got wind something shady happened to the dead woman, and they're all weirded out. Chef insisted on keeping his meat cleaver with him. Nev will freak out if he sees him with that thing. He could hack through a jungle," he said. Angie smiled, picturing buttoned-down Nev encountering Clarice's warrior chef.

"I better go check my draftees. Make sure they haven't bailed and left the gates to the fort open. You need anything?"

"No. Thanks for asking though." Thoughtful kid. Angie liked him. Too bad Caroline, her college freshman daughter, wasn't along on this trip to meet him.

***

A chill travelled through Angie's body. Could she have done anything to prevent the woman's murder? She had no idea the quarrel would lead to a death. She knew couples whose relationship centered on keeping the emotional pot stirred up, but they never harmed each other.

Only a few minutes passed between the time Angie first heard the nasty quarrel and the time the man stopped yelling. In that scant window of opportunity, could she have intervened? Gone to reception and told Clarice? But by the time Angie navigated her way through the throng of guests, the woman would've likely been dead. What if she'd knocked on the door in an attempt to interrupt the man's intensity and prevent it from escalating to murder? On the other hand, if she knocked after the man strangled the woman, Angie might well have ended up on the floor beside her. What if...

Angie couldn't come up with a plan that seemed workable even now that she knew the unfortunate outcome. She'd never forget the sound of the woman's pitiful sobbing.

And speaking of *what ifs*--if George hadn't interrupted her, she might've seen the man leave the room and been able to provide a description of the murderer. If she couldn't save the woman, she could've helped identify her killer.

***

Police and emergency vehicles approached the inn with sirens wailing. None too soon. A smoldering revolt threatened to erupt. Agitated guests milled around, asking each other questions, hypothesizing and casting challenging glances at Nev.

Kate had disappeared from sight. Most likely Nev sequestered the doctor to keep the guests from bombarding her with questions. Good thinking on his part. If word of a murder got out...

Angie sat alone. Wrapped in a blanket of questions.

George didn't return.

Logic asked her if George could be the killer. Angie found the idea hard to reconcile. No more than minutes after the murder took place, George was composed, rational, unflustered and neatly dressed. If he got angry enough to work himself into such a violent state that he killed the woman, surely he would've shown signs of agitation and disarray. Could he have dished out that much rage and concealed it flawlessly? Angie didn't think it possible.

But she couldn't ignore that George popped up in the right place at the right time. More accurately, he was in the wrong place at the wrong time.

Chapter Three

By the time the police dismantled Nev's lock-down security force and replaced knife-wielding cooks with officers, the library was in an uproar. Agitated diners, all talking at once, mobbed the arriving police with requests to be released from their hostage situation. Immediately wouldn't be soon enough to suit them.

The tough-faced police chief, alert eyes taking in everything, got Nev off the hook and set everybody straight right off the bat. "Settle down, folks. A woman's dead. Nobody leaves here until we know what happened. Get yourself a drink, a seat and chill." With those brief words, he quelled the Lantern Inn Rebellion.

The crowd heeded the chief's advice and resigned themselves to their fate but not without plentiful grumbling among themselves. Scott, moving through the crowd delivering drink orders, flashed Angie a thumbs up, apparently a signal his ninja kitchen staff had been retired and replaced by policemen.

After speaking to Nev, the chief zeroed in on Angie and waved his hand, summoning her to come with him. "I understand you found the body." Nev led them down a hallway. "I'm Chief Roger Byrd. What's your name?" The chief was a man of few words.

Matching his brevity, she said, "Angie Stephens. Journalist." The chief grunted, either to acknowledge he heard her or express his displeasure at the journalism profession.

They entered a small parlor where Dr. Mahoney waited alone. The chief motioned for Angie to sit down and got right to the point. "What'd you think, Kate?"

"I only did a brief examination of the deceased, but I think a scarf, likely belonging to the victim since it matched her dress, was twisted around her neck. Death by strangulation." The chief's eyebrows shot up. "Time wise, she hasn't been dead long."

"Jenny Harden. That right?" he asked.

"Yes. Jenny Harden."

"I told a couple of officers to find Adam, get him away from the crowd and start putting a time line together. I want background about what he was doing tonight before I question him."

"Who and why would anyone kill Jenny?" Nev asked. "When Kate told me the woman lying on the floor had been--uh--murdered, I was certain it was one of the guests. People bring their problems with them even when they're on holiday, so I thought it must be something like that--some quarrel that got out of control. It's tragic enough for that to happen to a stranger, but Jenny?"

"Adam's wife, Jenny?" Angie asked.

Before anyone could answer, George tapped on the door and entered with a tray of cups and coffee. "Clarice thought some hot coffee might hit the spot, Chief."

"Damn right. Pour me a cup and load it with sugar, George. Tell Clarice thanks." Addressing Angie, he said, "You said you know Jenny. Miss—what's your name?"

Did he have a memory problem? "Angie Stephens," she told him again. "No. I don't know Jenny. I just got here this afternoon. I don't know anybody in Whispering Pines. It's just that while Clarice and I were talking at the dessert festivity, Jenny's husband, Adam, asked Clarice if she'd seen Jenny." Angie relayed details of the brief conversation. The chief's solemn gray eyes flickered with interest.

"George, get Clarice in here. And while you're at it, get some coffee for my men. They're damn near frozen from this god-awful storm." George dutifully hurried away.

Clarice appeared right away. "Hey," the chief said to her. "Notice anything going on between Jenny and Adam tonight? Argument maybe?"

Clarice held up her hand. "Let me save you some time, Roger. I only caught a glimpse of them when they arrived. Busy night. As for getting into a fight, give me a break. We're talking about Jenny and Adam, the most docile couple in town. I didn't see either of them after their arrival until Adam approached me in the library looking for Jenny." The chief asked Clarice what he said. "Just that he got separated from Jenny. I introduced him to Angie, and we talked about his antique sled collection for her article for a couple of minutes. After that, he sauntered off in typical slow-motion Adam style looking for Jenny."

"Did he seem nervous? Anything unusual about how he looked or acted?"

"For goodness sakes, Roger, Adam nervous?" Clarice said.

He asked Angie about Adam's nervousness. "I'd never met him until tonight, but he seemed pretty laid-back. He certainly didn't seem worried about his wife being missing."

"Okay, Clarice, you can get back to your guests. If they give you any lip, get one of my men to handle it. Kate, you can go home, but will you check on Adam first? He's bound to suspect something's going on, or maybe he's figured it out. If he needs medical attention, get him an ambulance, and I'll send an officer along with him. Don't talk to anybody about the case." She glared at him. Angie guessed the doctor figured that out by herself. The chief saw her reaction but ignored it and turned to Angie.

"Angie? Right? I understand from Nev and Kate that you found Jenny's body. Start at the beginning."

"After I finished my dessert, I browsed the library shelves. I'm an avid reader, plus the party atmosphere was fun and upbeat. I didn't want to leave. Certainly not to go back to my room. When I reached the side door--it's kind of hidden in the bookcases--I was curious about it."

"Exactly what about a door interested you?"

"Earlier this evening I heard a couple arguing in the room next door to the library. The man was--"

"Whoa," the chief interrupted. "You heard a couple arguing in that linen room where Jenny got killed? What were they arguing about?"

"I only heard a few minutes of it. The man kept telling the woman to let him alone and keep her mouth shut. He was furious at her. The woman cried and said a few words, but I couldn't catch anything she said because of her sobbing. The man finished his tirade, and I heard moving-around noises. Thinking they might come out of the room, I hustled down the hall into the library next door and out of sight."

"Did you see anybody come out of the room?"

Angie shook her head.

"Okay. You said you opened the side door from the library. Why would you, a guest in this hotel, open a closed door? Isn't that a little forward?"

"I was curious about the room because of overhearing the quarrel. I'm inquisitive by nature--it's why I majored in journalism. I turned the knob. The unlocked door opened. A light was on in the room. All I wanted was a quick look to verify the concealed library door connected to the room, not just to a closet or had been sealed off."

"Did you expect to find the couple still there? Or one of them dead?"

"Dead? Oh, my gosh, no. By then, I was pretty certain they were gone."

"Why so?" the chief asked.

"I left the library and went back to the door of the room a few minutes later. It was silent and the door was locked. I assumed the couple left."

"Of course, the man could've been in there."

"He wouldn't have opened the door with her body lying there." Angie shivered. What if she'd walked in the room while the murder or the man's departure was in progress?

"So, if I've got this right, you got fixated on the linen room as Clarice calls it because you overheard a man yelling at a woman? And you opened the library side door to nose around out of curiosity about the quarrel?" She resented his phrasing, which made her sound nosy, not journalistic, but she affirmed her statements. "Since you just got here, I don't guess you recognized their voices."

"No. I didn't see them either so I don't know what they looked like but..." Angie paused, and the chief waited. "When I left the linen room door the first time and came down the hallway and into the library, it was empty. Nobody there. Within a few minutes, a man, who'd materialized out of nowhere, spoke to me. Scared me to death actually. He didn't come through the main doors from the hallway because that's where I was standing. It seemed to me like the only way he could've gotten into the library was through the side door from the linen room. Which puts him in the right place at the right time to be the yelling man."

The chief's mouth twitched like he just tasted something yummy. "Can you describe the man?"

"Actually I know who he is. George, the trolley driver. He picked me up at the train station today."

"George? You think George and Jenny were fighting? What in the hell would they have to fight about?" How would she know? That was for the chief to figure out.

"All I know is that he magically appeared at the side door at precisely the right time to have been in the linen room verbally battering the woman."

"I'll damn sure check out George's story about what he was doing in the library."

Angie felt better telling the chief about George. If he were the yelling man, Angie would be negligent not reporting his presence so near the body. If he wasn't the man, he'd know she told the chief, and she could kiss good-bye the chance at getting to know a good-looking guy.

"One last question, Ms. Stephens. When you first opened that side door and saw Jenny on the floor, did you think she was dead?"

"Yes. Someone strangled her. I knew by the way her scarf was wound around her neck."

"How so?"

"It was looped around her neck and stretched tight."

"Did you ever see a strangle victim before?"

"No, but I have an idea what happens."

"Okay. Thanks, Ms. Stephens. Please go to your room now and stay there. Nev, show me where Adam is. I want to hear what he's got to say about his wife's death."

Angie didn't tell the chief about recording the quarrel between the man and woman. She hadn't played the recorder yet, and for all she knew, it didn't pick up anything. She'd listen to it when she got to her room, and if anything was on it, she'd hand it over to the chief.

That should cinch making her look like the nosiest person on the planet.

Chapter Four

Dragging her exhausted self down the hallway to her room, Angie thought she might have to resort to crawling on all fours. It seemed like the chief questioned her forever. Each time she thought he'd finished, he came up with something else. 'Oh, one more question, Ms. Stephens...'

Pooped and feeling she might have only enough energy for one bedtime ritual, she elected to hang up her beautiful new dress. After putting it on the hanger, she adjusted the V-neck and hand-pressed the tummy slimming front.

She barely mustered up enough strength to tug on her pajamas and fell diagonally across her bed like a dead tree. Groggy from a day of traveling and a night of murder, she expected to fall asleep.

Twenty minutes later, too agitated to sleep, she dragged herself out of bed. Without turning on the lights, she headed for the mini-bar and tripped over an ottoman. "Oww," she groaned, sprawling across the ottoman, the wind half-knocked out of her and her big toe feeling damn near broken. She stayed put until she could take even breaths and the throbbing in her toe slowed down. Pushing herself upright, she hopped the last few steps.

She opened the door to the mini-bar and grabbed a bottle of white wine. Of course, Clarice had thought of everything--a corkscrew, stemware and printed cocktail napkins lay arranged on a tray on a shelf. Angie used the light from inside the fridge to figure out how to work the fancy corkscrew.

Taking the open bottle and a glass with her, she hobbled to the fireplace and clicked on the gas logs. She crawled back into bed and sat in the dark facing the fire with her back propped against Clarice's plump pillows.

She intended to listen to her recorder, but she was totally too tired. Tomorrow...

Angie missed the soothing presence of her cat, Chaucer. She named him after her favorite poet in the spirit that intelligent names make animals smarter. Whether or not his name boosted his intellect, she loved Chaucer. He was her constant companion now that her children, Caroline and Jonathan, were both away at college. Cuddling with Chaucer always made Angie feel calmer, but tonight she was on her own. No Chaucer. No cuddling. No feeling better.

A light tapping on Angie's hotel door startled her. If her glass hadn't been nearly empty, she would've spilled wine all over her sheets. Who would be knocking on her door at this hour? Getting out of bed, she pulled her robe off the bedpost, her heart racing as she tiptoed across the room.

Mercifully, her toe had stopped throbbing. Never underestimate the medicinal qualities of a bottle of good wine.

Angie had no intention of opening the door to anybody, but when she looked through the peephole, she saw Scott. "Angie, are you awake?" he whispered.

She unlocked the door and opened it. "Scott, what is it? Is something wrong?"

"Clarice wanted me to check and make sure you're okay. You finding Jenny and dealing with the chief's questions and all. What a night."

"Yeah. I can't stop thinking about it," Angie said. Hesitating for a moment, she asked Scott if he wanted to talk. His company sounded like a good idea. She missed having her kids to talk to.

Sure. If I'm not keeping you up." Angie assured him she was wide-awake. The light from the fireplace cast a pleasant glow across the room so Angie didn't turn on the lights. Without waiting for an invitation to sit, a done-in Scott dropped into a comfy chair.

Angie retrieved her glass and bottle of wine from the bedside table and joined him in a matching chair. Seeing Scott take a longing look at the wine bottle, she asked, "How old are you?"

"Twenty-one last June," he replied. "Legal age if you're thinking about offering me a drink."

"Wine okay?" she asked.

"Better have a beer instead. Wine might knock me out before I get to my room in the attic." Passing out sounded good to Angie--that's the effect she was working toward.

"You live in the attic?"

"Yeah, in staff quarters. A good deal for staff who don't live in Whispering Pines. Private room. Private bath. Not like in those BBC dramas when the servants lived in unheated rooms with only a cold jug of water for washing up."

Angie started to get up to get his beer, but he stopped her, "Stay put. I'll get it," he told her heading for the mini-bar. "I'll replace these in the morning," he said indicating his beer and her wine bottle, "so you won't be charged." Angie asked if he'd get in trouble with Clarice. "*No problema.*"

Knowing Scott had just come from downstairs, Angie asked for the latest news about the murder. "I hoped to hear what the chief said after questioning Adam, but he explicitly instructed me to go to my room."

"You would've had a long wait. The chief's still talking to Adam. Even though Adam heard a woman was found dead, he didn't connect her to

Jenny until he ran out of places to look. I guess when he began to consider there might be a link, he came unhinged. Kate gave him something to calm him down."

"Doesn't it seem strange to you that Adam didn't wonder earlier if Jenny's disappearance had anything to do with the dead woman? After all, he was well into his solo search mission when the woman turned up dead," Angie asked.

"It does to me, but according to Clarice, Adam and Jenny get separated at parties all the time." Angie told him she heard Adam say the same thing. She asked if the chief considered Adam a serious suspect.

"Absolutely. All I've heard is that Adam repeated the story that he didn't see Jenny after they finished dinner. He thought she was talking with her friends. That could be true, but it sounds lame, don't you think?"

"Kind of. Seems like at some point, he would've started wondering. I know the inn was crowded, but shouldn't he have come across her or run into somebody who'd seen her?" Angie said. "Does Adam have an alibi?"

"Not one that's worth much. He talked to a lot of people tonight, but he wasn't with any one person for very long. Adam's not a big talker so he doesn't get caught up in lengthy conversations. A good many locals were here for dinner, so he knew quite a few people and chatted with many of them. Adam's problem is that he's got lots of gaps in the evening that he can't account for. Foggy time line. He doesn't remember when he talked to people or how long or in what order. That's understandable, but he may not be able to put together a satisfactory alibi since his contacts were so random. Maybe his friends can help by recalling some details."

"Adam seemed like a nice man when I met him, but that doesn't mean a lot. All too often women are murdered by *nice* boyfriends or husbands."

Scott nodded.

"Are the police still questioning people?" Angie asked.

"Some. A lot of people who were in the dining room during that time walked to the library in groups, so they have solid alibis for the evening. The chief sent them home or to their rooms. Because of getting ready for dessert, the staff was in and out of the library. From the chief's point of view, all of us fall into a category of possibly seeing something important or having the opportunity to commit the murder."

Curious about Scott, Angie asked, "Are you from Whispering Pines?"

"Sort of. My father works for the State Department so I grew up living all over the world, but my parents are from here. I have lots of relatives in the area and consider this my real home. I'm a graduating senior at Dartmouth with a light course load this semester so when I have a few free days, I work for Clarice and live in the attic. I'm so-o-o ready to graduate. In the meantime, being at the Lantern gives me a break. Nice arrangement except for my astonishing similarity to an indentured servant." Angie laughed.

"About the murder... Any idea why anyone would kill Jenny? Enemies?" Angie asked.

Scott answered no to both questions. He explained Adam met Jenny at college. "When they graduated, they got married and moved to Whispering Pines. Adam took over the hardware store from his father. Jenny's always been active in church and community projects. No children. Nice house. Quiet life."

Angie wanted to tell Scott about the argument between Jenny and her killer. She needed a confidante to share her thoughts and suspicions, but she didn't know him well enough to trust him. Jenny was killed because she wouldn't agree to keep quiet. But what did she know that was bad enough to get her killed? Angie needed local knowledge, but it was too soon to make a decision.

"I better get up to my room," Scott told her drowsily. "The beer's making me sleepy, thank goodness," he said, draining his second can. Angie said goodnight to her young friend. She liked him.

***

Angie locked the door behind Scott and was barely snuggled under her covers when she heard another light tap on her door. Scott must've forgotten something. She couldn't find her robe so she dashed to the door and opened it without checking the peephole. It wasn't Scott. It was George.

"I was on my way to my room in the attic and saw a light under your door," he said.

Finding George, not Scott, at her door rendered Angie momentarily speechless. Puzzled by the light he saw under the door, she remembered she'd left the gas fireplace on for company and comfort.

"How did you know where my room is?"

"Simple. I checked the computer in the office. You're traveling alone so I wanted to let you know a couple of officers are patrolling the inn tonight. Call downstairs if you see or hear anything. It's been a hell of a night, hasn't it?

"It's definitely been a hell of a night. Thanks for checking on me, George. I'll call if I hear the slightest sound, believe me. Good night." She started to shut the door.

"Hold on a second, Angie. Could we get together in the morning? Maybe meet for breakfast? Talk a bit."

"Why?" Did he want to pump her about what she knew about Jenny's murder? Like, for example, anything that involved him. True, she wanted a confidante, but she could guaran-damn-tee it wasn't going to be George. No, sir-ee. Not if or until the chief got to the bottom of his flimsy story about how he got in the library.

George ignored her obvious attempt to get rid of him and continued, "It's about the magazine article you're writing. Clarice told me. It's going to be amazing publicity for the town. You can't imagine what the carnival means to us. I've worked with it from the beginning, and I can save you some time honing in on things."

She could use all the information she could get, and George seemed to have a connection to everything and everybody. "Like where?"

"Fitzgerald's Café, a couple of doors down the street."

Should be safe enough. Plenty of people around. She wanted a chance to pump him about what he was doing in the library and how he got there. "Okay."

"Great. Good night. Around nine?" he said. George's tie dangled loosely, his jacket hung over his shoulder. A wilted version of the impeccable man he'd been earlier in the evening.

Standing in the doorway in pajamas, Angie couldn't fail to notice that George hadn't failed to notice how thin her pjs were and how much of her body they revealed. Carried away by her enthusiasm for this trip, she bought skimpy bikini underwear instead of her usual *granny panties* as Caroline called them. Right now the bikinis were clearly showing through her pajama bottoms. And for all her pj top covered up, she might as well have answered the door topless.

Just before he turned to leave, George gave her an appreciative head-to-toe once-over. A look of satisfaction replaced his dog-tired look of weariness and exhaustion. Instead of feeling annoyed by his boldness, Angie felt sensual. How long had it been since a man looked at her like that? She was flattered, but she planned to keep a safe distance.

Chapter Five

Angie stepped out of the elevator into the familiar hum of friendly chatter and clattering dishes drifting from the breakfast area.

Clarice greeted Angie in her charming signature manner, but her weary, puffy eyes told the story of a sleep-deprived night. "Are you off to see the town? Get started on your article?"

"Yes. Have a nice day." With that, Angie dashed out the door before Clarice could ask more questions. She didn't want to raise any speculation about her and George having breakfast together. She was here to research and write a magazine article, and that was it.

Today was clear and sunny, a thumbs up change from yesterday's blizzard. Angie was grateful those ballistic ice missiles attacking her at the train station had moved east to assault the faces of residents of Vermont and New Hampshire. Better them than her.

But in spite of the sun, the temperature was frigid. Colder than the worst winter day Angie had ever endured in her North Carolina mountains. She heard on TV that last night's low was below zero. She believed it. It felt below zero now.

On a more positive note, yesterday's fresh coating of snow made the town as wintry-perfect as a Thomas Kinkade painting. The snow, plus wintry decorations and twinkling lights in shops, inspired Angie to get started on her assignment, just as soon as she took care of one little piece of business down the street.

Angie wore jeans, a bulky sweater and low-heeled suede boots since she planned to walk around town. Bundled in her warmest coat, a knit hat and mittens, she set off for Fitzgerald's Café. Just as George said, it was a couple of doors down the street from the inn. Angie entered the warm, homey café full of friendly people. From the looks of it, this is where the locals came for breakfast. Every small town has a favorite hangout, the place where everybody gathers in the morning to hash over the latest news. Angie didn't have to guess today's topic. Snippets of conversation bounced around the room. Jenny--strangled--murder--Adam--suspect.

George stood and waved Angie over to his table. Dressed casually, he wore jeans, a red cable knit turtleneck sweater and everyday leather boots. He looked outdoorsy handsome as he pulled out a chair for her to sit. Nice manners too. That, no doubt, came from working at the inn. Clarice didn't strike Angie as the kind of boss who'd settle for anything less than perfection from her employees.

A waitress, wearing a short pink uniform that showed too much of her pudgy knees, shuffled from table to table carrying pots of regular and decaf coffee, exchanging friendly banter with the customers as she refilled their cups. "Hey, Jackie, come over here," George called to her. She worked her way to their table, setting down one of the pots and handing Angie a menu she carried tucked under her plump arm. "This is Angie Stephens, Jackie. She's writing an article about Whispering Pines for *American Scene* magazine. How 'bout that?"

"Yeah, I heard. Awesome. Let me know if I can help, Angie. I know everybody in town. I can tell you tales that'll make your pretty red curly hair even curlier!" Jackie laughed out loud at her own joke.

"It's not that kind of article," George said. "It's about the winter carnival. Besides, I'm helping her."

"Heaven help us all. We'll have to leave town if she listens to you." Jackie rolled her eyes. "By the way, George, how many of your part-time jobs are you working at today?" Jackie's loud, brassy question halted other conversations.

A male customer at a nearby table added his bit. "I heard Nev had you out delivering flowers at the crack of dawn. I didn't know you were in the business of hauling around posies." The customers laughed heartily at news they hadn't heard. In good-natured response, George toasted the group with his coffee cup.

Jackie topped off their coffee before she moved to the next table. "I'll be back in a minute to take your order."

The heat of the café, or maybe it was heat coming from across the table, caught up with Angie, and she stood to remove her coat. George rose from his chair to assist her, folding and draping her coat over a spare chair. Clarice had trained him well.

Choosing breakfast was easy because Angie indulged herself with the works when she ate out. Her only regret was that there were no southern grits on this New York menu to top off her morning feast.

After Jackie took their orders and toddled off to the kitchen, George sat looking at Angie with the now familiar amused expression. She enjoyed the way he looked at her. It was sexy, even in the morning.

Anything new about Jenny's murder?" Angie asked. Realizing she'd asked a downer question, she watched his expression change from hot-blooded to cold serious.

"The police still have the linen room blocked off and an officer, who isn't talking, posted outside the door. Clarice is in a fix because that's where all our tablecloths and napkins are stored. Looks like she'll have to slum it today with paper products." So un-Clarice-like.

"What about Adam's interrogation? I heard it was long."

"Adam's got a lot of questions he can't answer. I find it hard to believe he killed Jenny, but how naïve for him not to wonder if his missing wife and the dead woman were connected? It's worse than naïve, it makes him look guilty."

"Yeah, Scott and I talked a little about that last night."

George arched an eyebrow. "I didn't know you and Scotty were friends. So he's who told you about Adam's interrogation?"

"Yeah. Nice young man."

"That he is. Speaking of interrogations, I just finished one with the chief. He was interrogating me, not vice-versa in case you're wondering," George said, teasing her. "Seems somebody told him about my presence in the library right after a man and woman had a volatile argument in the linen room. The chief has an eyewitness who says I didn't enter the library through the main doors. The eyewitness suggested I slipped through the side door from the linen room into the library, putting me at the site of the murder about the time it took place. Wonder who that witness could be." George looked her directly in the eyes. He didn't sound like he felt threatened or angry with her. In his place, she'd be damn mad if somebody accused her of being a murderer.

"Stop playing games, George. I know you know it was me. I'm the only person who could've told him because I'm the only one who saw you. I told the chief because you weren't in the library when I first went in, and then you magically appeared. You absolutely didn't come through the big doors from the hallway."

"I didn't come from the linen room either, and that's the truth. I swear to you I had nothing to do with Jenny's death. The extent of my relationship with her was 'Hello, how are you? Have a good day.' George sounded emphatic. "And we might as well get everything out in the open. I told the chief you came flying into the library looking like a hungry bear chased you down the hall."

"You did what? How dare you suggest I had anything to do with Jenny's murder?"

"Hold on. I didn't say you killed her. I said you looked like you were running away from something or somebody. At any rate, the chief wants to talk to you again. He said you didn't mention running down the hall during your interrogation. Like me, you were in the immediate area when the murder took place. That makes both of us legitimate suspects."

Well, damn George for getting her switched from finding the body to the suspect list.

"I'm brand new here. I assure you I didn't know Jenny and had no reason to kill her."

"Then we agree that neither of us did it?"

"I agree I didn't do it. I don't know about you."

"Yes, you do. I just told you."

"I'll keep the source in mind. Putting this in perspective, I came here to write a colorful article about a winter carnival, not end up on trial for the murder of somebody I didn't even know. And since my goal is get back into serious journalism, I'm going to get a jump on it by investigating Jenny's murder and removing my name from the suspect list."

"FYI, I don't like being on the suspect list either. What do you say we work together? Two heads are better than one and all that stuff. Like it or not, we're stuck in the same suspect boat. We were closer to the murder scene than anyone except the killer."

Angie hesitated. She didn't want to work with George. He still hadn't explained his presence in the library to her satisfaction, and, as far as she knew, the chief hadn't dropped his interest in George--or in her. Maybe working with George made sense. She could use his insight into the local psyche, a big time saver for her. "So what were you doing in the library?"

"The kitchen staff finished setting up for dessert. I was doing the final check. Heaven forbid the lemon drop cookies are too close to the triple chocolate bonbons."

"But how did you get in the library?"

"Trust me. I was already there when you came in. I had nothing to do with Jenny's death. That's the truth."

He sounded sincere, but she was wary. "We'll give working together a shot. If it doesn't pan out, we'll go our separate ways. Okay?"

"Yeah, but I think we'll make a good team," George said.

***

"I'll show you around town. Help you get your bearings. But first, I have to run over to Nev's greenhouses." She asked if he meant Clarice's husband. "Yeah. He's the only Nev in town."

George explained that Nev, a retired horticulture professor, began a new career growing flowers for the Lantern Inn as well as a lot of other businesses in town. "I'll just be there for a few minutes to check something. You can look at Nev's flowers. They're beauties. Then I'll take you downtown. Help you get your bearings so you can take off on your own this afternoon and interview people or whatever you need to do. I have to make the trolley run later, but I'll get you oriented before I leave."

Jackie arrived with their breakfasts and more coffee. While they ate, Angie asked George how the winter carnival began. "Out of necessity. The town's main employer, a paper mill, folded ten years ago. Its outdated machinery and technology couldn't compete, and it shut down, throwing most of the town's work force out of a job with no prospects for anything else. We needed to build a new, different economy," George said, "but nothing seemed viable. The town kept trying to attract businesses to the mill buildings. Factories around the region weren't looking for places to relocate. They were shutting down too."

"So where did the carnival idea come from?"

One night a bunch of us gathered in Clarice's kitchen to have a few drinks and try to come up with a solution. Nev jokingly pointed out that we had more snow than anything else. Maggie Thurston, who was busy thinking while the rest of us fooled around, pointed out that the town, with its Victorian buildings, was everybody's stereotype of what a small town looks like in winter, and we should capitalize on that.

"We decided to put on a winter carnival with the hope of bringing in a few dollars to tide us over until we thought of something better. We searched the internet, borrowing ideas from other towns that had carnivals, picking and choosing what we thought we could pull off.

"Everybody pitched in. Laid-off mill workers cut evergreens from the woods and brought pickup loads for merchants to decorate their stores. We strung white lights everywhere. That first celebration turned out to be a good moneymaker. Its success gave us encouragement that we might be on to something."

"Sounds like a miracle."

"It was a miracle," George said. "If the carnival hadn't worked, the town would've died."

George changed the subject and asked Angie about herself. She told him about her home in the small town of Forest Gate in the North Carolina Great Smoky Mountains and her children, Jonathan a sophomore at Princeton and Caroline a freshman at Georgetown. She mentioned, without any of the ugly details, that her husband, Jack Stephens, walked out on her when the children were babies leaving her as their sole support, her boring job as a children's magazine writer churning out stories about volcanoes, icebergs and earthquakes for the past eighteen years, her children's paternal grandmother's generous bequest which opened a world of opportunities for her and the children and the latest chapter in her life--her college friend Ted's amazing magazine assignment which brought her to Whispering Pines to write about the winter carnival and the chance to enter journalism after a twenty-year postponement.

Normally a private person to the point of paranoia, Angie immediately regretted her willingness to bare her so much of her life to a man she hardly knew and resolved to be more guarded.

George picked up the check from the table and helped Angie with her coat. "Let's go look at some flowers. You wait in here where it's warm. I'll pick you up out front."

While he was paying the check, Jackie yelled across the diner, "Angie, if you're going to hang out with George, you better watch yourself. Before you know it, he'll have you driving that trolley bus or delivering flowers." Her comments brought robust laughter from the other patrons. George ignored them, seeming unperturbed by the good time they were having at his expense.

Angie waited on the sidewalk, expecting George to drive up in the golden *Sleigh Bells Express* with its stenciled snowflakes and scrolled black lettering. Instead, he waved to her from a tan mini-van with Lantern Inn artistically painted on the doors.

Chapter Six

"Are you sure it's okay to barge in on Nev? Shouldn't we have called first?" Angie asked.

"Nah. He's expecting me. He'll gladly show off his flowers to you. His business has mushroomed, and he ships all over New England. Busier than before he retired."

"People dream about that kind of unexpected success," Angie said.

"Yeah. Nev loves his work at the greenhouse. He helps out some at the inn, but he doesn't really like it. That's Clarice's business. Not Nev's cup of tea. He was born to dig in the soil."

Angie grasped the scope of Nev's business success when George pulled into his parking lot. She expected a couple of makeshift greenhouses cobbled together from scrap materials. Instead, rows of modern facilities stretched before her.

George prepped Angie for the greenhouse visit with a word of caution. "Don't ask questions or you'll be setting yourself up for a crash course in Hort 101." George backed the van near the door and stopped. Angie noted a silver Porsche convertible parked next to them. Nev was doing well indeed.

A burst of color and delightful fragrance greeted Angie when she entered the front greenhouse. A lush garden flourishing in the midst of a frigid New York winter. From behind a bank of flowers came a voice, "That you, George?"

"Yeah, it's me. Come out and meet Angie Stephens. She's writing the article about the winter carnival."

"Splendid," Nev said, emerging from behind rows of evergreens in gallon pots. Even dressed in faded jeans and a red and black plaid flannel shirt, he was as striking and distinguished-looking as he'd been at the Lantern Inn the previous night. Warm eyes softened an angular, intelligent face. "Nice to meet you, Angie. I'm afraid we didn't have a proper introduction last night." She agreed it'd been a chaotic night.

"Hey, George, start loading the van, will you? All those boxes by the door are ready to go. I'll show Angie around." With a look of resignation, George picked up the first box and trudged out the door with it.

Nev was charming in the role of host, as proud of his beautiful blooms as a parent of a precocious child, volunteering the names of some of the flowers for her.

When Angie and Nev finished touring the greenhouse, she asked if the chief came up with anything after she went to her room last night. "I heard he talked to Adam a long time."

"It was a long interrogation. Adam's the number one suspect at this point, although the chief said a couple of other suspects were near the linen room around the time of the murder. He's looking into their stories too."

Nev didn't appear to know that she and George were two of those suspects near the linen room. Angie kept quiet. She didn't want that to get out. Everybody thought she was an angel sent to save the town, and she liked the image. Her goal was to help this quaint town, not get immersed in a scandal.

"There's not much to Adam's story. He said after he and Jenny finished dinner he went out to the reception area to take a cell call. Business, he told the chief.

"Jenny remained in the dining room to have coffee. Several of the wait staff remembered seeing her sitting alone when they offered her refills. Unfortunately no one remembers seeing her leave the dining room. The staff was busy, and she apparently walked out unnoticed. The last I heard, nobody had reported seeing her in the reception area or hallway or anyplace after she left the dining room. That is, until you discovered her lying on the floor of the linen room."

"So before Adam went out to take his call, he settled their bill?" Angie asked.

Adam put it on his credit card before he left the dining room so he didn't need to return. Like you said, Jenny just got up and walked out when she was finished."

"Seems like with all the talk about her murder, someone would remember seeing her after she left the dining room. It might help the police if somebody noticed whether she was upset or angry," Nev said.

Angie didn't mention to Nev about hearing the woman crying or telling the chief about it. She wanted to keep her name out of the investigation.

"What about Adam? Didn't anybody see him after he left the dining room? Like while he was talking on the phone? Was he upset or angry?" Angie asked.

Nev shook his head. "Nobody seems to remember seeing him. One of the diners thought she saw him in the reception area, but she can't remember when. Saturday nights are madhouses."

A phone rang somewhere among the flowers. "Back in a sec," he told her, excusing himself to answer the phone.

Angie didn't know about Adam's movements, but she had a good idea why nobody saw Jenny. Quite simply, when she left the dining room, she angled across a corner of the reception area and walked the short distance down the hallway. She'd arranged to meet someone in the linen room and went directly to it. With so many people milling around, it wasn't surprising nobody noticed her during the few minutes it took her to make her way from the dining room down the hallway. If Jenny was meeting a man, she probably hurried, not drawing attention to herself by engaging in pleasantries. Poor Jenny. What was she thinking on that short walk?

As for Adam being a suspect, it didn't make sense to Angie that Jenny sneaked out to meet her own husband. If they were arguing, why not wait and settle it at home in private? Angie didn't think Jenny met Adam in the linen room. Whoever she met was already angry with her or got worked up to a rage pretty quickly. On the other hand, Adam could've killed Jenny at the inn to deflect suspicion from himself.

Angie's head spun with theories about Adam and even George. But clearing herself was her priority. George and Adam were on their own.

When Nev finished talking on the phone, Angie heard him clicking switches, adjusting various systems critical to keep his flowers flourishing. George, on the way out the door with another box of flowers, flashed Angie a grin to which she automatically responded in kind. The more she saw him, the more irresistible he became. Cool down, girl, she told herself. Along with being hot, he may be dangerous.

Pushing a cart loaded with boxes of neatly packed flowers, Nev rejoined Angie. "Where's George?" he asked. Angie explained he was taking out the last box. "Good. That was Sherry, a local florist, on the phone. She needs an extra order right away. Will you tell George to load these too?"

Angie relayed Nev's message to George about loading the boxes. He gave her a comic look of hopeless resignation.

Angie laughed with him, but she felt sorry for him too. She hadn't been subjected to orders from a boss since she worked as a hotel maid back when her husband walked out on her, and she was desperate for a job. She had to get up at five o'clock to get the babies fed and dressed, delivered to day care and get herself to work. After she slaved until she could barely lift a mop, her supervisor kept telling her to work faster and do more rooms in less time. The children's magazine job, boring as it was, rescued her from backbreaking drudgery. Her year as a maid was, without equal, the darkest time of her entire life.

Taking pity on George, Angie pitched in and gave him a hand loading the flowers. She put down her purse, picked up a box of flowers and followed him outside to the van. They repeated the process until the flowers were loaded. "Hey, thanks," he said.

Nev appeared in coat and hat and met them outside when they were done. George asked, "Have you talked to the chief yet?"

"Not yet. I'll do it today."

"Good. The sooner you do it the better. You don't want him to hear that stuff from somebody else." Nev assured George he'd call. Did Angie imagine it or did Nev's self-confidence reveal a little crack?

Angie ran inside the greenhouse to get her purse. George checked a computer screen of numbers, turned off the lights and locked the door. The temperature outside felt even colder after being inside the tropical heat and humidity of the greenhouse. Angie was in a hurry to get into a warm vehicle and started toward the passenger door of the van.

"Over here, Angie," George called to her. "We're taking the car," he said, opening the door of Nev's Porsche. He didn't have to force her. She got in the car quickly, settling into the luxurious leather seat. The interior was toasty warm. George must have started the engine and turned on the heater while he was carrying boxes. Angie expected Nev to drive her back to town, but George hopped into the driver's seat and put the car in reverse. In seconds they zipped down the drive toward town. Angie looked back and saw Nev lagging along behind them in the mini-van loaded with flowers.

Angie said, "I thought you were going to make the flower deliveries."

"Me? I've done my share, thank you. After being up nearly all night because of Jenny's murder, I didn't get tucked up in my comfy servant's room in the attic until the wee hours. I no more than got to sleep when Clarice called me at five o'clock to get my butt out of bed on the double and see what was wrong at the greenhouses. There was a problem and, of course, I got elected to solve it.

"I ended up staying here and making early deliveries for Nev because he was behind schedule. He usually cuts and packs flowers at night if they have to be delivered or shipped first thing in the morning, but he didn't get back here last night because of the problems at the inn. I swear he and Clarice can think of more work for somebody else to do. Anyway, that's why I needed to stop by and check the greenhouse temps and make sure they're okay. Then, Nev put me to work again loading the van."

Angie was glad she didn't work for Clarice and Nev. Her boring job, as unglamorous as it was, didn't look so bad compared to George's multiple jobs.

It wasn't any of Angie's business, but she thought George ought to get one full-time job instead of three part-time jobs. He could probably make more money, plus have simpler schedules to keep up with. Talk about juggling.

"I'm off duty now," George said. "The greenhouses are toasty warm. Nev's caught up on packing and loading, so he can make his own deliveries." Angie didn't think George should feel too badly about his situation though. He was driving Nev's Porsche, not a bad payment for hauling some flowers around. If Nev needed any more deliveries made, Angie would volunteer. What she wouldn't give to drive this car. George handled it expertly, whetting Angie's appetite to slip behind the wheel.

"What was that exchange back there about Nev talking to the chief?"

"This is just between us, but several years ago, Jenny started making moves on Nev. She sent him emails at the greenhouse so Clarice wouldn't see them, but Nev showed them to her anyway. No secrets between them. However, Jenny became more persistent and invited Nev out to dinner with her. A date. Not a couples' get-together. This went on until Nev told Jenny in blunt terms not to contact him anymore, that nothing was going to happen between them."

"So that was the end of it?" George replied as far as he knew. Nev didn't mention it again. "Did anybody else know about the emails?"

"Not unless Jenny told someone, or she kept the old emails on her computer. Chances are the police will check it right away. That's why Nev needs to tell the chief before they do. I don't know if Jenny and Adam were going through a bad patch or if she found Nev's English accent irresistible, but she made his life uncomfortable for several months."

"And Nev didn't reciprocate her advances?"

"Absolutely not. He and Clarice have a deep love and respect for each other. I'm not sure of many things in this topsy-turvy world, but their commitment and fidelity are unshakable." Something of a cynic about love and marriage, Angie wasn't sure about unshakable marriages. She'd known devoted couples that fell apart. It depended on the force of the hurricane that struck them. Nev looked capable of staying clear of strong storms, including a relentless female one.

Angie relaxed and enjoyed the ride. This assignment was getting better and better. Here she was tooling around in a Porsche convertible with a good-looking guy. Two unexpected and pleasant additions to her journalism fantasy unless George's assertion of his innocence of Jenny's murder was bogus, and her intuition was wrong. She'd be wary until the chief removed him from the suspect list.

Chapter Seven

"Any idea what you want to see first?" George asked, driving back to town. Angie barely heard him because her mind was on Nev's Porsche, instead of topics for her magazine article. An aficionado of cars since childhood, she grew up hanging around with her father in the family garage where he restored classics from the 1950s and '60s. His passion and hobby had given her the chance to drive some of the most powerful street cars ever built in the US. Angie didn't mind bragging that she knew her way around fast cars. When it came to cars, being labeled a *redneck* didn't bother her at all.

Reluctantly dragging her attention away from the car, she replied, "It was snowing so hard last night, I didn't get much of a look at how big the town is and where things are. Maybe we should start with an orientation. And keep in mind, I'll be starting out from the Lantern."

"Everything's an easy walk from the Lantern. And this is a small town. No getting lost."

"I know Adam's store is closed today, but will you point it out so I can take a look at the sleds in the windows?"

"Sure thing," George replied. As they drove down Main Street, he asked, "So what do you think of Whispering Pines?"

"I'm impressed," she told him, marveling at the quaint buildings all decked out for the carnival. "The town's charming. I love that the original architecture survived. So many towns tear down or modernize their old buildings into nondescript glossy boxes."

As Angie expected, Harden's Hardware was dark and unoccupied. Poor Adam. Chief suspect in his wife's murder. Ample opportunity and no alibi.

Would the chief uncover the clincher, a motive?

George pointed toward a bundled-up woman arranging display racks outside a shop. "Sunny and her sister, Prissy, turned their parents' little grocery store into a book and gift shop. Mostly gifts now. Sunny tries to be friendly, but she always looks like she had a bowl of sour cherries for breakfast. She's hard to take at her best. Prissy inherited all the personality genes. Angie made a mental note to make sure Prissy was on duty before she wandered in to shop.

At the end of the three-block business district, George made a U-turn and drove slowly down the other side of Main Street. "That's all there is to town. Hey, if you don't mind, I've got another quick errand before I get ready for the trolley run. People have been seeing lights at the old mill that shouldn't be there. It's just up the road." Angie opened her mouth to object, but George whipped a right turn and sped away. "Granted, the mill's not much of an asset, but I'd better check it just in case..."

It made Angie uneasy to watch the town and sidewalks bustling with tourists fade behind her. They gave her a feeling of security, kept her from being alone with George. And she definitely wasn't interested in seeing the closed mill. She'd seen enough shutdown cotton mills in the south to know what old abandoned factories looked like.

George turned onto a straight road with no traffic and let the Porsche do its stuff. Without slowing down, he deftly dodged potholes, zigzagging with precision down the narrow road. Angie wanted to concentrate on the thrill of riding in this car, but losing control over where she was going unnerved her.

When the road dead-ended, George swerved into the old mill's parking lot. It was snow covered and undisturbed except for a big circle in the center scooped out by a snowplow. Angie asked why anybody bothered to clear the parking lot since the mill was closed. "For school buses. This is the end of the line for them, so they have to turn around."

Several large, dreary brick buildings loomed ahead of them. Age and idleness had wreaked their damage on the old paper mill. Vandals had added touches by breaking windows and spray painting undecipherable layers of colored messages on the sides of the buildings. Actually, when Angie took a closer look, the *F-word* was readable in an array of colors and handwriting styles, the universal first choice of graffiti artists and just plain hoodlums.

The mill was in sad shape. George's assessment that this place didn't have any economic possibilities was right on. Unlike southern cotton mills that were being torn down, the bricks salvaged and sold as historic building material, this place was just plain ugly and undesirable in any form. Angie didn't envision this mill's dismal bits and pieces ending up as accent walls admired during the cocktail hour in upscale Atlanta suburbs.

That's strange," George remarked. "See that four-wheel drive parked in front of the main mill? What would somebody be doing here on a Sunday morning?" Clearly obsessed by the vehicle's presence, George eased the car through the clearing left by the snowplow. At the edge of the cleared pavement, he stopped the car and turned off the engine. He got out and opened Angie's door. "Let's take a look at what's going on."

"Hold on. I don't care why that vehicle's parked here. This place and who's here is of no interest to me." In fact, she didn't see why it was any of George's business either unless shutdown-paper-mill-security-guard was listed on his already crowded job resume.

"It'll just take a minute to check. We keep advertising the mill for sale. Maybe this is a prospective buyer, and I can point out the buildings' assets." She told him quite truthfully, it didn't have any assets.

Seeing that George was determined, Angie reluctantly got out of the warm car to keep from being left alone in the empty parking lot. She didn't want to go to the mill either. She'd have to walk through cold, deep snow. At least she'd worn low heel boots after learning some slippery lessons about the hazards of high heels when she'd arrived at the Amtrak station. Her boots today were designed to look hot, not to keep her feet warm slogging through unplowed snow.

George put on spare boots stashed in his car that looked Arctic hardy. Angie started to ask if there was a pair for her, but the lack of them was obvious. After George changed into clunky lumberjack boots, he volunteered to make tracks for Angie to step in so she wouldn't sink in the snow. That would keep her new boots from getting messed up, but she still didn't like this side trip. Why should George care why a vehicle parked outside an old abandoned mill mattered? It wasn't like anyone could do the old place any more damage or make it less marketable.

George's stride was longer than Angie's so she held onto the back of his jacket to keep her balance. At least her boots didn't sink in the snow. So far, so good.

"Well, no question whose vehicle this is," George declared when they got close enough to see the license plate. It was personalized *MAYOR*.

"Mayor Cliff? I met him and his wife last night."

"Let's hope Adam talked to him or his wife last night, and they can help with his alibi. Polly's a sweetheart. If she saw Adam, she'd stay awake all night trying to remember every detail to tell Roger."

Angie said, "Frankly, the mayor looked like he could take care of things by himself. Let's go."

"Whoa. Not so fast. Let's see what Cliff's up to," George said mischievously. "Our mayor might be here on business or, more accurately, monkey business."

She looked at him questioningly. Monkey business? Was he suggesting the mayor was involved in some kind of hanky-panky? The same formal mayor she met at the inn last night? The one with cute bubbly Polly? No way. The mayor didn't strike Angie as a womanizer, and she knew a few things about married men on the prowl. As a divorced woman, she'd been a magnet for them. Her womanizer radar could pick them up walking down the street. Married men in her town used to be after her like a duck on a June bug until she systematically repelled their philandering advances. What she didn't need in her life was somebody's cheating husband who would cheat on her the first chance he got. No, thank you.

Of course, she had to consider that this was George's turf, and he knew the locals' foibles better than she did. Maybe Yankee cheating husbands were different from southern cheating husbands. She had no experiences for comparisons.

And if the mayor was up to something, was it smart for her and George to surprise him in the middle of whatever kind of business he was engaged in, monkey or otherwise? George charged toward the closest building, following a path of trampled snow from the mayor's vehicle to the mill. From the number of footprints, somebody or several somebodies had made more than one trip in and out of this building.

"George, I think this is a bad idea. Let's leave." Interrupting what might be an embarrassing situation for the polite mayor was nowhere on Angie's to-do list. His love life wasn't of interest to her. He didn't strike Angie as the Romeo type anyway.

"Patience. It won't take but a second."

George tugged at a garage-sized door that stood partially open. As it slid aside, more light entered the dim interior, and Angie got her first look inside the defunct mill.

"Where's the equipment?" Angie asked.

"Sold," George said, "to a mill in China."

Everything was gone except miscellaneous trash tossed here and there. All that remained was a vast, silent space, which had once hummed with the clatter of machinery and provided a livelihood for hundreds of employees.

"Cliff, it's George Satterfield!" George yelled loudly. "Where are you?" Startled, Angie pulled her head into her shoulders as George's voice reverberated through the cavernous space. He yelled again but no answer. "Maybe he's in the back," George said, leading the way. Angie was frightened. She didn't want to go further into the building with George, but she didn't want to stay by herself. She'd gotten herself into a mess with no good options.

Angie's fears about catching Cliff in a compromising situation diminished the longer she remained in the building. If the mayor was up to something amorous in this icebox of a place, he was a lot more hot-blooded than he looked. If tomcatting wasn't his motive, what was he doing here?

At the back of the building there were no windows at all, and the light became so dark that Angie could barely see George directly in front of her. He swore because he hadn't brought a flashlight from the car. Angie silently joined him for more reasons than the lack of a flashlight.

Without warning, Angie's left boot toe caught on something on the floor. She grabbed onto George's jacket with both hands, hopping on one foot while she struggled to free the other. "What're you doing?" he asked.

Before she could answer, her foot slipped loose, and she lunged forward into George. "What's wrong?" he asked, turning around and trying to get a hold on her to steady both of them.

"I tripped," she murmured.

"Are you hurt?"

"No. I'm okay. Sorry I smacked into you."

"You sure have a knack for running into me. You nearly knocked me down at the station yesterday," he said in a teasing voice. He had noticed when she fell over her suitcase and crashed into him. "Next time, let me know, and I'll brace myself," he joked.

More seriously, George said, "I'll open a side door so we can get some light in here. If there's trash on the floor, we'll need to get somebody to clean up. Wait here."

He didn't have to worry. She was too scared to move. Angie could hear George's footsteps walking away from her, followed by the sound of metal scraping against metal as a large door strained on rusty rollers. A thin shaft of sunlight crept across the room. When it reached Angie's feet, she screamed. In the triangle of light she recognized the object that tripped her. Mayor Cliff Schouten lay flat on his back. The front of his shirt and jacket soaked with blood. The overflow puddled on the cement floor.

George was at Angie's side before she stopped screaming. He knelt beside the mayor, felt for a pulse and shook his head. "I don't feel anything. I'm no doctor, but I think he's dead. He's ice cold."

Angie thought so too. She didn't know a human held as much blood as had poured out of Cliff.

George stood and quickly circled the mayor's body, returning to where Angie waited, stunned and silent. He held her arm with one hand and pulled her close to him. He put his other arm around her shoulders and held her firmly. "Are you okay?" She wasn't okay, but she pretended. "I had no idea we'd find something like this. I'm so sorry. I thought people were seeing lights from kids fooling around or burglars thinking there might be something of value in here." He searched his pockets. "I can't find my cell. Go to the car, and call the police. Stay put until they get here. I'll stay with Cliff."

Angie turned and ran, but an unnerving sensation seized her. Someone's gaze followed her. Creeped out, she tried to shake off her invisible stalker, but the feeling travelled with her.

Maybe it was George. Why would he be watching her? He knew where she was going. She shouldn't have listened to him. Shouldn't have allowed him to drag her along on his snooping venture. Shouldn't have entered this building. Shouldn't. Shouldn't. Shouldn't.

Angie ran faster than since she was a kid. With every step, she was grateful for her efforts, half-hearted though they were, to trudge along on her treadmill on a semi-regular routine. She kept telling herself to keep her eyes focused on the door. Each step brought her closer to it and further away from the bloody body lying in the back of the mill.

When Angie reached the door, she held onto the frame to steady herself for a second to catch her breath. She wanted to yell to George for reassurance, but she was too frightened. She was afraid of everything and everybody. Maybe the town, the complete bunch of them including George, were maniacal killers.

Aiming to keep her erratic feet on the tromped-down pathway to the car, she veered off it, plopping her feet in deep snow. It was all she could do to stay upright. Icy snow spilled inside her boots. Her feet were freezing, but they kept moving. Almost to the car, she kept telling herself, almost...

Angie struggled to open the car door, panicked that George might have locked it from habit. It swung open unexpectedly, almost knocking her down. Clinging to the top of the car with her fingertips, she stayed on her feet and swung her body around, landing butt first in the driver's seat. Before she could get the rest of herself into the car, colored snow on the ground caught her attention.

Where she'd been standing was red, blood red. "Damn!" she shouted as loudly as she could. Cliff's blood had soaked into her boots when her foot caught on his body in the mill. While she was getting in the car, the blood leached into the snow dyeing the snow red. Angie screamed. "Somebody, please help me! Take these awful boots off my feet. I can't do this."

But there was no one in this deserted parking lot to help her. On her own as usual, her crying notched down to sniffles. With closed eyes and mittened hands, Angie pulled off her spoiled boots and tossed them out the door. However, her relief was momentary. Blood transferred to her mittens while she was taking the boots off. She pulled them off without letting the blood touch her bare skin and lobbed them into the snow. She turned sideways in the driver's seat and faced the opposite direction so the boots and mittens were not in her line of vision.

Angie slammed the car door and locked it, shutting out everything to do with bloody boots and mittens and a dead mayor lying on a cold cement floor in the mill.

Her own boots ruined and her feet damn near frozen, she spotted George's ankle boots on the passenger floor. Half-dazed and teary-eyed, she fumbled until her numb feet slipped into them. Leather provided no warmth, but the boots provided a covering for her feet.

Recalling George's instructions to call the police, she reached for her purse to retrieve her cell phone, but where was her purse? She looked on the floor of the car and ran her hand under the seat. She clearly remembered taking it with her when she and George had gotten out of the car to go into the mill. She'd slung it across her shoulder, but she didn't have it now.

Maybe it fell when the car door almost knocked her down. She lowered the window, hoping to see her purse lying on the ground. "Don't let it be in the bloody snow," she said, pleading to the Universe. It was bad enough to ruin her boots and gloves but not her purse too. The Universe heard her plea. Wherever it was, her purse hadn't landed in the nasty red snow.

Angie stepped out of the car, careful to avoid the bloody areas, and checked the path. Her purse wasn't there either. Could she have dropped it when she tripped over the mayor's body and bumped into George? Please let it have sailed far away from Cliff's oozing body. George's phone must be in the car.

She got back in the car and, with shaking icy fingers, searched the storage cubbies. George must have it with him after all. Did he pretend not to find it to get rid of her?

One thing for certain, the car keys, whether George meant to take or leave them lay on the console in clear sight. If Angie didn't have a phone to call the police, she'd go get them. She started the engine and gunned it.

Glancing in the rear view mirror, she caught a fleeting image of George emerging from the front of the mill, waving his arms like windmill sails. She wanted to drive on, get away from him and this horrible place of death. In another second, she would've been gone and blissfully unaware he was frantically waving and galloping behind her. Angie stopped the car and backed toward him.

George, arms swinging, plodded sluggishly through the snow in Nev's heavy boots. Fright had replaced his familiar amused expression. What on earth sent him flying after her in such a hurry?

Angie reached over to open the door and George hopped in the passenger seat, snow flying all over her. "Get the hell out of here." Without waiting for him to close the door, Angie spun out of the parking lot and onto the road.

When the paper mill disappeared from sight in the rear view mirror, she asked, "What happened?"

"Can't--talk," George said, waiting until his breathing slowed.

"Something pretty freaking unbelievable. After you left, I walked over to the side doors to wait for the police. I thought the sunshine would be warmer. I only took a few steps when I heard a noise that sounded like rustling paper. I stopped and turned around. When I did, somebody took a shot at me."

"A shot? Like with a gun?"

"Damn right, like with a gun."

"So the whole time we were in the mill, somebody else was in there with a gun?"

"Yeah. He had to have been there when we entered. If he'd come in later, we would've heard him. Sounds in that big old empty building echo."

"Wait a minute. Does that mean somebody shot Cliff?

"Looks that way. When we found Cliff, I thought he'd committed suicide. But he'd always struck me as being too full of himself to take out his favorite person, but who knows what's going on in somebody's mind? Finding him dead on a Sunday morning at the mill reeked of suicide. I was shocked and didn't think to look for a pistol or whatever he'd used. But I felt sure Cliff did himself in. No way would I have hung around making a target out of myself if I thought somebody killed him. God, I'm not that dumb!"

Angie swallowed hard. She'd been right. Cliff's killer was watching her when she ran out of the mill. Maybe he even considered taking a shot at her.

"The killer must've seen us come in the front door and knew he was trapped. He couldn't make a run for it while we were in the building so he laid low waiting for us to leave. Unfortunately, I didn't leave. He must've assumed you'd call the police, and it wouldn't be long until they arrived. Probably tried to sneak out and accidentally kicked a piece of paper. I turned around at the sound, so he took a shot at me. I don't know if he tried to hit me, but he sure scared the hell out of me and got me out of the mill so he could get away."

Angie listened in disbelief. Arriving in Whispering Pines less than twenty-four hours ago, she'd found two dead bodies. If that wasn't enough, somebody had taken a shot at her wanna-be tour guide who, like herself, was a suspect in a strangling death.

This couldn't be for real. This perfect, magical town, the site of her long-awaited rendezvous with a journalism career, the town that looked like everybody's idea of a winter wonderland, was turning into the scene of a murderous rampage.

"I don't guess you saw anyone," she said, fairly certain the inside of the building would've been too dark.

"No. As soon as I heard the gun, I ran like hell and didn't look back. The shot hit something metal, probably the sliding door hardware. Sounded like a church bell clanging. All I cared was that it didn't hit me." George paused for a couple of quick breaths. "These boots weigh a ton. It's a wonder I could pick my feet up. When I got out of the building and saw you leaving, I panicked."

"Didn't think you could catch a freaked-out female driving a Porsche?"

George shook his head. "Didn't want to have to try. You took off like you meant business." He still looked ninety-nine percent shell-shocked, but his amused expression was kicking in again. "That was some quick maneuvering you just did. Where did you learn to drive like that?"

"I grew up behind the wheel of fast cars," she said and left it at that.

"George, this probably sounds wacko, but when I ran out of the mill, I felt like someone was watching me. Don't make fun of me, but I sensed an evil presence."

"It *was* an evil presence, and it took a shot at me."

Angie tried to remember hearing a loud noise that could've been the gunshot. It didn't happen while she was running to the car. She would definitely have heard it then. The front door of the mill was wide open, and the sound of a gunshot would've boomed all over the parking lot. Maybe it happened after she got in the car. Doors and windows closed, the engine running, the heater fan on high and her crying would've muffled outside noise. Enough to block out a gunshot?

Would it prove anything if she'd heard the gunshot? For starters, it would mean that George was telling the truth about a gunman. She wanted to believe him, but caution reminded her to temper her romantic notions with the reality of the situation.

"By the way," he asked, "why were you leaving the mill? I told you to call the police. Not go get them."

Angie explained her missing purse and her cell phone inside it. "I went through all the storage cubbies and couldn't find your cell either."

"Oh, hell, the last time I used it was to call Clarice when I was getting the van to pick you up in front of the café. I must've left it in the van instead of putting it in my pocket. It got you out of the mill and away from that gruesome scene. My only mistake was not going with you."

"Why didn't you?"

"I guess I thought Cliff deserved to have somebody stay with him. Watch over him. Old-fashioned, I guess." No, just thoughtful and respectful.

"Well, what now? Stop at one of these farms and ask them to call the police?"

"Waste of time. Most folks are at church or out having breakfast. Keep going toward town." Angie guided the Porsche onto the narrow road, driving at a more subdued pace than when George flagged her down.

"Angie," George asked, looking puzzled, "why are you wearing my boots? What happened to yours?" She explained about the blood, and he made a face. "I'm sorry I got you into this. I'll replace your boots." Angie thanked him for the offer, but she knew the cost of her boots was way out of his working-class price range. Still, it was a sweet gesture.

When Angie reached the edge of town, George told her, "Pull over at that convenience store. I'll run in and call Roger. This news isn't going to set well with him."

George returned a few minutes later and instructed Angie to drive back to the mill. "The chief's on his way. I was right. He's madder than hell."

"At us?"

"We'll do for starters," he told her.

"Why? We didn't kill Cliff. We just found him."

"After last night, I think the chief would've preferred we let Cliff lie in repose at the mill until he gets Jenny's murder straightened out. Don't take that seriously because Roger's a good cop. It's just that he's never had a murder like this to deal with and now he's got two," George paused. "Angie, you better face up to the fact that it's going to look suspicious that you found another murder victim."

"Why?" she asked indignantly. "I only got here yesterday. I'd never even heard of Whispering Pines until a week ago. Does the chief think in seven short days, I put together a plot to kill off the population of the town, and along with them, my chance for a career in journalism?" Her voice trembled with indignation. "This is my big moment. My editor friend is considering me for a permanent job. This is what I want to do with the rest of my life, not write kids' articles about volcanoes and icebergs." On the verge of tears again, she fought to hold them back.

George reached over and lightly caressed the back of her neck. "Just watch what you say, okay? The chief's calling you *that writer woman* and he's not pleased you turned up in the wrong place again." There was truth in what he said. She was new in town and doing an extraordinarily good job of locating recently murdered townspeople. That had to look like more than a coincidence to the chief. It looked fishy to her, and she knew she didn't kill anybody. If she'd ever thought about killing somebody, it would've been her ex-husband.

Still under the wheel, Angie turned the car around and pulled onto the road back to the mill. What the hell, she thought. She gunned the Porsche, dodging potholes as nimbly as George had. He gave her a grin full of admiration. "Nice maneuvering, lady. Pull over at that clearing ahead. We don't want to run into our paper-kicking, gun-blasting enemy until the police get here."

They sat in the warm car waiting for the wail of sirens. "George, why were you so hell bent on seeing what Cliff was doing in the mill? Do you have a connection to him?"

"No connection. The truth is Cliff's always had a reputation for liking the ladies, although as far as I know he's never been caught. Since he was out here at an unusual hour, I thought I might catch him fooling around and discover who the mystery woman was."

Angie wrinkled her nose in disgust.

"Just hold on. There's another reason I'm interested in Cliff, more important and serious than fooling around..." George's sentence was interrupted by the sound of sirens rapidly approaching. "I'll tell you the rest later. I'm not going to mention my plan to spy on Cliff to the chief. I'll just say I swung by to check the mill. When I saw Cliff's SUV, I was concerned so we went inside to check. Caring neighbor kind of stuff. Okay? It'll look better for both of us.

"If Cliff had a girlfriend, and if she's the one who did him in, the chief will figure it out. I've learned one thing--being nosy can get you into a heap of trouble." In spite of the seriousness of the situation, Angie laughed. She knew all about being nosy.

Chapter Eight

A police car skidded to a stop in the cleared area. Chief Roger Byrd jumped out before the siren stopped screeching. "What the hell's going on, George? The dispatcher said you reported Cliff Schouten's dead." George reiterated the story of finding the mayor's lifeless body in the mill.

The chief interrupted, "Cliff dead? Nonsense. The EMS people are right behind me. They'll be able do something for him." Angie hoped they brought a long tube and a truck tanker full of blood if they planned to revive Cliff.

"Not likely," George said. "Cliff was shot, and I'm pretty sure he's dead. And, somebody took a shot at me while I was in the mill."

"What?" the chief said, bellowing. "You're telling me somebody shot Cliff and then took a shot at you? That's the damnedest thing I ever heard, George. If Cliff's dead, he probably died from a heart attack, and you probably heard a car backfire!"

"Cliff bled all over himself and the floor. People don't bleed when they have heart attacks," George said, snapping back at the chief. "I can't swear he was shot, but since somebody took a shot at me, I'm assuming... And, Roger, I know the difference between a gunshot and a backfire!" The chief's expression indicated he didn't believe a word about shots being fired.

"Let's go. Show me where Cliff is." Turning to Angie as he walked away, he said, "Okay, Miss, you stay here in the car where it's warm. As soon as the paramedics and my officers get here, point them toward the right building. Tell them to hurry too." Relieved not to have to go back into the mill, Angie assured the chief she'd be glad to direct the emergency people when they arrived.

"What on earth was Cliff doing out here on a Sunday morning?" The chief asked George as they started toward the mill. "Don't Cliff and Polly always go to church? For that matter, what're you doing out here with that writer woman?" George's voice trailed off as he explained he'd been helping Angie with her magazine article and wanted to check on the mill before his trolley run. The chief turned and gave Angie an accusing look that she was responsible for all current mayhem.

Two police cars, an ambulance, and several emergency vehicles with lights flashing and sirens blaring arrived in a speeding caravan. Angie stood at the edge of the clearing, motioning them toward the main mill building. The police cars stopped in the circle, but the four-wheel drives plowed through the snow to where Cliff's vehicle was parked. Grabbing their equipment, the paramedics swarmed into the building.

Angie was grateful to get inside the car out of the bitter cold. She started the car's engine, and the heater warmed the interior quickly. She sincerely hoped she wouldn't have to see the mayor's body again, but she expected the chief would have questions for her. She was certain he was grilling George now. After all, the two of them were suspects in Jenny's murder and had just stumbled over another dead body. In her case, stumbled being the operative word.

Angie heard another siren. It was a police car followed by Dr. Kate Mahoney. Angie got out of the car and pointed Kate toward the right building. The police car pulled in behind the other cars, but the doctor forced her four-wheel drive SUV through the snow and parked beside the increasing contingent of emergency vehicles. A male officer and a female officer caught up with her, and the three hurried inside the mill. If any more vehicles were expected, somebody had better call for a snowplow because the cleared area was full.

Angie waited twenty minutes before George and one of the policeman emerged from the building, talking earnestly as they walked. George opened Angie's door. The policeman introduced himself as Andy and addressed Angie. "The chief wants you to come inside, Ma'am." Having no choice, she got out of the warm car and, still wearing George's oversize boots, clomped between the two men into the building. She wanted to ask George what the chief asked him, but she suspected Andy wouldn't allow him to tell her. In fact Andy must've read her mind. "George, don't discuss the crime with Ms. Stephens until the chief okays it."

Andy led Angie to the place where the mayor's body lay in the little slant of sunlight. George followed behind her. Kate and the paramedics stood near the sliding door George opened earlier. The chief, partially blocking Angie's view of the body, stepped aside and asked her to look at the mayor. Angie steeled herself to be calm and composed. In spite of her efforts, she gasped.

The chief glanced at her feet, swimming in George's boots. "Those your boots and mittens I saw in the parking lot?" Angie nodded. "Mind telling me why you left them in the middle of the parking lot in the snow?" Fighting a queasy taste at the back of her throat, she detailed the events from the time she stumbled over Cliff's body to her horror at discovering her boots leached blood into the snow. During her meltdown, she threw her bloody boots and mittens away from her and the car.

"I didn't think you were trying to hide them since they're visible from out on the road. We'll collect them with the rest of the evidence. Let's get on with the rest of the questions. First of all, is this the way Cliff looked when you found him?"

Angie took a deep, steadying breath. "No. I tripped on something, and George opened the side door so we could see what was lying on the floor," she said pointing to where the paramedics stood. "The mayor was lying on his back, and I was looking straight down into his face." The chief asked what happened next. "I screamed, and George ran over and knelt beside Cliff for seconds or maybe minutes. I don't know how long and felt for a pulse. He told me he didn't feel anything and thought Cliff was dead."

"Then?"

"George didn't have his cell phone and told me to go to the car and call the police. He stayed here with Cliff."

"You both agree he was on his back when you found him. He's on his front now, but neither of you turned him over?"

Angie and George reaffirmed they didn't turn him.

"Maybe the person who shot at me waited until I ran out of the building and turned Cliff over. Maybe the killer was looking for something." The chief rolled his eyes at the mention of someone shooting at George. He apparently didn't accept that at all. Angie couldn't help him with that one. She didn't know if she believed it.

Turning back to Angie, the chief said, "Kate was leaving the hospital when the call came in. She came along to see if she could help. Doc, is there any chance Cliff was still alive and turned over by himself after George and Angie left the mill?" Angie wasn't a doctor, but she figured she could answer that one.

"No, Roger," Kate said. "He was hit in the chest at close range and suffered massive damage to the heart area. He didn't survive the gunshot."

The chief pursed his lips. "What time did you say you found Cliff?" he asked George.

"I don't know." George looked at Angie questioningly.

"About ten forty-five," she replied, explaining she knew because she glanced at the car clock when they pulled into the mill parking lot around ten-thirty.

"So, Kate, what time do you think Cliff died?"

"Angie and George's time line sounds right. I'd say Cliff died around ten-thirty, give or take. This probably won't help with your time line, Roger, but Cliff goes to Ben's Diner every morning for breakfast. Maybe Ben can tell you something about what he was doing."

"And you don't have any doubt he died from a gunshot?" the chief asked.

"No doubt at all."

The chief said to the doctor, "I guess we'll have to wait to see what the autopsy and forensics turn up. As soon as we finish processing the crime scene and the photographer gets here and takes photos, I'll send the body to the hospital. Appreciate you taking your time to come out here, Doc."

"No problem. Sorry I couldn't help. When the call came, I thought Cliff had another heart attack. I sure didn't expect to find him murdered. It's going to be tough on Polly. You going to tell her, Roger?"

The chief groaned. "No choice. As soon as we're finished here. George can come with me. He's good with people."

George clenched his fists. Good with people or not, this wasn't a message he wanted to deliver. Neither would Angie.

***

"Find anything?" the chief asked his officers, Andy and Brendan, after they completed an inspection of the premises.

"The other buildings don't look like anybody's been inside them for years. But this building where Cliff died has recent trash--take-out food bags, sandwich wrappers, paper cups. They're not left from back when workmen moved out the paper equipment. They don't look that old. Doesn't make sense. Nobody's worked here since then. I don't get who would've been here long enough to bring burgers and fries with them," Andy concluded.

"As far as I know, nobody's got any business out here. Plus, the buildings stay locked to keep teenagers from coming in here to screw," the chief said. "Anything else?"

"There's something out back that doesn't make sense either. I think you better take a look, Chief," Brendan suggested, leading the way. Angie and George trailed along to see what the officers discovered.

At the back of the building, the officers had propped open a door. "When we opened this door to let some light in, we found these," Brendan said, pointing to the ground. "Looks like there's been foot traffic in and out of here. We didn't disturb the tracks. It's pretty obvious they lead to the service road behind the Stop'n'Shop Supermarket. Seems pretty strange somebody would've parked over there and walked through knee-deep snow to come in the back of the mill. They could've saved themselves a lot of trouble by parking out front."

George spoke up, "Somebody didn't want to take a chance of having a vehicle seen here."

The chief stuck his head out the doorway and looked around. "No tracks going to the front of the building, so whoever it was entered through this door. No damage to the door. Must've had a key. We get reports of teenagers partying out here, but they wouldn't have parked on the service road and walked through the snow. From the trash they leave, we know they park out front in the clearing.

"Andy, when the photographer gets here, I want him to take some close ups of these tracks. Have forensics examine them too. They may not get anything out of them, but it's worth a chance. After everybody finishes, you and Brendan follow the tracks. Look for anything that might've been dropped along the way. When you get to the service road, take a good look there too. Maybe we'll get lucky and match some tracks."

The sound of footsteps echoing in the hollow building announced the arrival of the anticipated photographer. After instructing her, the chief turned to George. "Okay. Let's go, buddy. I need your help on this one. Polly likes you. It'll help her to have you there when I tell her about Cliff."

George let out a defeated sigh. "I'll go out of fondness for Polly, but my being there won't help. This news is going to kill her." George started toward the front door. "Let's get it over with. Come on, Angie. We'll follow you, Roger."

"You can drop me off at the Lantern Inn," Angie told George when they got into the car.

"No way. You don't get off that easily. You're part of this deal as much as I am. Besides, Roger and I may need a woman's help."

"I think it'd be better if you got one of Polly's relatives or friends. I'm sure she'd prefer someone she knows to a stranger."

"First of all, we don't have time to try to track anybody down. It's Sunday, and they're asleep, at church or out eating," George said. "All these sirens are going to make the town mighty curious, and word's going to start spreading. We've got to get to Polly before she begins hearing bits and pieces. She needs a first-hand account from you, Roger and me. At least, what little we know at this point. Besides, you're not a stranger. You said you met Polly and Cliff last night."

"Yeah. For about two minutes. George..."

"We're here." George pulled in behind the police chief who was already halfway out of his car.

The chief opened Angie's door and handed her purse to her. "You dropped this inside the mill. Nothing to do with Cliff's murder." Angie inspected it for blood or other gross stuff stuck to the leather. No worse for its ordeal than a little trash she flicked off.

Reluctantly, Angie walked up the sidewalk, lagging behind the chief and George. Wearing George's boots made her feel awkward and poorly outfitted for the occasion. But even proper dress wouldn't improve this situation. Any way you looked at it, they were bearers of devastating news. Here to tell Polly her husband had been murdered.

The mayor's Victorian house looked like it had been plucked off the cover of a travel brochure, fresh snowfall included. With a white picket fence and inviting porch, the house looked like the last place violence would intrude.

Polly, dressed in Sunday church clothes, answered the door right away. Worry lines on her forehead deepened when she saw the three of them. She blurted out, "Oh, no! Did Cliff have another heart attack?" With tears forming in her eyes, she looked from the chief to George to Angie, waiting for confirmation.

George moved to Polly's side and put his arm around her shoulder. "We've got bad news, Polly. Cliff's dead," he told her in a tender voice.

"Dead? No!"

"It's true, Polly. It happened out at the old paper mill."

Through tears, Polly's expression changed from sad to confused, "What? Cliff had a heart attack at the mill?"

The chief gave Polly a brief accounting of what happened, including the news that Cliff had been shot. "He was shot deliberately," the chief added for clarification.

"Why would anybody shoot Cliff? There's a mistake." Polly asked, her voice wobbling.

"Polly, I know this is hard to take in. I was out at the mill and saw the murder scene with my own eyes, and I can barely believe it," George told her.

Angie sensed Polly was verging on hysteria. "Can we call a friend or family to come and be with you?" Polly composed herself long enough to recite her cousin's phone number. Trembling, she flopped down on the sofa.

Nicely dressed, she wore a pricey burgundy suit and gold jewelry. Comparably pricey two-tone tan suede knee boots completed her outfit. A tan wool coat lay draped over the back of a chair with purse and gloves neatly laid out on the cushion. Polly was ready to leave for church except her escort failed to show up. In fact, he wouldn't show up ever again.

George stepped into the kitchen and made the call on Polly's land phone. "--yes, Lillian, I said Cliff is dead--no--not a heart attack--shot--"

He repeated parts of the brief facts. Apparently Lillian was too shocked to accept the horrific news. When George returned to the group in the hallway, the chief was questioning Polly about when she last saw Cliff.

Angie visualized Cliff's movements as Polly filled in the timeline. "Cliff's an early riser, but I like to sleep late on the weekend so he got up this morning at six o'clock, his usual time, got dressed and went to town. He eats breakfast at Ben's Diner every day. He likes to read the paper and talk to the usual crowd that gathers there." Kate, the doctor, had said that too. "When he's finished, he goes to his office and works," Polly added.

"The mayor's office?" Angie asked.

"No. His professional office. Cliff's an optometrist," Polly explained. "On weekend mornings, he likes to catch up on checking new glasses and..."

"A quiet time to work," Angie added. Polly smiled vaguely at Angie for finishing her sentence. Taking advantage of having Polly's attention and her tenuous composure, Angie asked, "When we arrived, you were certain something had happened to Cliff. Why was that?"

"The sight of the three of you meant bad news. You see, I was already worried about Cliff. He had a bad heart attack a year ago. When he was overdue coming home to leave for church, I got uneasy. Cliff's terribly punctual. I waited here by the phone expecting to hear from him any minute, telling me he was on his way home. I got so worked up, I didn't leave the house, even to run outside and get the paper. Afraid I'd miss his call. You see, Cliff uses landlines because he can hear better on real phones. A little hearing loss," she said, pointing to her ear.

"Did you call anyone trying to find him?" George asked.

"Oh, yes. I called the diner first, but Ben hadn't seen him since early morning. I called his office too and left messages, multiple times, but he didn't pick up. He doesn't like to take calls when he's working."

"Sounds like Cliff put in a lot of overtime," George commented. Polly volunteered that not only did Cliff work weekend mornings but some evenings as well. George raised his eyebrows at Angie.

Talking about daily routines calmed Polly. Angie ventured a question. "Can you think of any reason why Cliff went out to the old mill?"

"No. Not unless he went out to check on it. Sometimes locals call him if they see cars or people hanging around out there."

"Polly, do you have a key for Cliff's office? We'll need to search it."

"Oh, no," she replied. "Cliff didn't allow me to intrude in his professional business. He was adamant about handling his practice by himself."

"Polly," Roger said, "What did you do all morning? From the time you got up until we showed up? You said you didn't leave the house. Didn't you go anywhere looking for Cliff? In short, can you verify your whereabouts before we got here?"

"I did normal Sunday morning things-- straightening up, getting dressed, and waiting for Cliff to walk through the door any minute. When he was overdue, I started calling his office and leaving messages. I thought if he was there, he'd realize from the number of times I called that I needed to talk to him. I didn't go anywhere. Like I said, I didn't even go outside to get the paper."

"Did you talk to anybody else or see anybody?"

"No. Just the one call to the diner. Oh, my sister in Providence called me. We didn't talk long because I was waiting to hear from Cliff. We cut it short."

Roger asked for her sister's phone number and wrote it down. Angie noted that Roger was thorough in his interrogation.

The front door opened and Polly's cousin, Lillian, arrived. Polly fell into her arms sobbing. Roger, George and Angie retreated. Relieved at Lillian's arrival, Angie hurried down the sidewalk, barely able to hold back her own tears of compassion for Polly.

Angie and George stood with Roger beside his police car. "I'm going to have a talk with Ben and see if he remembers when Cliff was at the diner. Like Kate said, it was probably too early to do us any good, but it'll help fill in his movements this morning. If you two think of anything else you saw at the paper mill, call me. In the meantime, don't discuss the case. Before you go, I need an accounting of your movements this morning so I can verify them. Did you go anyplace other than Fitzgerald's Café and Nev's greenhouses?" Apparently, George had already told Roger about those. Angie added that they rode around town a short time before going out to the mill.

"I almost forgot," George added. "I've been to the greenhouses twice this morning. One of the alarms went off at five o'clock and Clarice, as usual, called me to go see what was wrong. Nev showed up about six to start packing flowers. He was behind schedule. Because of Jenny's death, he didn't get back to the greenhouse to pack them last night. So while he packed, I put the boxes in the van and made a couple of deliveries for him."

"A burglar alarm?" Angie asked.

"Nothing so exciting. A heater shut off and the temperature dropped enough to set off an alarm. The computer program for the heaters has a glitch in it. I got it working on my first trip at daylight and checked it again when you were with me. I hope it doesn't trigger the alarm again tonight. I need my beauty sleep. I'm about dead." Angie added another job to his resume, alarm repairman.

Since George had been out and about in the wee hours, could he have gone to the mill too? Did he have anything to do with Cliff's murder?

Roger had a few more questions. "For the record, George, did you see anybody while you were out the first time? What I really mean, did anybody see you?"

"Sure. I stopped by the Pine Tree Inn, Green Gables Inn and let's see... Oh, yeah, I stopped at the Lantern Inn, but I didn't see anybody there. I just stuck the flowers in the service entrance. Then my last stop was the parcel office to ship a load of flowers."

"Did anybody see you at the first two inns?" George replied the front desk clerk at the Pine Tree and a kitchen worker at Green Gables. And, of course, Charlie at the parcel shipping office.

"Okay, we'll check them out. You making the trolley run today?" George replied he was.

The chief asked Angie if she'd been anywhere before meeting George for breakfast. She shook her head, gave him her cell phone number if he had more questions and let him know she'd be walking around town gathering material for her article.

She hoped, instead of questions, the chief would call to say he'd solved both murders, and she and George were off the hook.

Chapter Nine

George pulled into a convenience store parking lot. "Man, I need a cup of coffee. It seems like a week since breakfast. I'll run in and get us a couple of coffees, and then we'll find a quiet out-of-the-way place to talk." George got out of the car but leaned toward Angie and spoke before he shut the door. "We need to level with each other. This is deadly business and, like it or not, we're in the middle of it, together." He was right. She'd held back and suspected he had too. She had doubts about sharing, but maybe it was the sensible thing to do.

***

George drove a block from the main drag and parked on a side street. Angie took the lid off her coffee, added two sweeteners and relished the first sip. Coffee hit the spot. Angie glanced around and understood why he'd chosen this place. The buildings in the area housed professional offices so it was quiet on Sunday. "Well, Miss Angie, where shall we begin?"

"For one thing, why the surprised look on your face when Polly was telling us about Cliff's extra work hours? What gives?"

"Remember out at the mill, I told you Cliff might be up to monkey business? In Whispering Pines, everybody keeps up with everybody else's business, but Cliff got away with fooling around with women without ever getting caught. Lots of talk but no sightings. When Polly told us about Cliff working weekend mornings and late evenings, it hit me that he did it in his office, right under our noses.

"I'm sure Cliff didn't have so much business that he had to work those extra hours. To begin with, Whispering Pines isn't very big so there's only so much eye business here. Besides, a lot of people go to malls where glasses are cheaper. When the police get around to going through his accounts, I bet Cliff was just barely making ends meet. Polly's the one with the big bucks." George took a long drink of coffee. "By the way, Cliff's office is in that building."

Angie's head swiveled. "Which building?"

"The two-story red brick building." George pointed across the street. "Cliff has the first floor and an architect has the second. In the back, there's a parking lot and entrance."

"Can we drive around back?" Angie asked.

George put the car in gear and pulled out of the parking place. He made a left at the first intersection and another left down an alley. Halfway down the alley, he turned left into a small parking lot immediately behind Cliff's building. "No wonder Cliff did his fooling around here," Angie said, checking out the area. "This is perfect. Pine trees surround the parking lot. It's like a secret place." The tree branches blocked Angie's view of the windows in adjacent buildings, so chances were people looking out couldn't see the parking lot. "Even someone driving down the alley couldn't see cars parked in the lot. Give Cliff credit for finding the perfect hideaway."

George pulled the car into one of the parking places. "And to cover his absences from home, he bluffed Polly into believing he's an overworked optometrist."

"Wouldn't you love to go in and take a look?" Angie said. George asked what she thought she'd find.

"I don't know. Records? Appointment books? Something that proves Cliff was using his office for romantic rendezvous purposes. The reason you dragged me into the mill was to catch him with a woman and find out who she was, right?"

"Not exactly but... Hop out of the car." George had a mischievous glint to his eye.

Cutting edge investigative journalism was what she wanted, so she might as well go for it.

"How do you propose we get in? I'm sure the doors are locked nice and tight. I doubt there's a convenient key tucked under the doormat. Polly doesn't even have a key. Do you plan to knock the door down?"

"Of course not. I'm exceptionally mechanically inclined. If I can't open a seventy-year-old lock... Shall we go?"

"Why not?" If George could open the door, which Angie doubted, it would only take a few minutes to look around. Then her good sense kicked in. "Hold on a minute. Maybe this is carrying your interest in Cliff's love life just a bit too far. You're in kinky territory."

"Nonsense. Cliff's love life is intriguing, but something a lot more serious is going on than fooling around, and I think our old buddy Cliff was up to his steely blue eyeballs in it. Considering Cliff's sudden and bullet-assisted demise, I think there was a falling out among thieves, not lovers. Let's hustle while the police are tied up at the paper mill."

Angie had to run a few steps to catch up with him. By the time she reached him, he was already manipulating the door lock with a thin knife blade. To her surprise, the lock clicked. George opened the door, and they were in Cliff's office. The waiting room was typical of doctors' offices, coordinated sofas and chairs and accessories in soothing colors.

Once she was inside Cliff's office, Angie expected to be scared, but she wasn't. She was excited. This was the kind of adventure she'd dreamed about as a college journalism major. Snooping. Uncovering critical information. Putting clues together to come up with answers. That's what journalism was all about. Except for the breaking and entering part. That wasn't covered in any of her courses. "You don't think Roger will come here to search?"

"Not yet. He's got his hands full at the mill. Besides, he can't get a search warrant for Cliff's office today so he'll have to put off this search until tomorrow. Judge Rothschild's in Boston this weekend for his baby granddaughter's christening, and he won't be back until tomorrow to issue a warrant. Nothing to worry about."

"We might as well skip the waiting room," Angie said. "Too public. Cliff wouldn't keep anything incriminating here."

As they walked past the dark examining room, George muttered, "If these walls could talk..."

"What does that mean?" Angie asked.

"I told you there were rumors that Cliff liked the ladies. Well, this is no rumor. It's true. Cliff liked teenage girls too." A queasy feeling crept into Angie's tummy as George pointed toward the dark examining room. "When I was in high school, a girl who was a close friend of mine told me that while she was alone in that room with Cliff having her eyes checked, he took her hand and pressed it against his crotch."

"Oh, my gosh, George, that's disgusting! What did the poor girl do?"

"She was naive and unsuspecting and didn't realize for a few seconds what was going on. But when she figured out where her hand was, she jerked it back and bolted out the door."

"Good for her. Was anything done about it?"

"No. She was too embarrassed to tell anybody besides me. We were like brother and sister. Shared all our secrets with each other. And it wouldn't have done any good for her to report it. That kind of thing wasn't taken seriously then. Cliff would've denied it, and that would've been the end of it."

"Thank goodness times have changed. Don't you wonder how many times he tried it with other girls?"

"Probably a lot. Got away with it too. I'm sure any other girls were like my friend, too ashamed to tell anyone, felt like it was their fault." That was true. Angie remembered a friend who was touched by an older man, and she was afraid to tell anyone.

"Let's divide the room. I'll take this half with the filing cabinets," Angie said.

"Okay. Look for Cliff's personal files and Winter Carnival Committee records dealing with their funds," George told Angie. "Grants and profits from the carnival have allegedly disappeared. Big sums of money."

"What does that have to do with Cliff's murder?"

"Cliff was treasurer. His hand was closest to the till."

Angie quickly went through the drawers. "These are patient files. Wouldn't his staff have access to these? Doesn't seems like a good place to store anything secretive." She moved on.

George tried a plain, inconspicuous door labeled *Inventory* that led off from the lab where Cliff checked–glasses. The door was locked, but George opened it in seconds with his knife blade. He wasn't kidding when he said he was mechanical.

"Holy crap! Cliff made himself a little love nest," George said. He took Angie's hand, tugging her into a small, nicely decorated bedroom with an attached neat bathroom. This was not the kind of room a busy eye doctor threw together to catch a well-deserved nap. Nothing haphazard about this room. It was intended for entertaining. Although the room was immaculate, a rumpled, unmade bed gave testament to its use.

"Start on that side of the room. If he hid anything, it's in this room. He wouldn't keep secret stuff in the office where a staff member might stumble across it." George found a couple of clean cloths in Cliff's workroom. "Wrap these around your hands. You don't want to leave fingerprints. It'd look bad if the chief found your prints and thought Cliff lured you into his web during the few days you've been in Whispering Pines," George said with a twinkle in his eye. Angie made a *Yuk* face. "It'll be interesting if any of the prints in here are identified. Like if some of the local ladies have to explain what they were doing in Cliff's private boudoir."

Angie thought George was enjoying this too much. He was way over the edge of kinky. George picked the lock on a cabinet and exclaimed, "Uh, oh, Angie, look at this, DVDs with handwritten labels. These didn't come from Red Box. Looks like Cliff recorded his romantic escapades and wrote the woman's first name on the label. Maybe I spoke too soon when I said he wasn't killed in a lover's quarrel. If one of his girlfriends found out about these, she might've been mad enough to put a bullet in him."

Angie backed away from the DVDs as cautiously as if the cabinet was filled with striking rattlesnakes. She hoped George wouldn't play them, but he was already inserting one into the player. Angie didn't want to watch, but the erotic scene mesmerized her. The male was undoubtedly Cliff, but Angie didn't recognize the female. George's pop-eyes said he did. He stopped the DVD after a few minutes, put it back in its labeled case and inserted it into its proper spot. "I got an idea," George said, rifling through the other videos.

"What's that?" Angie asked, reluctant to ask and reluctant to hear the answer.

"This one says *Jenny*. What you want to bet its Jenny Harden?" he asked, inserting the disc into the player and pushing Play. Although Angie had only seen Jenny in death, she had no doubt the woman on the screen was the same person. The real-life graphic sex scene that took place on the bed was hard to watch. What a bastard Cliff was. Jenny, happy and passionate, responded to Cliff's lovemaking. As Angie watched the video, she couldn't help noticing Cliff was considerably more animated in bed than when she met him at the Lantern Inn.

"Do you think Jenny knew she was being recorded?" Angie asked.

"Not likely. A married woman with a lot to lose wouldn't knowingly let herself end up in a porn video." His answer made sense.

"What if Adam found out about Jenny and Cliff?" she asked.

"I think his motive for killing both of them trumps anybody else's."

"Of course, it could've been one of Cliff's other women. Maybe one of them found out about Jenny and was jealous." Angie dropped the suggestion. It wasn't nearly as good as Adam's motive.

"Let's put the videos back where we found them. If Roger finds them, he can figure it out. I hope he doesn't have to make them public though. It's going to wreck some marriages and lives." George was quiet. "But I guess these women should've thought twice before they got involved with Cliff. The person who'll be most hurt is Polly. She'll be humiliated in front of the whole town."

"You don't think she ever suspected anything?"

"No. Polly's sweet and fun to be around, and she'd do anything to help anybody, but she's not got much on the ball. She has a ton of money, but her daddy made it, not her. He was one sharp old man, but frankly Polly didn't get her daddy's smarts."

George focused his attention on the wall. "You know, I think the examining room is on the other side of that wall. I'm going to take a quick look. Be right back. Keep looking."

Angie did as she was told. She rummaged through drawers and ran cloth-coated hands around nooks and crannies. She didn't know what she was looking for and wouldn't know if she found it.

George was back a few minutes later. "Well, I was right. Cliff mounted a video camera on the other side of this wall in the examination room. It blends in with all those eye-examining machines and looks like it belongs there. Only difference, there's a nice little hole in the wall with the camera aimed through it at the bed. What a low life! Since the camera's hidden, I'd bet Jenny didn't know she was being recorded."

Angie felt queasy. She already knew more about Cliff's sex life than she wanted, and the more she learned, the sleazier it got. She tried to put the memory of those few minutes of video out of her mind and concentrate on finding whatever it was George thought Cliff was doing besides screwing half the town.

Worry about the police catching her nibbled at Angie. Her friend and editor of *American Scene*, Ted, would never forgive her if she got arrested while she was working on an article for his magazine. It went without saying he'd never hire her to write for him again. Of course, that wouldn't matter because she'd be in jail and unavailable for assignments anyway. Why did she get into this?

Before she figured out the answer, her hand touched a loose piece of board in the back of a cabinet drawer. She tugged at it until it jerked free. Grasping the object lodged behind the board, she pulled out a manila envelope. "George, come here. I think I found something. Cliff went to some trouble to hide this. It didn't stuff itself behind this board."

George hustled over and opened the envelope. "Good job, Angie. You're a first-class burglar. Put the board back like you found it, and come see what I found."

Angie forced the board into place at the back of the drawer and followed George into a closet. "Squat down so you can see better," he told her. Angie obeyed, wondering what perverted sense of adventure prompted her to suggest breaking into the office of a lecherous optometrist who got himself murdered that morning. What was she doing watching his porn videos, rummaging through his files and squatting in his closet with a man she barely knew?

George pointed to an open safe filled with stacks of cash. "Good Lord," Angie said.

"You said Cliff was just getting by in his optometrist practice. Looks to me like he was doing pretty good."

"Cliff didn't make this kind of money checking eyes. It came from someplace else. Knowing about this cash and what's in the envelope will give us answers to a lot of questions."

Angie heard sirens. They made her nervous, considering she was guilty of breaking and entering, tampering with evidence and who knew what else.

"The police cars are busy running back and forth to the mill. They won't search Cliff's office until tomorrow."

While George was tidying up evidence of searching Cliff's vulgar office, Angie, still worried about getting caught, opened the outside door to listen. The sirens were louder and getting closer.

"George," she yelled, "the police are coming this way! What should we do?"

He ran to the door and handed her the car keys. "Get the car out of the parking lot and go back the alley the way we came in. Turn left at the first stop sign. Remember, turn left. Go up the street out of sight and wait for me."

Angie ran to the Porsche, started it, put the car into reverse, turned around and shot out of the parking lot. Slow down, she told herself. Don't attract attention. She turned left and found herself on a quiet side street with stately homes set well back from the road. She pulled over and stopped, choosing to park under a clump of trees that seemed to partially hide the car. She willed George to hurry. She felt exposed and vulnerable.

The passenger door opened and George, breathing heavily, collapsed onto the seat. "Take off," he told her. Resisting the impulse to gun the engine, Angie forced herself to drive at an acceptable speed for a residential street on Sunday. The last thing she needed was somebody calling the police to report a speeding silver Porsche. How hard would that be to track down in a small town like Whispering Pines? "Turn left at the next street. That'll put us back in town. I've got to get ready for work. What are your plans? Where do you want me to drop you off?"

Pooped, Angie said, "The Lantern Inn. For a nap."

"I wish I could join you," George replied. Did he mean he wanted to take a nap in general or with her in particular? She glanced at him, but his face, looking straight ahead, didn't answer her question.

Besides, she had another bone to pick. "George, we almost got caught in Cliff's office. You said Roger couldn't get a search warrant because the judge was in Boston at his granddaughter's christening. You said..."

"Chill, Angie. I know what I said. I'm sorry. Roger must've figured out some other way to get a search warrant. In this day of electronic communications, who knows?"

"You said you knew! Silly me thought you knew what you were talking about. Remember what I'm supposed to be doing here? Writing a sweet little winter carnival story but, guess what, I'm driving a getaway car!" She laughed at the incredulity of what she said. She was irritated at George for almost getting her arrested, but she had to admit, breaking into Cliff's office was the most exciting thing she'd done in years or maybe in her whole life. She needed to be zapped out of her complacency, and Whispering Pines had delivered one bolt after another.

"Here's a flash for you. I don't want to get caught either. I got my reputation to protect."

Angie ignored him. She doubted he had any reputation to protect.

"What did you do with the manila envelope I found in Cliff's drawer?" she asked. "That was my big discovery. I hope you didn't leave it behind."

"No way. It's zipped securely inside my jacket. This is what I came for," he said patting his chest. "I hope you don't mind, but I'm going to drop you off at the back entrance of the Lantern. I don't want to run into Clarice. If she sees me, she'll know I'm late for the trolley run and jump all over me with both feet."

"Wait a minute. How am I going to get in? Are you going to pick the lock of the back door of the Lantern too?"

"Don't need to. It's daytime. The door's unlocked." George gave Angie a quick tutorial how to navigate the inn's hallways and service stairs to get to her room. "Clarice annexed houses adjacent to the Lantern to triple the number of guest rooms and add passageways for the staff to get around without being intrusive. You'll be fine."

As soon as Angie stopped the car, he promptly came around to take over driving. She couldn't believe she was sneaking in the back door of the hotel where she was a paying guest so a trolley driver wouldn't get caught for being late for his run to the train station.

Before he got in the car, he told her, "If I don't have a heart attack from chasing after you in a speeding car all day, I'm going to the greenhouse when I get back from the trolley run and make photocopies of these documents we borrowed from Cliff's office. I want to return the originals as soon as things cool down over there."

Angie asked why the greenhouse. "Nev leaves about six to come to the Lantern for dinner and dessert. I can have the place all to myself and use his photocopy machine. I don't dare take these to one of the commercial photocopy places. I don't want anybody to see what's in this envelope, and I especially don't want anybody to see me with it. Plus, photocopies are free at the greenhouse." Angie asked when he was taking the envelope back to Cliff's office. "I don't know yet. I'll wait for the right time. Then I'll slip in and out like a cat burglar," he joked, wiggling his fingers wickedly at her.

"George, this is serious. A man was murdered today."

"Indeed. And somebody took a shot at me. Remember? I could be lying beside Cliff right now dreading for Kate's colleagues to begin my post-mortem." Angie didn't share his autopsy humor. She didn't want George to be dead.

"Roger may already wonder if we're the guilty parties who coaxed Cliff out to the mill and offed him. He just might figure we reported his murder to take the suspicion away from us and conclude we broke into Cliff's office to destroy incriminating evidence. Seems like a solid case against us to me."

"Except we don't have a motive. I've always known Cliff was a sleaze ball. If I ever thought about taking him out, it was when he made his sick move on my friend. You just got here, what motive could you have? Don't worry about getting caught. As long as Cliff got away using that alley and parking lot for his escapades, we should have no trouble getting away with being there once. Try to get some rest. I'll be in touch." With that, he sped away. One thing for sure, George looked a whole lot better behind the wheel of a silver convertible than he did driving the *Sleigh Bells Express*.

Angie stood listening to the sound of the car's powerful engine. Her father would've loved that car

Chapter Ten

Caught in the clutches of a vivid nightmare, Angie heard a man's voice calling her name. In near hysteria, she popped up to a sitting position, convinced Cliff caught her prowling during a snoop visit to his office. He pointed a pistol at her head.

At such close range, he couldn't miss hitting her. Poor Caroline and Jonathan wouldn't have a mother, and she wouldn't get to see them graduate from college. And sweet Chaucer. He wouldn't have anybody to take care of him and would have to fend for himself. Poor kitty.

But the voice belonged to George, not to the villain threatening to pump her full of bullets. Angie summoned him, "Help me, George! Break the door down!"

When Angie awakened enough to identify her surroundings, she was in her room at the Lantern

Inn, not in Cliff's office. No Cliff. No pistol. And it was George who hovered over her. "You okay, Angie?"

"No. I'm not okay." She broke into tears. George sat down on the side of the bed and put his arms around her, holding her close to him.

"What happened?"

"I had the nightmare from hell. Cliff caught me searching his secret bedroom. He was so hateful and kept saying I wasn't a journalist. He said awful things about Polly too. I thought you were in Cliff's lab calling my name. I was screaming for you to save me. Oh, my gosh, I can't stop shaking."

"You're okay. I'm here," he said stroking her hair. "Cliff's dead. He can't hurt you."

"Are you back from the trolley run?"

"I got back a little early and decided to check on you. Lucky me. I got here just in time to rescue you," he said, flashing a sweet smile.

Angie regained some of her composure, but she made no effort to move away. She liked the way his arms held her, strong and confident. She liked the way he smelled, clean and masculine. She liked the way he looked, even if he was wearing that silly coachman's outfit. Sans monster stovepipe hat. Thank goodness.

George gently put his hand on her cheek and tilted her face toward his. For the first time in years, Angie wanted a man, this man, to kiss her. And he did. Soft, gentle kisses exploring her lips.

Angie's arms automatically embraced him, and she eagerly responded to this kiss and the next one.

She snuggled against George's chest and closed her eyes to capture the memory of this moment with this man. Whatever happened or didn't happen with him in the following days, she didn't ever want to forget the desire she felt for him right now. She wanted him more than she'd ever wanted any man. Part-time jobs and all.

George spoke softly, "Angie, I hate like hell to break this up, but I've got to get going. Lord knows I'd love to spend the rest of the evening holding you in my arms, but I need to take the envelope from Cliff's office over to the greenhouse to copy the contents. By the time I get cleaned up and changed, Nev ought to be leaving to come here to the inn."

Was it that late? Between her dream-induced near death standoff with Cliff and her fantasy-come-to-life kissing session with George, she didn't have any idea what time it was. "I wish you didn't have to leave."

"Me, too, but I don't want to get caught with these documents." When Angie threw the covers back to get out of bed, George said, "Do you sleep in your clothes? Frankly, I liked those pjs you had on last night."

"I only sleep in my clothes on days when I trip over dead bodies and break into lewd optometrists' offices. It's a wonder I didn't keep my shoes on."

At that, George glanced under Angie's bed and reached to retrieve his boots she'd put on after throwing her bloody boots in the snow. "Maybe I better take these with me. What will people say?" he asked, pretending to be shocked. "For my part, I like the looks of my shoes under your bed."

In spite of her wariness, she liked George. He was fun and exciting and sexy, and he was some kind of good kisser. She, too, would like his shoes under her bed.

"Hey, George, hold on a second. Just for the record, how did you get in my room? I'm sure I locked the door."

"You have to ask, my partner in crime?"

"You mean you picked the lock?"

"Well, it was more subtle than knocking the door down as you were loudly demanding. I thought something awful was happening to you."

Angie remembered screaming for George to knock the door down and save her, but always in her dreams, she was never able to make a sound. "You could hear me?"

"Everybody on this floor could hear you and probably in the basement and attic too. You were screaming to the top of your lungs. I didn't want anybody to call the police so I let myself in to see what was wrong with you."

"Oh, my gosh. I guess having a woman scream for you to break her door down doesn't help your reputation."

"To the contrary, my dear. Makes me sound studly!"

"Are you ever serious?"

"I try not to be," he said seriously. He was serious about not being serious?

"Anyway, thanks for saving me from Cliff. That dream was too real." Trying not to sound overly hopeful, she asked, "Are you working at dessert tonight?"

"No rest for the weary. Clarice will have no sympathy for the rough day I've had, which started at five o'clock at Nev's greenhouse."

Before he left, worry lines clouded his face, and he asked, "You sure you're okay now?" She was definitely okay. She was better than okay. He gave her a soft, sweet kiss on the lips and let himself out the door.

Bone-weary, Angie fell back in bed. Her nap had done nothing to rest her. Being accused, threatened and almost shot by Cliff wiped out the effects of resting.

Drifting and dozing, Angie enjoyed a half-sleep until a knock on the door woke her. Groggily, she made her way to the door where Scott stood with his face screwed up. "Hey, I just saw George in the kitchen, and he told me a little of what happened today. Are you okay?"

"Sort of. You got time to come in?" she asked. Angie kept coming back to Scott as the most likely confidante of her few acquaintances. His youthful age seemed to eliminate him from Whispering Pines' lethal middle-aged romantic entanglements.

"Yeah, sure, I'm off duty for a while. News about Cliff has spread like wildfire through town. I was worried about you." She appreciated his concern. She and Scott took the same chairs they occupied the night before. Angie clicked on the fireplace, feeling chilly now that she was out of bed.

"Scott, I know something about Jenny I didn't tell the chief, and I desperately need to confide in somebody. I had a reason, maybe not a good one, for not mentioning it so I don't know how to tell the chief now."

"I'm good at keeping secrets. I'll try to help," Scott said. "How could you know anything about Jenny? I thought you said you didn't know her or anybody else here."

Angie told Scott everything about her eavesdropping episode and recording it. "I told the chief about hearing a man ranting at a crying woman in the linen room less than an hour before I found Jenny's body. The reason I opened the door from the library was curiosity about the room. It doesn't make sense a woman sobbed her brains out, and a second one got strangled in the same room in such a short time. Too much of a coincidence."

"Yeah. But Angie, why didn't you just tell Roger you recorded a man yelling at a woman around the time Jenny was killed? Why keep it a secret?"

"Last night I was too embarrassed. But it keeps gnawing at me. I haven't listened to my recorder yet so I don't know if it picked up anything. But if it did, it might help the police identify Jenny's killer."

"You got it here?" Scott asked.

"It's in the drawer."

"Do you want me to listen to it with you? See if there's anything on it?"

"Okay, I'll get it."

Angie retrieved the recorder from a purse in her dresser drawer and pressed *Play*. Nothing happened. She cranked up the volume. After a few moments of silence, a man's voice exploded in the room. Angie and Scott jumped from its loudness and venom. Scott grabbed it and turned down the volume. Angie rubbed her neck to ease a minor case of whiplash. The man's hateful words flowed from the recorder. The woman's sobbing rose and fell in the background. Angie could barely endure listening to that despicable diatribe again. She knew the answer to one question--her recorder had done its stuff.

Scott sat with his head bowed, his face in shadows. When the recorder stopped, he looked up at Angie, eyes wide open. "I'll be damned," he said, almost in a whisper.

She tried to read his face, afraid he was going to name the sexy trolley driver. "Is it George?" She could barely wait for his answer and, at the same time, she couldn't bear for it to be George.

Scott's expression changed from astonished to puzzled. "George? Why would you think it's George?"

Angie explained about finding George in the library, standing at the side door to the linen room right after Jenny was killed. "He wasn't in the library when I went in, and he didn't come though the hall doors. He just kind of magically appeared."

"Hell, that doesn't mean anything. He helped set up dessert, checked everything and probably took a little nap on a sofa until you came in and woke him up."

"Napping when he was supposed to be working?"

"He does it all the time. We all grab a little snooze or hide from Clarice when we get caught up. If she saw us with nothing to do... But I give her credit, she works harder than anybody."

"The man on the recorder isn't George. Positively. Absolutely. No doubt." Scott said. "But I know who it is."

"Hell, Scott, out with it."

"Cliff Schouten. Whispering Pines' honorable mayor who isn't so honorable." Angie asked if he was sure. "That I am. I heard him yell like that once. When I was about ten, we kids were doing some batting practice in the street, and a ball hit his car. It didn't dent it or anything, but Cliff let loose on us. Sounded just like he did on that recorder. Hearing him yell makes me want to grab my catcher's mitt and go home as fast as my legs will move," Scott said laughing. "I kept my distance from the mayor after that. Put your mind at ease, Angie. That's not George's voice."

"I'm so relieved. I didn't want George to be the yelling man. How do you suggest I get this tape to the chief? It'll clear George and me of any involvement in Jenny's death."

"Here, I'll dial the chief's number for you, and you can tell him what you have." Roger was out so Angie left a message for him to call on her cell ASAP.

"If I'd given the recorder to the chief last night, Cliff might be alive."

"None of this is your fault. It was in motion before you got here. You arrived just in time for the explosion."

"I hope you're right. There's something else, Scott. George and I discovered today that Cliff and Jenny were having an affair."

"What? Cliff and Jenny?" Scott asked, his mouth and eyes wide open. Angie assured him they were deeply involved, but she didn't say how she knew. "I've heard gossip about Cliff screwing around. But with Jenny? She's like the perfect wife," Scott said, rubbing his forehead in disbelief. "I don't get it. Even if Cliff and Jenny were fooling around, what could go so wrong that he got angry enough to kill her? Are you sure about the romance?"

Angie assured him she was. "I'll fill you in on the details later."

"Okay. I'll take your word for it," he told her. "New subject. What were you and George doing at the old mill when you found Cliff?"

"George showed me around town to help with my magazine article, and then he said he wanted to check the old mill. Something about people seeing lights that shouldn't be there. When we arrived, George got over-the-top interested in why Cliff's SUV was parked there on a Sunday morning. It was George's idea to go inside. He hinted Cliff might be with a woman."

"Instead of being with a woman, you found him dead. You think it's related to Jenny?"

"It seems probable. He and Jenny had a connection."

Scott looked at his watch. "I gotta go. I'm late going back on duty. Clarice'll be doing a room search for me."

Angie was glad she didn't work at the inn. Her hotel maid job years ago had been bad enough, but those expectations were nothing like Clarice's.

Chapter Eleven

Angie lay down again to rest, drifting between daydreaming and dozing. Nightmares about Cliff shooting her were blessedly replaced by sexy images of George kissing her.

She glanced at the clock expecting it to be time to get dressed for dessert, but it was only seven-thirty. She drifted off again. No need for her to hurry and get there a half-hour early like last night. That hadn't turned out well.

Her cell phone rang, interrupting her pleasant interlude. She answered on the second ring, expecting to hear Jonathan or Caroline. "Hey, Angie, how's it going?" boomed the affectionate voice of the editor of *American Scene* magazine, Ted Merrell. She, as well as the rest of the students in their journalism class at Western Carolina University, weren't surprised at Ted's stellar career in publishing. They recognized his rare gift for bringing a story to life the first time they read one of his assignments.

Excited to tell Ted about her progress, Angie told him her research in Whispering Pines was going great. "Word's spread that I'm writing an article about the winter carnival for the magazine. I'm practically a celebrity. The town is over the moon about the free publicity."

"Yeah, I bet they are. Should be good for their business. Is the town as good as I was told?" Angie assured him the inn and town were perfect, deliberately omitting she'd found two bodies in the two days since she arrived. She didn't want Ted to think she was bad luck. As long as she was careful what she said, he would never hear about Whispering Pines' murders. News of her unfortunate discoveries in the snow-drifted boonies would never make it up to Ted in his New York City skyscraper office.

The din of voices on Ted's end drowned him out so he shouted above them. "Staff meeting starting. Gotta go, love." And with that, he clicked off. Angie felt elated. The brief chat revitalized her enthusiasm for her mission. She resolved to exceed Ted's expectations for her article. Ted's rescue offer, the ticket to escape her dreary job, came just in the nick of time. A few more years would permanently snuff out her creativity.

Not only did she love this first assignment, but Ted covered her expenses and paid a generous fee for freelancing. How good was that? Not counting the two murders, the adventure had been amazing.

The phone rang again. This time it was George. "Hey, Angie. I photocopied Cliff's documents. I got big news. Let's get a bite of dinner someplace and sneak into dessert later." Angie asked if he wasn't supposed to work. Wouldn't Clarice miss him? "I'm sure she will, but it won't kill her if I'm a little late." He asked how quickly she could get ready and arranged to pick her up at the back entrance of the inn.

Angie replaced the recorder in a purse in the back of a dresser drawer. When Roger returned her call, she'd get it into his hands and out of hers. Plus, she'd explain the recording by telling him that, as an investigative journalist, it was her habit to record interesting bits and pieces of information as she encountered them. And, when she discovered the recorder had information likely relevant to Jenny's murder, she contacted him. Simple.

***

Angie felt guilty winding her way through the kitchen again. A paying guest, she was yet again dodging her hostess to sneak out with a staff member. Scott saw her and mouthed *George*. Angie mouthed *yes* back. Scott laughed. She didn't understand why he found it funny and wasn't sure she wanted to know. She accepted

Scott's certainty that she captured Cliff's voice on her recorder, not George's. Scott better be right.

Angie emerged from the Lantern's back door into a dimly lit employee parking lot. She expected to see the sports car, but George pulled up in a four-wheel-drive pickup. "Hop in. It's supposed to snow again so I brought the truck. Plus, I think the Porsche's been seen too many times today." That was probably true, but Angie preferred the car. At least the pickup was nice and warm inside.

George had changed into a dark gray suit, white shirt and red and gray patterned tie for dessert. He looked studly indeed.

"I think we'll run over to Maple Grove. It's about fifteen minutes away. We can talk in private."

***

Maple Grove was smaller and considerably less festive than Whispering Pines. The buildings looked old and rundown, not quaint. George parked in front of a diner, his pickup in line with several others already there. Other than a take-out pizza parlor, Angie didn't see anyplace else to eat.

A waitress waved them to sit wherever they liked so George guided Angie to a booth in the back, out of sight if any Whispering Pines residents strayed to Maple Grove. The waitress brought menus before they got their coats off so they placed their orders promptly. Cheeseburgers, homemade fries and beer for both.

As soon as the waitress left, Angie blurted out she had big news too. "I didn't tell you something earlier... I recorded a few minutes of the tirade in the linen room. I didn't tell the chief either, but I will. This afternoon, Scott and I listened to the recorder for the first time, and it picked up voices. Scott said the yelling man was Cliff. No doubts. Roger's supposed to call me, and I'll offer to turn the recorder over to him."

"That's good news, Angie. Roger can cross our names off Jenny's suspect list."

"I hope it's enough to clear us. I'm not so sure about Adam. You know, it's possible he saw Cliff and Jenny going into the linen room together since he was wandering around the inn at that time. Scott and I think Adam's high on the list for both murders."

"Doesn't look good for him," George said in an uncharacteristically pessimistic voice.

The waitress brought their beers, and they both took long sips.

"Okay. Come on, tell me your news. I shared mine. What was in the manila envelope?"

"Account numbers and passwords to both the Winter Carnival Committee's records and Cliff's personal accounts. Nev left the greenhouse early so I went straight there after I left you. I made extras of everything and dropped off a couple of copies for Maggie Thurston. She's chairman of the

Winter Carnival Committee and the one who clued me in last week that she suspected the treasurer, good ol' Cliff, was dipping into the funds."

"So she's why you were snooping on Cliff?"

"Yeah. About a week ago, Maggie stopped by my place with something gnawing at her. Turned out to be Cliff's wonky bookkeeping. Maggie knows better than anybody how much we've received in grants and how much has been expended to help merchants and businesses capitalize on the carnival trade. She asked Cliff about some of the figures, and he exploded. Scared her. She tried to defuse the situation by telling him she was probably mistaken.

"I didn't think Maggie would cower to anybody, but Cliff's meltdown shook her. By being so outraged, he convinced Maggie something shady was going on with the finances so she came to me for help."

"Why you instead of the police?"

"She trusts me to be discreet. If she'd gone to the police and been wrong, Cliff would've made her look like a fool. Not Maggie's style. Plus, after her encounter with Cliff, she was afraid of him. She knew I'd look into the money matter without Cliff knowing. Aside from trusting me to keep quiet, I handled the committee's finances in the early years and know something about them. She thought I might recognize irregularities if I could get a look at the accounting records. I was trying to find a way to get a look at his records when he got himself killed and made it easier."

"Did Maggie ask you to break into Cliff's office?"

"She's too subtle for that. Let's say she knew I'd find a creative way to get a look at the real records, not the bogus monthly reports Cliff submits to the committee. So now, Maggie has copies of the accounts and, at her request, I faxed a copy to an auditing firm in Boston when I went home to change clothes.

"You went home? I didn't know you had a home. I thought you lived at the Lantern."

"Why would you think I lived there?"

"Because you said you were going up to your room in the attic last night?"

"Oh. I have a room in the attic for when I work late. After having to stay so long last night because of the murder, I didn't feel like driving home. But I do have a home. Small, but comfortable.

"Like I was saying, I didn't have much time to study the deposits and expenditures, but I could tell that a lot of money's gone through the committee account. It's going to take somebody with more accounting experience than I have to trace the intricacies of the committee's business in the three years Cliff's been treasurer. From what I saw, it looks like our buddy Cliff was embezzling funds right and left. He should've known he couldn't pull anything on Maggie. The carnival's her baby."

"Sounds like he thought he was smarter than anyone else."

"That's Cliff, all right. I assumed he had a partner in his embezzling venture, which ended in a falling out and Cliff getting shot. I was certain I had the embezzling case solved except for identifying his co-conspirator. When we saw Cliff's car at the mill, I hoped that's who would show up, and I could find out who it was."

"So you were focused on Cliff's embezzling activities more than his love life. That's a relief. That was a little too weird for my taste."

"Yeah, but it was a tantalizing sideshow," George said, eyebrows raised. God, he was cute.

"I don't know about the embezzling end of this, but from what we learned in our brief, illegal foray into Cliff's office, I say he's committed more than enough sins to make a lot of people mad enough to shoot him. Maybe his enemies formed a secret alliance like in *Murder on the Orient Express*, and they all did him in. Cliff's *Real Housewives of Whispering Pines* had a pretty good mutual motive too," Angie said.

"Lots of good motives," George said as the waitress arrived with their food. "This place isn't much on ambience, but the food's always good," George said.

"Um-m-m," Angie said after trying a bite of the thick fries. "Getting back to Cliff, when you think about it, his behavior could have set off any number of people. Videotaping his romantic interludes would make a woman furious if she found out."

"Enough to kill him?"

"Enough for a mountain girl like me. But suppose Cliff carried this further and told the ladies he recorded them and demanded payoffs to keep the videos secret. Then any one or all of the *Housewives* would have a double motive--retrieving and destroying the tapes to save their reputations as well as putting a stop to the blackmail. And firing a bullet into Cliff might make someone feel pretty good about getting even with him once and for all. I'm sure if these ladies found out about the videos, there was some downright, old-fashioned desire for revenge. By the way, you said you'd tell me who the other woman was in Cliff's video."

"Have you met Martin Vanderwelde, the pharmacist?"

"No, but I saw his drugstore when we were riding around town today."

"That was Karen, Karen Vanderwelde, his wife, on the video. You know, I always figured Cliff picked up women in bars. I had no idea he was fooling around with his and Polly's friends. Cliff saw his girlfriends and their husbands every day and carried on like nothing had happened. That takes a lot of gall."

"When I take the envelope back to Cliff's office, and if Roger hasn't beaten me to it and removed the tapes, I'm going to play all of them and see who else got caught by the candid camera."

"Uh, oh, George, you're back in kinky territory."

"It's not like I'm watching them for thrills," he said in protest. "We need to know who's involved."

Angie liked his reference to *we*. She and George--they were in this together. "Just thought of something--maybe, that cash in Cliff's safe is proceeds from his blackmailing scheme. It was all in tens and twenties, wasn't it?"

"Yeah. It's certainly too much cash for a small business like Cliff's to keep on hand. Boy, I can't wait to get back in Cliff's office and take another look. Want to come?"

"Just tell me when."

"This time I'll be more careful finding out where Roger is." Angie made a face at him, remembering the sound of police sirens coming toward Cliff's office and how close they came to getting caught.

"Do you think any of the cash in Cliff's safe came from embezzled Carnival Committee funds?" Angie asked.

"No. If I'm right, that's small potatoes compared to what he dipped out of the fund. It's either blackmail money like you said or Cliff's own money he stashed away for some nefarious purpose. Maybe he had more than one scam going. Who knows?"

"I just thought of another possibility connected to Cliff's sordid love life. What if one of the husbands found out his wife was fooling around with Cliff and was jealous or just plain mad about it? We can't rule out riled husbands. From the number of videos in Cliff's office, half the town could be suspects. Oh, by the way, George, will you stop by my room when we get back?"

"Are you inviting me over for a bit of dalliance?" he asked as his lips curled into his devilish grin.

"Speaking of dalliance--you aren't married, are you?"

"Angie, I assure you that I wouldn't have been in your bedroom kissing you if I were married. No, my dear, I'm single. And very available," he told her. Damn, she liked this guy.

"Now that your marital status is settled..." she said. "I want you to hear the recorder before Roger picks it up."

"Believe me, I want to hear it."

***

The kitchen staff at the Lantern bustled with dinner preparations as Angie and George negotiated another secret entrance. George acted like a naughty ten-year old as his eyes darted around looking for Clarice. She wasn't in sight, and they made it to Angie's room undetected.

Angie opened a dresser drawer and retrieved her recorder from her purse. George followed her movements with intense interest. She rearranged chairs, gestured for him to sit, put the recorder between them on the table and turned it on.

George jumped halfway out of his chair. "That's Cliff! No doubt about it! Whoa, I've never heard him mad though. He's always kind of robot calm and even-tempered." When the woman's sobbing became audible, George scooted to the front of his chair to hear better and clenched his fists. "Oh, my god. Does she say anything?"

"A few words but they're inaudible, at least to me. I only caught a few minutes of the argument. The woman cried the whole time."

"How did the eavesdropping and recording come about?"

"First of all, let's call it investigating, not eavesdropping. Nice southern girls aren't raised to eavesdrop, okay?" George widened his eyes in mock horror at her *Scarlett O'Hara* breach of etiquette. "Back to my story. I was exploring the inn, and while I was walking down the hallway, I heard a man's angry voice coming from the linen room. Investigative journalist that I am, I stopped and listened. Then I remembered my new high-powered recorder so I put it up to the door and started recording. Just a little innocent snooping on my own, a harmless game to get back into the investigating mode. The man's hatefulness gave me chilly bumps, and I wasn't even in the room with him. I didn't know if the recorder would pick up the voices. And certainly no idea the woman would be dead a short time later."

"No wonder you had nightmares about Cliff. It wasn't just about finding his body. You heard him in person."

"From my brief meeting with him at dessert, I would never have recognized his droning monotone as that violent voice. When the couple stopped quarreling, I thought they were going to come out the door and catch me so I ran down the hall and into the library. The reason I hid in the library was so I could see them when they came out the door, but you butted in before I had a chance."

"Oh-h-h. Sorry for ruining your plan. You might've seen Cliff leave the room, and when you saw him at dessert, you would've recognized him. At the time, I couldn't figure out for the life of me why you came barreling into the library like that."

"I told Roger about you being in the library because I thought you were the man yelling at the woman."

"I'm a gentle man and don't yell. I don't run around with married women either. Someday I might even tell you how I materialize and vanish." Angie started to tell him that Scott already told her he was napping.

George moved on to another topic. "What on earth did Jenny do or say to make Cliff so mad? She sounds pitiful. Why didn't she yell back at him or something?"

"Maybe she did at the end, and it got her killed."

George asked if anyone else knew about the recording. "Just Scott. Since I didn't tell Roger about it, I had to talk to somebody, and Scott seemed like a good choice. I figured he was safe from being entangled in middle-age love affairs gone wrong."

George nodded and looked at his watch. "We better get downstairs. I'm sure my tardiness has Clarice fuming." He held his arm in the English gentleman style, but before Angie could slip her arm through his, he pulled her close and kissed her.

What a kisser, Angie thought as they walked down the hall, her arm in his.

Chapter Twelve

Dessert was in full swing when Angie and George approached the door to the library. Angie attempted to pull her arm away from George, but he caught it and held it firmly in place.

"Ready?" he asked.

"Yes," she said without hesitating, and they walked into the crowded room as a couple.

Clarice's gaze dropped to their arm-lock, but she didn't react. Whatever she thought of Angie and George being together didn't register on her face. Clarice greeted Angie in her typical, cordial manner and then asked, "Will you excuse us for a moment, my dear? I need to talk to George."

As Clarice and George walked away, Angie heard Clarice ask, in a most un-Clarice-like tone, "Where the hell have you been? I've been trying to call you all afternoon. We're short-staffed, and you show up hours late."

Clarice's voice trailed off as she and George headed for the kitchen. George turned around to Angie and silently mimicked Clarice's harping. Angie laughed. Clarice would probably fire him before the night was over. At least he had his other jobs to fall back on.

"Looks like you believe me that George didn't kill Jenny," a voice whispered behind Angie. She turned around, recognizing the voice of her confidante. "You and George are getting pretty friendly," Scott teased. "I noticed Clarice didn't give you a disapproving once-over when you came in the library together. That's a big positive for you. She's madder than hell at George though."

"Poor George. I like him, but it's hopeless," Angie told Scott. "Not only do we live hundreds of miles apart, he's not what I had in mind."

"As for the distance, that's why the Wright Brothers invented airplanes. I don't know what you're looking for in a man, but women around here consider George a top-of-the-line catch." Angie wasn't surprised. She knew from her own experience that small towns offer few opportunities for forty-something romance. In her hometown of Forest Gate, older single women chase any unattached man who can hobble along. As for dating by airplane, Angie couldn't see George's budget stretching to include plane trips to North Carolina.

Scott scanned the room while they talked. When Clarice returned from the kitchen, he scurried away without a word.

Angie sampled a few bites from the dessert table, but she was stuffed from dinner at the diner. She wandered around the library, catching a glimpse of George working now and then. When he caught her eye, he made silly overworked-underappreciated faces at her. Aside from being handsome and thoughtful, he was funny. She observed how he was meticulous about arranging desserts, replacing used plates and silverware. He would be a good employee if he weren't so irresponsible.

A woman approached Angie. "Hi. I'm Sadie Parker. I hoped for a chance to meet you. I own the Shear Magic Beauty Shop."

Angie liked this woman on sight. Under a beehive of teased bleached hair, she had a soft, cheerful face that exuded good humor. A low-cut leopard-skin print top was filled to the max by a hefty push-up bra, and black velvet stretchy pants hugged her shapely derriere. Gold stiletto heels completed Sadie's version of a *Sex and the City* look.

"I can't believe what's happened to you since you got to Whispering Pines. You must think we murder each other at a pretty fast clip. That George ought to be shot for taking you into the old mill, suspecting Cliff was there and all. Lord knows what Cliff would've been doing if he hadn't been dead."

"I can think of one thing he wouldn't have been doing in that frigid mill," Angie said. Sadie gave Angie a gentle, knowing nudge and laughed.

George approached them from behind. He put his arm around Angie's waist and gave Sadie a friendly peck on the cheek. "If you want to know the real scuttlebutt about Whispering Pines, Sadie's your girl," George told Angie. "Just don't listen to what she says about me," he joked and moved on to his duties.

"Looks like George has taken an interest in journalism," Sadie said in a mischievous whisper. "Good luck to you. You'll need it. Oops, I gotta go. My ride's leaving. Stop by my shop. You can't miss it. I want to help with the article." Angie waved good-bye as Sadie's behind swayed rhythmically toward the door.

Why did Sadie say she needed good luck if she hung out with George? The man was a puzzle. She couldn't tell if the people who knew him even took him seriously. Did they even like him?

Taking advantage of a break while George and Scott cleaned up and carried trays of dishes to the kitchen, Angie went to her room to touch up her make-up. As she turned on the lights in the dark room, she was struck again how beautiful it was. Large urns of natural greenery filled the room with the fragrance of a forest. Angie liked sitting in front of the fireplace, but her favorite place was the turret with high curved glass windows. The view down Main Street, especially at night, was worth whatever Ted's magazine was paying for the room.

Angie sat down at her dresser. When she opened the drawer to get her make-up bag, she instinctively jerked her hand back. Something was wrong. Her belts and purses were scrambled. Checking the other drawers, she found her folded clothes helter-skelter. Someone had rifled through her belongings. She couldn't believe a maid dared do such a thing. The flawless Clarice would never put up with an employee who went through guests' possessions. Angie felt dirty knowing someone had prowled through her stuff, especially her new sexy underwear. She hoped they didn't touch her bras and underpants.

Who could it have been? She was a stranger in town. Nobody knew anything about her except she was writing a magazine article and that she found two dead people. She didn't think anyone was curious enough about what she had to say about the Winter Carnival to go to this much trouble to preview her notes. That left the murders.

While Angie ran questions through her head, she heard a rustling noise in the bathroom. It sounded like someone brushing against the shower liner. Had the drawer searcher hidden in her bathroom? What should she do? Anxiety gripped her. If she attempted to pick up the phone, the intruder could hear and get to her before she dialed downstairs. By the same token, he could catch her before she could escape from the room.

She heard the noise again. She looked around for a possible weapon, but there was nothing within her reach except her makeup pouch lying on the dresser. A lot of good it was. She spotted her beautiful heels underneath her bed, better weapons than the makeup. She clenched one shoe in each hand with the heel pointed outward. With a good, strong grip on each of them, she eased toward the bathroom. Slowly she opened the door a few inches and felt for the light switch. Using the heel of one of her shoes, she flipped the light on. Nothing moved in the room so Angie pushed the door open. She'd left the shower curtain bunched up at one side and could see no one was hiding in the shower.

She heard the noise again. Hot air blowing from a ceiling heating duct rustled the plastic shower curtain. Mesmerized by the rhythm, Angie watched. Each time the heat came on, the liner fluttered and swished. She leaned against the doorframe, frightened and limp but relieved she didn't have to attack anyone with nothing more lethal than her high heels. Even worse, she didn't want to break her heels over some hoodlum's hard head.

One thing for sure, she planned to buy some of that self-protection spray stuff Caroline carried with her. When she had a chance, she'd ask Caroline what it was and how to order it. Then she'd do some serious damage if anybody got in her way. The next time would be--don't-mess-with-Angie-time.

Anxious to get away from her room, Angie ran to the elevator and pushed the button repeatedly until the doors opened. Before she got in, she stuck her head inside to make sure no one lurked in the corners. Justified paranoia. In the reception area, she bumped into Dr. Kate Mahoney coming in the door. "Hello, Angie. Are you okay?" she asked. "You look a little flushed."

Without stopping for a breath, Angie blurted out the story of her room being messed up. It wasn't like she knew the doctor well enough to confide in her. She just happened to be the first person Angie encountered that she knew at all.

"Gosh. I'm so sorry. Did they take anything?" Angie replied that she didn't bring much with her, and it all seemed to be present--costume jewelry, shoes and clothes. "Let's find George. He'll know what to do. Besides, I've got a bombshell of my own." As they walked quickly down the hallway, Kate remarked, "You can definitely rule out staff going through your possessions. Clarice would have them tarred and feathered." Angie's opinion exactly.

They found George in the library removing the tablecloths and putting them in a laundry cart. "Evening, Kate. Angie, you look like you've seen a ghost." George looked at her with worry lines marring his handsome face. "You didn't find another body, did you?" he asked in a timid voice. She and Kate explained what happened, talking at the same time. "Are you sure about this?" George asked.

"Yes. Everything in my dresser drawers was topsy-turvy. Then, I heard a noise in the bathroom and thought somebody was hiding in there." Her voice quivered. No wonder. Every time she turned around, she ran smack into another catastrophe. George drew her close to him and cuddled her.

How good to have someone care about her feelings and offer soothing words and comfort. Having to be self-sufficient and brave for herself and her children had exhausted her.

George gave her back a gentle caress and released her from his embrace but not before Scott exchanged glances with the doctor, glances emitting dark nuances.

"We need someplace to talk. I've got big news, and I do mean big news," the doctor told George.

"The linen room?" George asked.

Angie and Kate turned on him in unison.

"Are you crazy?" Kate asked. "Do you remember what happened in that room?"

"Yeah, George. Kate and I already got a good, long look at it. We don't plan to go back."

"Sorry. How about your room, Angie? I'm finished here." Eager to hear Kate's news, she readily agreed.

As they walked through the quiet reception room to go to the elevator, Clarice and Nev were huddled together behind the desk. Separating quickly and looking sheepish, Angie wondered if they were making out. Middle-age newlyweds? How cute.

Angie unlocked her door and flipped on the light. "I don't think I've ever been in one of the Lantern's guest rooms before," Kate said. "It's lovely."

George turned on the fireplace. Angie offered drinks. George and Kate helped themselves to beers from the mini-bar, and Angie opted for white wine. George deftly opened the bottle and poured a glass for her. While they were getting settled, someone knocked on the door.

It was Scott. "I came up as soon as I got the table linens down to the laundry room. Why did you three leave together? What gives?"

"Hey, Scotty," George greeted the young man. "Kate's got news. And by the way, Angie had an intruder earlier who nosed around her room. We need to do something about the lock."

Scott frowned, but before he could question her, Angie changed the subject by offering him a drink. "Thanks, I'll snag a beer."

Drinks in hand, the group settled into chairs in the sitting area of Angie's room. Kate opened her mouth to reveal her big news but stopped at the sound of another knock on the door. "Who can that be?" she asked in a whisper.

George peered through the peephole. "Oh, hell, it's Clarice. What are we going to do? We can't jump out the window. It's too high. Brace yourself. We'll have to face her." George's jokes and Scott's collusion annoyed Angie. In an exaggerated gesture, George stepped away from the door. "Let her in, Angie. There's one of her and four of us, but those aren't good odds."

On the other side of the door, Clarice shot back in a sharp tone, "Shut up, George and Scott. I can hear you."

That left no doubt Clarice heard their remarks. Angie already felt guilty that she offended Clarice's hospitality by slipping in and out the back door like a common thief. Now, this. She expected Clarice to evict her and put her out on the icy streets to look for another place to sleep.

When Angie opened the door, not only was Clarice there, but Nev stood beside her. Clarice surveyed the group. "So this is where you all are. May we come in?"

"Join the gathering, folks. Kate's got news to tell us," George volunteered.

Unsure how to handle Clarice and Nev's presence in her room, Angie settled on playing hostess and offered drinks. George continued his role as bartender, pouring wine for them.

"Okay, Kate, you've got the floor at last. I don't know anybody else who might crash our little party." Angie chanced a peek at Clarice and Nev who didn't look offended, although George just called them party crashers. True, they showed up uninvited, but it was their inn. Angie kept hoping there wouldn't be another knock on the door. The only other possible interested person was the police chief, and she didn't want to do any talking in front of him.

With the stage set and her audience settled, Kate announced, "Jenny was pregnant--three months when she died."

The group was stunned. They looked from one to the other without saying anything.

Clarice was first to speak. "Are you sure, Kate? Adam and Jenny couldn't have children."

"Everybody in town knows about Adam's problem with the mumps when he was young," Nev added.

Kate said, "All that means is that Adam couldn't father children. Nothing to do with Jenny conceiving. Autopsies don't lie, especially when it comes to the presence of a three-month-old fetus. It speaks for itself.

"In case you think I'm revealing confidential medical information, I'm not. The autopsy results leaked all over the hospital. I got my information from overhearing some volunteers talking about it, but I confirmed it. Of course, news is out, also, that Jenny was strangled, but we already knew that."

"Whew-w-w." George released the word slowly. "Jenny pregnant after all these years? She must be about forty-five."

"Forty-six," corrected Kate.

Angie barely heard the age discussion because her mind was preoccupied with what Kate had just said. "That's it!" Angie shouted at the group.

"That's what?" asked Clarice, startled by Angie's outburst. The others looked at Angie with question marks on their faces.

George intervened. "Hold on a minute. Angie and I know a couple of things about Jenny's murder that the rest of you don't know. I think we should tell them, Angie. We have some of the missing pieces to the puzzle."

"For goodness sakes, tell us," Kate urged, impatience speeding her words.

"As long as everyone agrees to keep what they hear in this room among us until we can talk to Roger," George said. "Okay?" Everybody agreed. Clarice glared at George, suggesting she suspected he was mixed up in some kind of mess. "All right, Angie, go ahead."

In a matter-of-fact voice, Angie told how she heard a man raving at a woman in the linen room and how she recorded the one-sided tirade. She told the stunned gathering that the woman cried and said a few words, but Angie couldn't understand them. "Separately, Scott and George both identified the male voice on my recorder as Cliff, so he was the man yelling at the woman. Plus, George and I learned that Jenny and Cliff were romantically involved." A collective gulping followed that revelation. "Now that Kate told us Jenny was pregnant, I think Cliff was the father of Jenny's baby, and Saturday night, she either told him for the first time she was pregnant or she was pressuring him to do something. From what y'all just said, she couldn't pass the baby off as Adam's. And considering Cliff's angry reaction and the almost immediate strangling of Jenny, he didn't take to being a daddy."

"That's for damn sure," Kate said. "What he really didn't take to was losing Polly's money." The group made consenting noises. "You see, Cliff and Polly lived way beyond Cliff's income. He didn't have much of a business anymore, and he liked the good life Polly's inheritance provided for them." Creep, Angie thought. Cliff valued his easy life more than helping Jenny, whose pregnancy was his responsibility. Angie felt sorry for Jenny getting herself into such a mess. On the other hand, Jenny was a big girl and knew the consequences of fooling around. It went without saying she should've been more careful.

"George, what makes you so sure Jenny and Cliff were carrying on?" Clarice asked.

"Angie and I paid a little visit to Cliff's office yesterday afternoon." Clarice rolled her eyes at

George. "Cliff has a secret bedroom behind his lab where he entertained his lady friends. And a secret camera for recording when he entertained them."

"That's sick," Kate said with a groan.

"Gross." Scott added.

"Hold on. You haven't heard it all. I think Cliff targeted well-to-do women like Jenny. He had a lot of cash in a safe in his bedroom. My guess is that it's blackmail money." George paused. "Scotty, run down and get some more wine and beer, will you?"

Angie waited for Clarice to object to George ordering Scott to help himself to her booze, but she ignored it. Instead, she asked, "George, did you actually see proof that Cliff was involved with Jenny and actually see the cash?"

"Yes, to both questions. I don't know how much clearer I can make this, Clarice, but Cliff made videos of himself and Jenny rollicking around in bed. And not just Jenny but other women too. His DVDs are organized and labeled with the woman's first name. Meticulous, Cliff was." Clarice made a face.

"Local women?" Kate asked.

"Yes. Local women." Clarice shook her head, her expression morphing from disbelief to disgust. "Cliff has more videos, but I didn't have time to look at them. But, yes, Clarice. Angie and I both saw proof of Cliff and Jenny.

"A DNA test will establish paternity easily enough," Kate said. "I'll alert the coroner. She expected Adam to be a dead end paternity wise. She'll still have to test him, of course, but you folks have hastened the medical investigation along. Thanks for telling me."

George reminded her. "Just keep quiet where you heard it."

Scott returned with a bag full of drinks. He and Nev poured rounds for everyone.

Kate asked, "You know what's sad about this situation? Aside from Jenny Harden being dead? Jenny and Karen Vanderwelde married busy men who didn't spend much time at home with them. Lonesome wives are easy targets for sleazebags like Cliff. It's bad enough if he was on the prowl for sex, but if he targeted them because they had money and then recorded them with the intention of getting money out of them, it's even more revolting."

George said, "Since you haven't heard enough, there's another angle to this story. Maggie Thurston suspected large amounts of money had disappeared from the Winter Carnival Committee funds. When she questioned Cliff, he blew up. Believe it or not, Cliff scared Maggie." That brought chuckles from everyone. Angie didn't laugh. She didn't get the joke.

"Anyway, Maggie asked me to do some snooping on Cliff." Clarice asked if he found anything. "Angie did. A manila envelope Cliff hid behind a false panel in the back of a file drawer in his secret boudoir. I figured if Cliff went to that much trouble to hide something, he considered it important, so I photocopied the contents of the envelope. From taking a quick look, I saw that a lot of funds didn't go for Carnival projects. Maggie hired an auditing firm in Boston, and I feel certain they'll trace a ton of money to Cliff's personal bank accounts."

"If I've got all this right," Nev said, "we assume Cliff killed Jenny because she was pregnant and about to upset his well-financed lifestyle. But who killed Cliff? The more we talk, the more suspects we come up with. It could've been any one of his girlfriends." George interrupted saying he and Angie called them the *Real Housewives of Whispering Pines*.

"Aptly named," Nev said. "You know, blackmail makes for a volatile situation. The victim is on edge because of the constant threat of exposure. The blackmailer gets greedier and ups his price. The victim gets fed up. Boom!"

"Maybe that's what happened. Cliff squeezed the women for more money, and one of them couldn't come up with it. She got caught in a situation with no way out except getting rid of the blackmailer. And, it goes without saying, the husbands of Cliff's women rank high on the list of suspects too. How about a husband who just found out his wife is pregnant, and he knows for a fact he's definitely not the daddy?" Angie asked.

"That points to Adam. It looks like he's the prime suspect as Cliff's killer," Clarice said.

"Yeah, but I can't see Adam setting up a meeting at the mill. Seems like he would've hunted Cliff down as soon as he found out about the baby and killed him on sight," Kate said.

"How about Maggie as a suspect? That carnival is dear to her heart," suggested Scott.

Kate said, "Maggie wouldn't have settled for anything less than having Cliff staked over a colony of fire ants so she could watch him suffer." The group laughed and agreed. Nev said crossing Maggie was a dangerous mistake. Angie wondered, in the absence of ants, might Maggie have settled for a gun?

Unless something surfaced to point suspicion, Angie was staying with her previous conviction. "I'm putting my money on one of the *Housewives*," she said. "Whichever one she was, she was getting even with Cliff for the humiliation she endured. She planned his murder, and I bet she gave him a piece of her mind before she shot him. I certainly would have."

"Well, right now, we know more than anybody about what happened, including Roger," George said. "One more thing, Clarice. Somebody came into Angie's room while we were at dessert and went through her things. Get the lock changed."

Clarice looked devastated. "Angie, I'm so sorry. Was anything taken?"

Angie had her mouth open to say *no*, but she remembered something. She went to her dresser and opened the drawer where she kept her purses. She opened her black leather purse, and her heart sank. "My audio recorder is missing. I put it in this purse, and it's gone. I didn't think to check earlier." Clarice said how peculiar for someone to take a recorder. "Someone thought I knew something. The recorder must've looked like the only thing in the room that could contain incriminating information.

"Now the chief won't be able to hear it, and it's such an important piece of evidence."

"At least, Scott and I can testify it was absolutely Cliff. We both heard it. It'll work out okay," George said.

"Oh, Angie, what a terrible experience you've had in our town," Clarice said, almost in tears. "I had so much hope your beautiful article would bring new visitors. I hate to think what you'll write about us now that two murders have been committed. On top of that, your privacy has been violated in my hotel."

"None of that will be in my article."

Clarice turned on George with full force. "George Junior, you should never have taken Angie into that mill." At the sound of George Junior, Scott and Nev and George broke into laughter. Clarice narrowed her eyes, staring at them until they abruptly stopped. She started on George again. "Why did you go in that building and take Angie with you when you knew Cliff was in there? He could've been doing," she said, struggling for words, "who knows what?" Clarice continued berating him until George held up his hand to stop her.

"Chill, Clarice. Sorry to interrupt while you're all fired up at me, but I've about had it for one day. Tell you what, I'll take you out for lunch next week, and you can turn loose at me. On second thought, let's make that drinks instead of lunch. It'll be easier for me if I'm sloshed." Nev and Scott laughed out loud.

Instead of being angry, Clarice said, "You're impossible. Okay. I'll settle with you next week. But it's lunch, not a few cheap drinks. And I'll choose the restaurant."

With that settled, Clarice turned to Angie. "I don't know what to say about someone entering your room. We've never had anything like this happen at the Lantern. I'll get maintenance to install a new lock right away."

"You aren't to blame, Clarice. Whoever broke into my room was targeting me. Somebody was snooping to see what he could find out about me. Since he looked through everything I brought, he should be satisfied. But a new lock will make me feel better."

"Oh, my goodness, I think our lovely town's falling apart," Clarice declared. "I guess we'd better call it a night. I don't think I can take any more news. I'm sure tomorrow will bring more revelations, none of them pleasant, I'm afraid." Everyone got up to leave.

Clarice started for the door, but George stopped her. "I talked to Mother when I went home to change clothes. I told her everything about finding Cliff's body. I figured she knew about it, but I wanted to tell her myself."

"Everybody in town knows about it. I'm sure she did too, but she needed to hear it from you and see for herself you were still in one piece. If we'd known you were nosing around Cliff's office and took Angie with you, we'd have had a joint heart attack. You're going to be the death of us."

"Sorry," George said, sounding sincere. Clarice leaned close to him and whispered in his ear. George gave her a gentle hug and a kiss on the cheek, whispering something back to her.

What was that tender exchange all about? It didn't fit their usual adversarial pattern. Angie felt she owed Clarice an apology. "I'm sorry about using the back door to avoid you. George and I couldn't face having to answer questions. We couldn't make sense of what happened at the mill, much less explain it to anyone else. On top of that, I was rattled, especially after the police almost caught us in Cliff's office." Clarice gave George a sharp look, and Angie remembered George hadn't mentioned their *Bonnie and Clyde* getaway. Uh, oh, she shouldn't have let that slip.

Clarice ignored the comment. "Oh, Angie, I don't blame you at all. I'm just so sorry you've seen such an ugly side of our town. We're not like that. At least, I didn't think we were." With that, Clarice wished Angie a pleasant evening and left.

Nev, Scott and Kate told them goodnight too. Kate thanked Angie and George again for telling her about Cliff and Jenny. "It'll save a lot of time in identifying the baby's father and solving Jenny's murder."

"What brought on that affectionate farewell scene with Clarice? I thought you didn't like her," Angie said after she closed the door.

"Oh, she's okay sometimes," George said. "When I'm not so beat, I'll tell you about it. Right now, let's just sit for a few minutes before we call it a night."

Chapter Thirteen

George and Angie sat on the love seat, staring dreamily at the flames. He turned toward her, his face relaxed and contented. "This is my favorite room in the inn. I'm glad you're staying in it. Did you know I grew up in this house?" She shook her head. "I did, and although I haven't lived here for a long time, I still remember every square inch of every floor, including some secret places."

"Secret places?"

"Yeah, the man who built this house either had a flair for whimsy or a desperate compulsion to hide from his wife. The tops of the front turrets appear to be sealed, but one of them has a secret entrance. When I was a kid, I figured it out while I was prowling around the attic. It took a while but I learned how to open the secret door. I started my breaking and entering career at an early age," he said smiling at Angie.

"I turned the turret into my clubhouse and spent hours up there, especially when I was hiding from Clarice," he joked. "I kept all kinds of things up there, snacks, drinks, books and my prized possession, some girlie magazines I found all tied up in a nice, neat bundle a neighbor put out with his trash. By today's standards, they were pretty tame, but they were racy stuff to my eight-year-old eyes."

"You must have been terrible. No wonder Clarice was after you."

Angie didn't want to embarrass George by asking, but she assumed his mother had been on the household staff with mother and son living on the premises. Curious about his family, she said, "You mentioned to Clarice that you saw your mother when you went home. Do you live with her?" He explained they lived on the same property but not together. "Oh, I remember," she told him jokingly, "you have a home, small but comfortable as you put it."

"Exactly," he told her.

"Clarice called your mother Francesca. Sounds Italian."

"And that she is. Beautiful, high-spirited and full-blooded. That's where I get my dark hair and eyes and my good looks," he joked. "Her Neapolitan genetics overpowered my father's Anglo-Saxon coloring."

"You look Italian."

"Except for my size and nose. I got Dad's height and his English gentlemen's nose." He traced his straight nose with his fingers to prove it. For a fact, this good-looking man got the best of the Italian-English mix.

"On a more serious note, when I went home, I stopped by my mother's house to tell her what happened today. I knew gossip was flying."

"You didn't tell her I went with you, did you?"

"Sure. It was your idea. I had to give you credit."

"Are you crazy? That makes me sound like a criminal, not a journalist. Everybody expects me to come up with an enticing story that will promote the carnival, not get myself put in jail for burglary." The town would turn on her if she let them down. "What did your mother say?" she asked tentatively.

"She thinks you sound interesting."

Interesting? "As in Billy-the-Kid-interesting? Lizzie Borden interesting?"

"Of course not. Mother's quite open-minded for her generation."

"Actually, George, breaking and entering is a criminal offense, not a generational issue."

"Mother doesn't think you're a criminal so don't worry. Guess what though? I found out why Mother disliked Cliff so much. She's always gone to Maple Grove to an optometrist, but I didn't know it had to do with how much she hated Cliff. I despised Cliff because of my friend's experience in his office, but my mother's contempt for Cliff was based on one of his early romances, pre-videotaping technology. Cliff had an affair with one of Mother's friends and promised they'd go away together, but he never made good on it. Eventually her husband found out about the relationship, and she had to make a hasty move to her daughter's home in Florida."

"Another angry girlfriend and another jealous husband? Please don't tell me they're in town."

"Nope, you don't have to worry. The husband's dead, and the woman's in a nursing home. In Florida." George smiled at Angie. "I better go so you can get some sleep."

"Please stay for a few more minutes but no talk of the murders. Let's enjoy the fire." Angie got up and turned off the lamps so the only light came from the flickering flames of the fireplace. The music of Chopin coming from a TV music channel filled the room. Snuggling in the crook of George's arm, Angie rested her head on his shoulder and wondered why she couldn't have found this appealing, gentle, teasing man when she was younger. Why did it have to come so late? And in this faraway place? She'd always dreamed of romantic scenes like this, but it didn't happen until she met this part-time... whatever he was. In spite of the improbable future of this romance, she was glad she came to Whispering Pines and even gladder she met George. At least she knew romance existed. On the other hand, sadly it would exist only a few days for her.

Sitting quietly, neither Angie nor George spoke. They didn't need words. Being together in their cozy world was enough. George kissed her in the same searching way he had this afternoon. Not demanding anything, he kissed her for the sheer pleasure of kissing. He was the sexiest kisser ever.

"I have to go now," George told her pulling away after a prolonged smooching session. "I'm exhausted," he told her, rising to his feet.

"Don't we have to take the envelope back to Cliff's office tonight?"

"Surprise! I took it back during dessert, slick as a ribbon."

"You did what? You weren't missing from the library long enough. I saw you every few minutes."

"Perfect alibi, huh? I sneaked out while dessert was at its busiest. Apparently it worked if you didn't miss me."

Angie pouted. "I wanted to go."

"I know, but you didn't miss anything. It only took a couple of minutes. Nothing happened that would've sparked your journalistic interest," he said. "I didn't take time to look at the videos of the other women. I still don't know who else is involved."

Angie walked George to the door. They kissed goodnight. "How about breakfast in the morning? We can eat here. Clarice puts out a nice spread. I'll have to make it kind of quick though so I can get over to the greenhouse and finish Nev's damn alarm system before it malfunctions in the middle of the night again. Breakfast at eight?"

Angie eagerly accepted. She wanted to be with him as much as she could these next few days. And when he went to work at the greenhouse, she'd work on her article.

***

Angie poured the last of the wine into her glass and sat on the antique fainting couch in the turret. Through the large windows, the length of Main Street lay before her. The lights in the stores shining on the blowing snow created a fantasy world equal to the one she was living. All due to a chance meeting with a quixotic man. Whoever and whatever he was, he definitely was not Jenny's murderer.

Angie heard a faint siren in the distance, but this time it didn't matter. She wasn't committing a crime, and the police weren't racing toward her.

Chapter Fourteen

Bright sunlight coming through the turret windows warmed Angie's face. "Where am I?" she asked aloud. It took a few minutes to for her to waken enough to tune in to her surroundings. As her brain clicked, she remembered dozing off on the fainting couch. The gas fireplace had kept the room warm and cozy, and a good thing that was. She'd slept all night with only a silky throw for cover.

Breakfast with George awaited her. She hopped up to shower and dress.

Bunching her auburn curls into a messy ponytail, and dressing in jeans, a pale aqua cashmere turtleneck sweater and gray low-heeled suede boots, Angie arrived downstairs promptly at eight. Clarice, looking refreshed and meticulously groomed, was giving directions to some guests about morning carnival events.

After they went out the door, Clarice called to Angie, "I hope you had a restful night." Angie assured her she did. "George is waiting for you in the Breakfast Room," she added cheerfully. Clarice made it sound like a date. Did breakfast qualify as a date? Angie wanted it to be a date.

George sat at a corner table with a newspaper open to the comics and a full cup of coffee in front of him. He glanced up as soon as she entered the room and rose to greet her. Wearing old jeans and an MIT sweatshirt, he was dressed to work at Nev's greenhouse. He looked hot even in faded jeans. Down-dressing didn't lessen his appealing good looks.

"Morning. How was your night?" he asked, taking her hands in his and kissing her tenderly on the lips. He tasted like fresh coffee. Yum.

"I slept like a rock. How about you?" George said he, too, slept like a rock until four o'clock when Nev's alarm system went off again. "One good thing about it, I got a head start on my day. Just think, it's only eight o'clock, and I've put in half a day already," he said, shaking his head. "Let me get you some coffee."

She was dying to hear if there was news about the murders.

"Nothing this morning."

Like everything Clarice choreographed, the breakfast buffet was superb. Angie and George ate until they were stuffed. Heads nearly touching and holding hands, they shut the world out, speaking softly in lovers' murmurs.

Too soon for Angie, George said he needed to get back to the greenhouse. He'd left Nev's alarm system in mid-repair. With a parting kiss on the lips, he left.

Angie lingered over coffee, sorry George had to leave but anticipating working on her article. With so many ideas bouncing around in her head, she hoped a stroll through town would help her focus. She faced the lucky dilemma of an abundance of material.

Angie had another cup of coffee and reviewed her draft outline, filling in ideas. George had covered Whispering Pines' economic downfall and the birth of the carnival. She didn't need any more about that. Besides, she had George handy. Just thinking about him made her glow. She'd waited a long time, but she was smitten and smitten badly. What a good feeling to care about someone and to have that someone to care about her.

Bundled in her coat, scarf, hat and gloves, Angie walked a couple of blocks from the Lantern to the town's shopping district. It was her first chance to stop and study the decorations. She was immediately enchanted and took photos, although Ted planned to arrange for a local professional photographer. In the meantime, her amateur shots could help Ted narrow his choices.

The first building Angie came across was Harden's Hardware. Dark and obviously closed,

Angie stopped to look in the windows at the wonderful antique horse-drawn sleighs. Although the interior was dim, revolving colored spotlights and strategically placed ceiling lights highlighted the sleighs. Smaller sleds filled the in-between spaces. Some were made of wood and more recent models made of both wood and metal. The collection didn't include any plastic sleds.

A movement in the store caught Angie's attention. Someone was coming toward the front. Uh-oh. She dreaded facing Jenny's husband, but it was too late to run away.

"Good morning," Adam said, opening the door.

Angie responded in what she hoped was a respectful and consoling tone. "Hello, Adam. I'm so sorry about your wife."

He bowed his head.

Caught in an awkward silence, Angie said, "I was admiring your window display. Nostalgic."

Adam spoke, his voice hoarse and weary. "I couldn't bear to stay at home today, so I came down here to rattle around. There's plenty of work to keep me busy, and it takes my mind off--what happened. If you have time, why don't you come in? I'll tell you about my family's sled collection."

Caught by surprise, Angie stepped inside the store. Adam locked the door behind her, prompting immediate misgivings about her situation. This was a bad idea.

"I just made a fresh pot of coffee. How about a cup?"

Angie stuttered and accepted.

"Be right back."

Angie pulled off her gloves and fished in her purse for her cell. She checked to be sure she knew where the 911 keys were and held the phone in her hand. As he walked toward the coffee pot, Adam flipped on the overhead lights, startling Angie. That was a small shock compared to Adam's appearance when he returned with coffee. He looked like hell. Puffy face, bloodshot eyes, unshaved, rumpled clothes. Instead of the plain but tidy man she met at dessert, this man looked like he hadn't slept or cleaned up in days. Was he a grieving widower or a guilty killer?

"I guess you've heard about Jenny's..." He struggled to find a word and whispered, "*condition*. I didn't know she was running around with anybody. I didn't have any idea. I loved Jenny. I thought she was happy, and we had a good marriage." With this baring of his soul, Adam turned away, sobbing quietly. Although Angie barely knew the man, she felt compelled to comfort him and placed her hand on his shoulder.

He got it together and apologized for breaking down.

"Do you have family or friends?" she asked. "I could call someone for you."

"I can't talk to them. I know what they're all saying. Jenny pregnant and everybody knowing it wasn't mine," he replied, shaking his head.

Stymied by what to say, Angie searched for a new topic and turned to the obvious, Adam's amazing sleds.

"Right. I'll give you the tour," Adam said with an underwhelming attempt at cheerfulness. For the next half hour, Adam led her through an assortment of every kind of sled she'd ever seen and even more she hadn't seen. She relaxed and listened to Adam's stories about their histories. Talking about them revived him. He seemed to forget about Jenny for the moment. When Angie started to leave, tears came to his eyes again. With seeming and genuine sincerity, he thanked her for coming to his store and for her company.

Angie hustled away from Adam, glad to depart his tomb of desolation. Out in the air, she breathed deeply, uncertain of what she thought about his innocence or guilt.

A car horn, loud and brash after the silence of Adam's store, caused Angie to jump. She turned toward the series of quick honks. Scott drove past in Nev's Porsche. He slowed down and made silly faces at her. Angie waved back. She remembered an old saying that you're not a tourist anymore when you start seeing people you know on the street. Good. She liked this town. And some of its people.

Angie located Sadie's Shear Magic salon, but to her disappointment, a sign on the door proclaimed the shop was closed on Mondays. She needed to talk to Sadie, but it'd have to wait.

The children's carnival activities were in full swing in a park between the one-way lanes of Main Street. Packed with families and kids, it reminded Angie of carnivals she took Caroline and Jonathan to when they were young. At times like this, she missed having little kids but not the hard work and financial struggles of the early years. The memory of the responsibilities she's carried on her shoulders by herself cured her yearnings in a hurry.

With camera in hand, she started checking out the activities. Pre-schoolers gathered around kiddie swimming pools filled with snow and dug with their hands for prizes. They could keep digging until they found a toy, one prize per child.

Standing beside the pool, a little girl cried. Between sobs, she said, "Dylan got a better toy than me." Dylan, apparently her slightly older brother, kept quiet, no way offering to switch.

How many times had Angie tried to resolve her kids' disappointments? She could've told this mom who was trying to fill King Solomon's sandals that these disappointments have no successful outcomes. Grateful not to be in the middle of this one, Angie moved on to the next event.

A line of small kids waited for a turn on a playground slide made of ice. Angie asked a dad standing beside her, "How did they make the slide?"

"They used a front end loader to pile up snow the right size and shape. Then the fire department sprayed it with water over a period of days until it was solid. The steps are from an old swing set. We tried ice steps last year to be authentic, but kids couldn't climb them. We had a pile of kids on the ground all the time. We had to hustle to find a substitute." The man laughed out loud, apparently remembering the calamity of little kids, heavy boots and icy steps. If they were anything like the steps at the train station platform, she fully sympathized with the little guys sprawled on the snowy ground.

Angie got a coffee from a street vendor and sat on a bench to watch young and old ice skate on an outside rink. Another fire department contribution. A mixture of music played over loud speakers. *Winter Wonderland* by Bing Crosby added an appropriate dose of seasonal festivity to the entire park area. Angie truly was in the middle of a winter wonderland.

Giggling came from behind Angie's bench. She turned around and watched older kids throwing plastic rings at little snowmen made of Styrofoam balls. Ring the Snowman--a cute winter version of a traditional carnival standby. With an unexpected smack, an errant plastic ring popped

Angie on the head. Too lightweight to hurt, it still startled her, and took some of the cuteness out of the game.

Surprised by the number of photos she had taken in the kids' area, Angie moved on to explore more of the carnival. She couldn't believe people were paid to do this job.

As she passed Ben's Diner, Angie glanced through the big plate glass windows and saw a familiar bleached blond beehive. Sadie spotted her at the same time and waved wildly, mouthing words to come inside. Angie didn't waste any time getting out of the cold.

Wearing jeans and an embroidered denim jacket, Sadie looked less exotic than she had at the Lantern Inn Sunday night in her stretch pants and low cut top. She wore her hair the same, piled high on her head, apparently her trademark.

Sadie chattered while Angie took off her winter garb. Pushing them and her purse to the far end of the bench, she slid in. "What're you doing?" Sadie asked.

"Having fun at the children's activities. I was more than ready for something upbeat after spending a half-hour at Adam's store--my vote for the most dismal place in New York State. But the good news is that I'm getting over finding Cliff's body. The more I learn about him, the more I'm surprised somebody didn't kill him sooner."

"That's a fact. Cliff was a no-good SOB. What gets me is why George took you inside that mill. I can tell you for a fact that if I'd known Cliff was in there, dead or alive, I'd have run the other way through ass-deep snow as fast as my boots would carry me."

Angie was so caught up in listening to Sadie that she didn't notice Ben approach their table. Eyes downcast and face expressionless, he asked, "Get you something, Miss?" Angie ordered hot chocolate.

"Sadie, does Ben always look so long-faced?"

"No. He's down in the dumps today. Not much of a talker in general, but he's always friendly and chats with his customers. I asked him if he was okay, and he mumbled something about not feeling well."

"Could he be upset about the murders? Was he close to Jenny or Cliff?"

"Nah. Cliff ate here every morning, but Ben and Cliff weren't friends or anything like that. I don't think Ben was close friends with Jenny and Adam either other than chit-chatting now and then." Angie studied Ben's face. He looked like a man in such misery, he might collapse from its weight.

Forcing her attention back to Sadie, Angie asked what she knew about Cliff's love life. "Does this have anything to do with the investigation of Cliff's murder you and George have going?" Sadie asked. "If it does, tell me what you're getting at, and I'll see if I know anything to help you. Keep in mind I would never betray a trust unless somebody's in danger. Just saying."

"Got it. How did word get out that George and I are investigating Cliff's murder? This entire town must be wired for video and audio. Like a creepy science fiction movie. Invisible eyes and ears taking in everything. It makes me wonder how some electronic busybody missed capturing Cliff's murder on video or audio or both."

Sadie laughed at the recording remark. "Don't worry about me knowing what you and George are up to. George and I have been buddies since we were in diapers."

Ben served Angie's hot chocolate and then eased himself onto the counter's end stool, the one closest to Angie and Sadie. He opened the newspaper, but his eyes stuck to one spot on the page. Angie shot a glance toward Ben and shook her head at Sadie.

Sadie whispered, "When we finish our drinks, let's go over to my shop where we can talk in private."

***

While Sadie was unlocking the door to her shop, Polly passed in a car driven by her cousin, Lillian. Angie gave her a polite wave, not wanting to look too cheerful under the circumstances. Polly, zombie-like, didn't return the greeting. Poor humiliated woman. At least she had someone to help her get through this ordeal. This was not going to be an easy time for her. And with all the unsavory news yet to come, it was only going to get worse.

Once Sadie and Angie were inside the shop, Sadie locked the door. She didn't turn on any lights, but sunlight coming through the front windows made it easy for the two women to make their way through the shop. "I never turn on the lights when the shop's closed," Sadie explained. "If I did, half the town would bang on the door wanting their bangs trimmed or their eyebrows waxed."

Sadie led Angie to a little comfy office in the back of the shop and pulled a curtain across the opening before clicking on a lamp. To complete her rituals, she put coffee and water in a coffeemaker. "Now, we're all set. So tell me, why are you interested in Cliff's love life?"

"His penchant for philandering may be linked to his murder. Any one of his girlfriends, or their husbands if they found out what their wives were doing, could easily have been mad enough to shoot him."

"Cliff's a low-life and always was," Sadie said with venomous contempt. "There's always been talk about Cliff fooling around. What are you fishing for?" With this great source of local gossip at her disposal, Angie was tempted to ask her about George, but she'd save that for another time. Right now, she needed information about the women in Cliff's life.

Angie took a deep breath and briefly told Sadie about her and George breaking into Cliff's office and the secret bedroom and videos of Jenny and other women. Angie revealed her theories about scorned women and jealous husbands and blackmail. Sadie listened with wide-open eyes. "So these foolish women went to a secret bedroom in Cliff's office to have a fling or maybe even a serious love affair with him, and the sleaze ball taped them? I thought I'd heard everything, but this beats it all. It's low-down even for an evil bastard like Cliff." Sadie stared into space, her face scrunching into a spiteful frown.

Sadie sure didn't like him. No sympathy from her that he took a bullet to the heart. Had Sadie been a girlfriend? Maybe a dumped girlfriend? Angie liked Sadie and hoped she didn't star in one of the videos.

"So, Angie, you think one of the girlfriends or their husbands killed Cliff?"

"Seems logical. But this is all new to me. In my hometown, when somebody gets killed it's generally a quarrel between two people who know each other. Sometimes the motivation seems trivial, but tempers flare. One of them pulls a gun out of a pickup truck, and the other one dies. Everybody knows who did it. In fact, the shooter stays around so he can tell his side of the story to the police. He wants to get it on record that it was the other guy's fault, and he was justified in shooting him. I'm sure we've never had a murder where half the people in town were suspects."

"So, you got any suspects not connected to Cliff's love life?" Sadie asked.

"Before Cliff was murdered, George had started looking into the possibility that Cliff was embezzling from the Winter Carnival Committee funds. George thought embezzling was the reason for Cliff's murder. But now he's not so sure since we uncovered the sex and videos. Wasn't that a movie title?"

"Yeah. *Sex, Lies and Videotape*. Same as here except for different technology. By the way, I know about the embezzling. George talked to me right after Maggie dropped her bombshell on him. He hoped I might pick up something on the grapevine, but I haven't heard a word. Personally, I think Cliff cleaned out the fund all by himself. As treasurer, he could do it without the risk of involving anyone else.

"Not to sound self-centered, although I am, but are you going to put all this Cliff-crap in your article? That'll kill the town worse than the mill closing." The effervescent Sadie had gone from anger at Cliff to depression.

Angie laughed at Sadie's defeated expression. "My article will be about the fun events of the winter carnival. Finding Jenny's and Cliff's bodies, plus my interest in serious investigative journalism, prompted me to get involved with George in looking into the murders. Of course, the chief included George and me on his list of suspects for Jenny's murder since we were both close by when she died. Same with Cliff's murder. We were in the wrong place at the wrong time twice."

Angie didn't add that she'd solved another murder or that her write-up of that one led to this assignment. If her efforts proved helpful in finding Jenny's and Cliff's killers, she might write an article about those too. Of course, she didn't want it to look like her presence, in some sinister way, triggered a rash of murders. People would start running like hell at the mention of her name.

"One other thing, Sadie, somebody broke into my room at the Lantern last night." Sadie leaned toward Angie. She patted her hand sympathetically and asked what was taken. "That's the strange part. The intruder went through every single thing I brought with me, but the only thing missing was my audio recorder. Saturday night at the Lantern, I recorded a man yelling at a crying woman in the linen room. George and Scott independently identified the man's voice as Cliff's. They couldn't tell anything about the woman. She cried all the time while I was recording. Because of the timeline, the woman was likely Jenny. I guess you heard she was pregnant." Sadie said the whole town knew.

Poor Adam. So humiliating for him. "My theory is that Cliff killed Jenny when he found out she was pregnant because she wanted his help.

Maybe she even insisted he divorce Polly and marry her."

"That sounds like something Jenny would come up with. Poor naive girl. No wonder she's dead if she thought Cliff would give up Polly's fortune for a baby. Anybody in town could've told her not to go that route.

"Hold on a minute here, Angie. If your room was searched Sunday night and the only thing taken was a recording incriminating Cliff, then it stands to reason Cliff was behind it. But he was already dead by then. So, that means he had a partner in his dirty deeds and Cliff had put him up to searching your room." Sadie asked if Cliff could possibly have known she recorded him.

"No, I'm certain he didn't know I was in the hallway. He was in the linen room ranting at Jenny with the door closed. When they stopped fighting, I ran to the library in case they came out of the room. He didn't see me in the hallway."

Sadie was clearly puzzled and intrigued. "Did you tell anybody about the recording?" Angie replied that she only told Scott and George. "Well, you can rule them out. Knowing what a loner Cliff was, I can't picture him having a partner. He's too paranoid. I don't think he'd trust anybody with his dirty secrets, especially with a lot of cash involved. He would've been afraid of somebody letting the cat out of the bag."

"So who searched my room?" Angie asked.

"Beats me. But it makes me uneasy that somebody helped Cliff. Whoever it was didn't do it out of friendship or loyalty to Cliff. You can be sure of that. Cliff figured out a way to force somebody to do his dirty work. Maybe that person killed him. Another suspect and another motive out there."

"Oh, please. No more suspects or motives. We have more than enough with Cliff's girlfriends, their husbands, blackmail and embezzling." Angie's voice dragged as she went through the list.

"It could easily be any one of them," Sadie declared. "They all have powerful motives to mow Cliff down."

"Believe me, Sadie, Cliff had these women trapped with those videos. They must've been desperate to get out of his clutches. George planned to see who else was on the DVDs when he went back to Cliff's office to return the manila envelope, but he didn't have time. Too bad. He could've identified other women and husbands with powerful motives." Sadie looked excited at the prospect of knowing which other women had been lured to Cliff's web as George called it. Maybe Sadie was kinky too. Maybe the whole town of Whispering Pines was kinky as well as homicidal.

"Well, Angie, you came to me for information, but you and George are way ahead of me. I do know one woman Cliff's fooled around with for quite a while. Prissy Wilken. Did George take you by the gift shop to meet the Wilken sisters?"

"We drove by while Sunny was on the sidewalk checking the display. George warned me to avoid Sunny. He said she doesn't live up to her name. So Cliff was involved with the other sister? Prissy?"

"Yeah. A couple of years ago Prissy, who is younger and considerably more cheerful than Sunny, started coming to the beauty shop to get her hair done every week. Keep in mind, this woman had never set foot in a beauty parlor in her life. Not only did she get her hair fixed but asked questions about choosing make-up and how to apply it. And she bought new clothes, expensive, in-style clothes. Another first for her. There's only one thing that can motivate a fashion-clueless old maid to glam up, and that's a man. I didn't see her around town with anybody, so that meant her boyfriend either lived somewhere else or was married. Since Prissy and Sunny never went anywhere, it wasn't likely she could've met anybody so I figured he must be local and married.

"One night, I was closing the shop a little late, around eight-thirty, when I saw Prissy drive past. I had a funny feeling she was on her way to meet her secret boyfriend, so I got in my car and followed her. You and George aren't the only snoops around here," she said. "Anyway, when Prissy drove down the alley behind Cliff's building, I turned my lights off and trailed behind her. When she pulled into Cliff's little parking lot, I was so discombobulated, I almost smacked my car into a tree trying to sneak past. I came within an inch of hitting the damn thing." Sadie bent over laughing.

"I figured Prissy was meeting up with Cliff so they could go to a nearby town on a date, but I guess she went to his secret bedroom. You know what makes me sick about this?"

"It all makes me sick. What gets you?"

"I've known Prissy all my life and to the best of my knowledge, she's never had a date. I just hate to think Cliff was her first lover."

Angie seconded it. "Gross."

Angie added, "Do you think Cliff deliberately hit on these women because they had money for his blackmailing scheme?"

"I doubt he thought that far ahead. Cliff was an opportunist. I bet he started fooling around for the heck of it and added the video recording for some extra thrills and eventually thought of the blackmail angle. And take the embezzling... I bet he didn't run for treasurer so he could embezzle the committee funds. He ended up becoming treasurer and found himself in the position of having the opportunity to do it. But who knows what went on in his warped mind?"

Angie glanced at her watch. "I better get back to work. Want to walk around town with me?"

"I'd love to, but I need to work on my books. Unlike Cliff, I actually work in my little back room." Angie liked Sadie's frankness. She zipped right to the point.

"What do you think Prissy's sister will say if she finds out about Cliff?" Angie asked while she put on her coat.

"I'm sure Sunny knows nothing about sex, so somebody will have to draw pictures to show her what Prissy and Cliff did. When Sunny sees them, she'll have a heart attack, and Prissy will end up with the family business all to herself. Then she can buy more clothes and make-up." The two laughed. "I'm going to seriously mull over what you've told me. If I think of anything that might help, I'll leave a message for you at the Lantern."

What better contact could Angie hope for than a beauty shop owner who sees and hears the town's secrets?

Chapter Fifteen

Angie strolled down the street away from Ben's restaurant and Sadie's salon. She found herself in front of Martin Vanderwelde's pharmacy. Curious about the man whose wife got mixed up with Cliff and unknowingly starred in one of his X-rated videos, Angie went inside to nose around. A tall, slightly built man in rolled-up white shirtsleeves and a patterned tie worked behind the pharmacy counter. Right away, he asked if she needed help.

"Just browsing," she answered and made her way down an aisle. From time to time, she stopped, pretending to examine a bottle of aspirin or a box of Band-Aids, and studied Martin. It was hard to determine much about him except that he seemed professional and efficient in his looks, voice and manner.

The front door opened and, as soon as the woman entered the store, Angie knew it was

Karen Vanderwelde. She looked the same as she did on the video except she was now upright, clothed and prettier in person.

The woman immediately approached Angie. "I saw you at the dessert Saturday night, but I didn't have a chance to say hello. I'm Karen Vanderwelde. Welcome to Whispering Pines. I'm thrilled you're writing an article about the town. It's going to be so good for the carnival."

Angie mumbled an affirming response. She didn't expect to see Karen in the drug store and certainly hadn't foreseen a conversation with her. Inwardly embarrassed that she'd seen such private moments of the woman's life, Angie wanted to get away before she blurted out something inappropriate.

Saving Angie grief, Martin called Karen to the phone. "I'll be there in ten minutes," she told the caller. She waved good-bye to Angie and went out the front door. Relieved she left, Angie trotted down a new aisle. Without paying attention to where she stopped, she picked up a package of the closest merchandise and ended up with a handful of condoms. Giggling like a teen, Angie put them back and hustled along to the less provocative vitamin shelf.

After snagging a few essentials on her shopping list and receiving advice from Martin, Angie hit Main Street again. She stopped at each store window, checked out the decorations, took photos and made precise notes of ideas to include in the article. At the end of the short business district, she crossed the street and walked up the opposite side to admire the decorations.

When she reached the Wilken sisters' gift shop, she debated going inside. Sunny wasn't in sight which meant all-clear for shopping, but after her chance meeting with Karen, she wasn't sure if she could face an encounter with another member of Cliff's harem. Of course, as many girlfriends as Cliff had, she might have to eliminate half the businesses in town. The appeal of the merchandise in the window display won out.

Sadie hit this nail on the head. Prissy was an improved version of Sunny. She wore a stylish blouse and slacks and flawlessly applied make-up. It was obvious she made the most of Sadie's advice. To Angie's relief, Prissy had a Meg Ryan flip hairstyle. She had wondered if all Sadie's customers came out of her shop sporting bleached, teased beehives. The possibility of a town full of Sadie look-alikes spooked her. Apparently Whispering Pines' premier hair stylist reserved the house specialty for herself.

Angie didn't know how Prissy looked before her makeover, but she was a decidedly attractive fifty-ish woman. And now that she'd dolled herself up and gotten some dating and mating experience behind her, Angie predicted she'd do okay with the opposite sex in the future, especially with Cliff out of the way. Prissy's emersion from her drab, celibate life looked permanent.

Prissy was busy helping another customer, so Angie headed for the cat boutique. Her neighbor, Grace, lovingly took care of Chaucer when Angie and the children traveled. Over the course of years, Angie developed a system of buying unique gifts for Grace and her cat, Snowball, which satisfied Angie's need to pay Grace for her kindness. Grace, who refused to travel, delighted in receiving surprises from places she'd never visit.

Both cats needed new collars. Angie usually bought a handful at a time for Chaucer--cheap with elastic release in case he got caught on a bush. Choosing one for him was easy--an inexpensive red one with rhinestones looked perfect for a slightly chubby gray tabby. Regardless of how cute the collar was, it wouldn't be long until he lost it.

Angie took choosing Snowball's collar more seriously and moved up in price range. Accepting of collars and even of an occasional bow clipped on her head, Snowball wore hers until Grace changed it. A bright green collar with white glittery snowflakes caught Angie's eye. Designed for a dainty white girlie kitty.

When Prissy finished with a customer, she joined Angie in the cat corner. Like most people in town, Prissy knew who Angie was. "How wonderful to have a journalist from a popular national magazine writing about our town. Goodness, I never expected something like this." It was an ego trip for Angie to hear someone refer to her as a journalist. It had been a long time coming and rewarded her optimism. The Universe listened to her, responding to her overwhelming positive vibes and ignoring her occasional lapses into despair.

Prissy accompanied Angie to the front door and held it while Angie balanced her purse and a large shopping bag. She stuck her notepad, pen, camera and cell in her coat pocket.

Based on her brief conversations with Prissy and Karen, Angie deemed them to be attractive, intelligent and likeable women. No doubt poor, dead Jenny was too. Why did they get mixed up with a loser like Cliff? A simple answer. Loneliness. Their common denominator. Unfortunately, they chose a poor way to relieve it and the wrong man to help them.

A pickup truck pulled up beside Angie. "Hey, Good-Looking," a man yelled at her. "You new in town? I can show you a good time."

Angie climbed in the cab of the pickup. "Clarice is right, George. You are impossible. How did you find me?"

"Easy. I drove up and down the street. I knew you were here somewhere. How about afternoon tea at the Lantern? I thought you'd like to go so I went home and changed clothes. Clarice can't throw me out for not looking presentable," he said with a smug smile. George had changed from jeans into a black suit, white shirt with lime green pin stripes and a tie with a black and white pattern on a lime background. He was better than presentable. He looked gorgeous. Not only was George a great kisser, he was a snazzy dresser. It was a pleasure to see a man who knew how to dress. George must spend all his income on clothes. Maybe not his smartest investment, but he sure did look hot.

"Wonderful," she told him. "But I have to change clothes first." George said he'd hang out with Scotty while he waited.

When they got to the inn and entered the reception parlor, Clarice called to them, "Hi, Angie. Oh, George, there you are." The polished lilting tone of her voice changed sharply. "I've called everywhere trying to find you. Where have you been?"

"What's wrong now?" he asked, the familiar tone of resignation evident in his question. Angie didn't blame him. Clarice looking for him usually meant work needed to be done. Work with his name on it.

"Brigitte's called here three times. She's been desperately trying to get in touch with you. She said you didn't answer your home phone or cell."

"Is she okay?" he asked, his anxious eyes fixed on Clarice waiting for an answer. Angie felt a strong pang of jealousy. Good grief, she hadn't been jealous since college. She didn't know she could muster up jealousy. It meant she was still capable of caring enough about a man to be worried about another woman in his life.

But who was this Brigitte? Clarice called her *Bri-gitte*, using the French pronunciation. Was she George's girlfriend? Ex-wife?

Clarice assured him Brigitte was fine. "Nothing that some money won't cure."

Money? George was paying money to a woman? For the moment she was going to disregard the obvious reason a man pays a woman. Scrambling to think of less disreputable reasons, did he have a demanding girlfriend or was he behind in alimony payments to an ex-wife? Late alimony sounded more likely because of his dicey job situation. A knot swelled in Angie's stomach, making her feel uneasy and a little nauseous. Although a romance with George was more or less doomed by the distance between North Carolina and New York, she didn't want it sabotaged by some greedy female named Brigitte who probably wasn't even French. Angie only had a few more days with George before she had to go home. She wanted those days to be fun, not to have him yanked away by a female from his past.

"Not to rush you, George, but Brigitte would like the money put into her account this afternoon, *s'il vous plaît*. That reminds me, I better call Francesca right away. Brigitte called her several times too." Brigitte hit up George's mother? "Francesca was flustered because Brigitte couldn't find you and volunteered to deposit the money on your behalf on her way into town for tea. Wouldn't Brigitte have a ball if you both put money into her account? Plus, you'd be in hock to Francesca. Double jeopardy." Clarice made it clear that she thought George getting the short end of the stick was a good joke on him.

Angie felt sorry for George. The women in his life sure expected a lot from him and didn't cut him much slack when things went wrong. In fact, Clarice seemed oblivious to his feelings. Who knew how George's mother treated him? Apparently the mysterious Brigitte's out-of-the-blue demand had thrown everyone, including George, into a tizzy.

Clarice handed George a hand-written note. He looked at the list, squinting. "I can't read this."

"Never mind. I'll rewrite it and give it to you later." Clarice snapped the paper out of his hand and wrote something on a sticky note. "This is the total Brigitte wants." George didn't react. Angie wished she could see how much it was, but she wasn't in the right spot to sneak a peek. "Here's the breakdown of Brigitte's request as per your previous instructions to her," Clarice added.

"Okay. I'll run to the bank and transfer the money now," George said, taking the list from Clarice. "Back shortly," he told Angie, giving her a kiss on the cheek.

"Clarice, call Mother, and tell her I'm going to the bank. If she's already made the deposit, call me right away. I've got my cell," he said, waving it in the air. George got to the door and then turned to Clarice. "And FYI, the reason I didn't answer my cell when Brigitte called was because I didn't hear it. I was crawling under dirty benches on dirty floors replacing Nev's computer cables. He'd nicked them all to hell, and I figured as long as I was there, I might as well put on new ones and save myself another trip over to the greenhouse at five o'clock some morning. So, there." With that said, he closed the door behind him and left.

Clarice totally ignored George's comment and went back to work. She didn't even roll her eyes, the expression of displeasure Angie had learned to expect from Clarice when George flubbed up.

Was it a good idea for George to provoke Clarice with his smart-alecky attitude? With the Brigitte financial crisis looming, he needed all his jobs and paychecks. These Lantern Inn people had strange relationships with each other. Angie didn't think they even liked each other.

Actually, this whole town was sort of loopy and maybe homicidal. Make that definitely loopy and definitely homicidal.

The furor over Brigitte and money puzzled Angie. Why did Brigitte garner this kind of response from George, Clarice and his mother? Brigitte wanted money and everyone was falling all over themselves to make sure she got it. Even Clarice, George's employer, was delivering messages and instructing him how to handle it. And his mother was mixed up in it by offering to loan George money, even planning to deposit it in the bank. Did she suspect or know George didn't have enough to take care of the Brigitte problem? Maybe Brigitte was an ongoing issue in George's life.

With George gone and Clarice talking on the phone, Angie started across the reception area to the elevator. She wanted to escape this talk of Brigitte. She didn't want to hear anything else about this woman who wielded so much leverage.

"Angie," Clarice called to her. "George's mother is coming to tea. She wants to meet you."

Angie politely said she looked forward to meeting George's mother, but she didn't mean it. In fact, she felt nervous about meeting George's mother. Geez, that was silly. Whatever was between her and George was mostly in her imagination. She felt certain his mother only thought of her as the magazine writer, not someone connected with George in a serious, romantic way.

***

After Angie showered, she flipped through her clothes and pulled out an emerald green dress with flutter sleeves and wrap front. She'd bought back it in the fall when she delivered Caroline and her belongings to Georgetown University in Washington DC. So far, she hadn't had any place to wear it. What better occasion for her classy dress than wearing it to an elegant tea at this beautiful and historic inn?

Angie put the dress on for an inspection. The skirt was a little shorter than she usually wore, but she had good legs so why not show them off? All too soon, they'd be old, lumpy legs, and nobody would want to see them.

When she tried on the dress at the store, Angie questioned if it was too youthful for a forty-three year old mother with two children in college. Caroline, her in-house fashion advisor and critic, insisted it was perfect and urged her mother to get it. Now, a couple of months later, Angie was glad she'd listened to her daughter. The dress suited the lifestyle of the woman Angie was determined to become, a successful female journalist with a polished sense of style.

Putting on make-up reminded Angie of Prissy who got a late start on her life. She hoped Prissy had a better future than past. Cliff? Yuk!

For jewelry, Angie wore a slim sterling chain with a contemporary pendant, long sterling earrings and discount store bangle bracelets. She finished off with her strappy heels. She wished she could wear these shoes every day.

All put together, it was time for a long, critical look at herself. The dress fit her beautifully, accenting her boobs and skimming over her tummy. Thank goodness she'd lost some extra pounds. Her long curly auburn hair, green eyes and a sprinkling of freckles gave her a youthful look. Well-cut, nice fitting clothes didn't hurt either.

Angie tossed her billfold and room key into a little black satin purse. She took one last look at her make-up in the bathroom's magnified mirror and declared she looked damn good.

***

Entering the main parlor for the first time during her stay, Angie felt dazzled by its sophisticated glamour. Nev's flowers and greenery embellished with exquisite ribbon complemented the decor. Spellbound, Angie stood just inside the doorway absorbing the understated elegance of Clarice's decorating savvy.

Angie spotted George, her boyfriend, talking with a dark-haired woman. As Angie approached them, the woman turned toward her. She had to be George's mother. He looked like her. The woman wore a rose-colored knit dress on a body that a forty-year old would envy.

George made the introductions. "Oh, please, call me Francesca," his mother insisted. Angie quickly found herself engaged in conversation with this animated woman who gestured in typical Italian fashion. She asked about Angie's children, her hometown in the mountains of North Carolina, her writing job and her current article for *American Scene*. Angie asked about Francesca's Italian heritage. Angie and the children had been to Italy several times, so she was interested and knowledgeable about *Italia*.

George tactfully excused himself and left the two women to get acquainted.

Clarice spoke to her other guests and eventually made her way to where Angie and Francesca were involved in a discussion of their favorite Italian cities. Clarice and Francesca, obviously good friends, stood with their arms around each other's waists like two schoolgirls. Their deep friendship was touching, but it didn't surprise Angie because George said he and Francesca had lived at the Lantern Inn when he was a child. Considering her exquisite looks, Angie suspected Francesca had worked at the front desk or as hostess in the dining room of the inn. She didn't look or act like maid material.

The tea ceremony began with Clarice presiding. Not usually a tea-drinker, Angie entered into the spirit of the afternoon ritual by accepting the drink of the day. She'd become a convert to scones when she and the children rented a house in England one summer, so she went for a plain one with clotted cream. George poured coffee for himself and took several pastries. He guided Angie to a small sofa where they sat.

Angie was still wondering about the mysterious Brigitte. As much as she wanted to ask who she was, she was afraid of the answer. At the same time, before she got any deeper she must know if there was someone else. She settled on an indirect approach to unravel the mystery of

Brigitte. "Did you get to the bank in time to take care of your business?" she asked.

"Just barely. Banks have such odd hours any more, I never know when they're open. Anyway, I got Brigitte's account squared away. Mother said she needs to change her travel arrangements for school break and leave tomorrow instead of the next day."

"Brigitte's in school?" Angie asked.

"Yeah, she goes away to school. Whispering Pines is good for little kids, but I wanted Brigitte to have more challenges in high school. Believe me, it was painful to let her go, but it's a tremendous opportunity for her. That doesn't keep me from missing her though."

If she was going to school, Brigitte obviously wasn't old enough to be a girlfriend or ex-wife. Hoping not to sound too nosy or too blunt, Angie asked, "George, exactly who is Brigitte?"

"Oh, I thought you knew. She's my daughter. Sorry, I keep forgetting that you don't know everybody's family history back to the Revolutionary War. Did you think I had a French girlfriend?" he asked, teasing dancing in his eyes. "Hey, I'm flattered," he added seriously. His daughter? Angie hadn't imagined he had a child. She asked if there were any more. "No. Just Brigitte. She'll be home next week for a short school break. I wish you could stay and meet her."

"I'd like to meet her," Angie said, regretting the things she thought about Brigitte being a greedy ex-girlfriend or wife. "I never guessed you were a father."

"Have been for sixteen years. See, I'm full of surprises," he said. "Later I'll take you over to my place and show you her photos."

It was Angie's turn to be mischievous. She looked at him with pouting lips. "For a minute, I thought you were going to invite me over for a bit of dalliance."

"That can be arranged."

Tea at the Lantern ended at six o'clock, a lovely experience, one of the most pleasant events of Angie's stay.

Francesca left in a flurry, explaining she was meeting Gordon Rothschild, and they were going to dinner and a play. George whispered to Angie, "Judge Rothschild is Mother's boyfriend." So that's how George knew the judge was supposed to be in Boston Sunday and not available to issue a search warrant for Roger. Angie shot George a sharp look as a reminder of how close they came to being caught in Cliff's office. George ignored the accusation and told her the family expected Francesca to marry the judge in the future. Angie thought it was a good idea for George to have a judge in the family. Maybe the judge could keep him out of trouble. On second thought, that was a big job even for a judge.

Angie and George said good-bye to Francesca. Noticing the time, Angie asked George, "Aren't you late leaving for the trolley run?"

George answered, "No, Dan Hall's better now."

"Who's that?"

"He's the regular trolley driver. He's starting back tonight. I filled in while Dan recuperated from a sprained ankle. You didn't think I was a trolley driver, did you?" he asked with a grin.

"What was I supposed to think? You were driving a trolley and wearing that goofy outfit when I first saw you. It seemed logical to assume that was your job. What do you do for a living?"

"Angie, Angie, didn't your mother teach you it isn't nice to ask a man about his finances?" George said, closing the topic. At least, she'd found out he was Brigitte's father. She wondered what else he was or wasn't, where he worked or didn't work. "Now that we've established I don't have to make the trolley run, would you like to have dinner with me?"

"Yes, that would be lovely," she answered.

Chapter Sixteen

Angie hadn't considered the possibility that George had a child. His erratic work schedule hardly lent itself to hands-on parenting. Maybe that's why he sent Brigitte away to school.

And where was his daughter's mother? Was a girlfriend or ex-wife, greedy or otherwise, still in the picture?

After George and Angie left the inn, he suggested they have dinner at a place called *Me Gusta*. He called on his cell phone and made a reservation for seven thirty. "We've got some time to kill. What would you like to do?"

"How about looking at the snow sculptures? Sadie said they're a must-see. I heard everybody in the stores talking about them."

"Good idea. I haven't had a chance to look at them except for a quick glance as I passed on the trolley. I'm glad I'm finished with the trolley runs.

I don't have time for another job. Of course, it was worth it. Look who I met..."

George drove into a neighborhood where snow people stood upright or sat or reclined on almost every yard. The only requisites to enter the competition seemed to be a hefty dose of imagination and the nerve to use it. George pulled up in front of a house with a snow babe wearing a bikini made from an old flowered bed sheet. Laughing, George put the truck in gear and drove up and down streets, frequently pulling to the curb to admire the artistry of a snow person or laugh at an outlandish creation.

Dozens of snow people later, George said, "It's time to eat. I think you'll like *Me Gusta*. It's booked every night."

The line of people waiting to get inside attested to the restaurant's popularity. Since he phoned ahead for reservations, George escorted Angie past the waiting line into an intimate lounge serving complimentary drinks while waiters prepared their table.

Fifteen minutes later, Angie and George were seated at a table in front of a window with a view of Main Street. Angie scanned the menu, surprised at its innovative offerings. It was the kind of menu she expected in some upscale eatery in Europe, and it was just as expensive. Could George afford this place? Didn't boys figure out how to handle dating and money, or lack thereof, when they were teenagers? To avoid an embarrassing situation, she'd follow his lead and order something comparably priced. Offering to split the check might be an iffy move. George didn't strike her as a man who'd allow a woman to pay. She'd go with the flow.

"Everything sounds delicious. What are you getting?" she asked.

"Caribbean Crab Cakes with Tropical Fruit Salsa," George said, making an immediate selection and putting his menu aside. "I love good crab cakes, and they're excellent here. What strikes your fancy?" Her ploy hadn't worked--he'd chosen one of the most expensive items on the menu.

She ended up choosing what sounded most delicious. Champagne Scampi over rice. It was a little less expensive than George's choice so she didn't feel guilty. Rather than having salads, George and Angie settled on a seafood appetizer sampler for two--smoked salmon, mushroom caps stuffed with lobster and spicy grilled Gulf shrimp. "I could do with a couple of orders of these for a meal," Angie declared.

Angie and George held hands while they waited for their meals. Conversation was light, the topics random. She liked this guy so much, the ease with which they slipped into a relationship, the lack of pressure to be talking all the time, the simple joy of being with him.

George's meal was served stacked on his plate beginning with a mold of saffron rice surrounded by slivered vegetables and topped with two generous size crab cakes. Tropical fruit salsa was spooned around the edge of his plate. Angie's shrimp were decoratively arranged around a bed of rice with a stack of vegetables on top of the rice. Angie and George both said the meals were too decorative to wreck by eating, but they dug in anyway. "This is even better than it looks," Angie said.

"I told you it's a great place." The line of waiting diners continued to grow longer.

"Can you remember the Seven Deadly Sins?" George asked.

"What a question! Some. Why?"

"I was just wondering if Cliff made it all the way down the list. Looks like he had a pretty good shot at hitting all of them."

Angie tried to name them but kept up coming up one short. "You know, I think Cliff might have been okay on Gluttony. As I recall, he didn't look heavy."

"True, but keep in mind, the man was getting an inordinate amount of exercise. He could've been guilty of gluttony and stayed thin."

"George, you're terrible. The way we're eating, we may be courting gluttony."

"I'm going to risk it. How about dessert?" Angie declined. "Chocolate cake with raspberry sauce," he told the waitress.

When George's cake arrived, Angie moaned. "That looks decadent. One little bite?" Teasing, he danced a piece of cake on his fork in front of her. She caught his hand and guided the fork to her mouth. "Umm, heavenly."

George offered another piece, but she stood fast. No way was she going to eat herself out of her new designer clothes. She lost twenty pounds after months of hellacious starvation, and they were going to remain lost.

Angie and George took long, slow sips of coffee. "You know, George, I keep having this sick stomach-churning feeling that I know something about Cliff's murder that I can't put my finger on."

"How so?"

"I'm certain I saw something yesterday that wasn't as it should be. Something that was out of place or in the wrong place. When I close my eyes I can almost see it, but I can't grasp it. It bugs me because I'm sure it's important."

George was interested. "Okay. Let's approach this logically. It would've been at the paper mill or in Cliff's office. Let's talk through what we did at both places. With both of us remembering, we're less likely to overlook anything." Together they retraced their steps, interrupting each other often to add a detail or ask a question.

"George, hold on a minute. I can almost see it." She closed her eyes and strained to dislodge the trapped clue.

"Anything?" Angie shook her head. "Well, if you think of what it is, call me on my cell day or night. It means something or it wouldn't nag at you." Angie promised.

When the waiter brought the bill, George scooped it up immediately and stuck a credit card in the leather folder. Who was paying for dinner had been resolved.

The *Sleigh Bells Express* passed as Angie and George left the restaurant. Dan clanged the bell at George and waved. Angie asked, "Isn't it late for the trolley to be getting back from the train station?"

"It's already back and shuttling visitors around town." George looked at his watch. "Hey, come on, and hop in the truck. I want to show you something. You'll love it."

As they drove toward George's surprise, Angie recognized Cliff and Polly's house. Its bleak darkness was a stark contrast to the neighbors' over-the-top lighting. Angie wondered if Polly was inside the house. She hoped she'd gone to stay with her cousin or a friend. What a sad night to be alone when the entire town reveled in the carnival. George held Angie's hand, a warm reminder she wasn't alone tonight.

George headed out of town toward a bright glow of lights in the countryside. "What are those lights, George? We're in the middle of nowhere."

"Hold on a minute. You'll see."

George pulled into a large area that was sort of plowed. He parked his truck and grabbed a flashlight from the glove compartment. Following the crowd, he and Angie trudged toward a steep hill dotted with lights. Confused, Angie didn't know what they were supposed to see or do.

Taking Angie's hand, George led her to an empty standing spot behind a rope. A loud speaker warned, "Ladies and gentlemen, choose your standing place now. For your safety, do not move after the show begins."

"What on earth?" Angie asked. Just then, the lights illuminating the hill went off and darkness fell over the area. George stood slightly behind Angie with his arms around her waist. She wrapped her arms over his and cuddled against him.

One by one, flames flared at the top of the hill. A group of skiers carrying torches wended their way down the hill. Slow-moving, the two rows of skiers crisscrossed back and forth, interweaving in perfect synchronization.

"That was wonderful," Angie told George when the show ended. "I've never seen skiing by torchlight. Quite beautiful."

"If you want to see races or jumps, they go on at the ski slope every day. Downhill, cross-country, tubing, snow shoe. Times and places are on your program." Angie put them in the *maybe* column. She preferred unusual activities. "Speaking of races, check your schedule for dog sled races. You can get a ride on a dog sled too." That was more her speed.

On the ride back to town, Angie and George caught a glimpse of the nightly fireworks display. "Do you want to go and watch?" he asked. Angie passed on the fireworks. She'd taken her kids to multiple July Fourth celebrations. Jonathan and Caroline loved them, but fireworks didn't do much for her.

George parked his pickup so that he and Angie could stroll through downtown. "Look at the Wilken sisters' gift shop windows."

George said, "Sunny's quite artistic."

When Angie suggested that Prissy's talents took a different form, they giggled.

Martin's drugstore displayed an old-fashioned Victorian winter scene with animated characters dressed in velvet and fur. "Those must have set him back some bucks," George remarked. Angie wondered if efficient, precise Martin knew his pretty wife was one of Cliff's lovers. Underneath his calm, professional exterior, was he an angry, jealous husband? Angry enough to blow Cliff away?

As sad as it was, Harden's Hardware looked as festive, or more so, than its neighbors. What would Adam do now? His embarrassing personal life was fodder for the local gossip mill. Could he pull his life back together after his and Jenny's secrets had been bandied around town? Any way Angie looked at this case, Adam had the strongest motive for strangling Jenny and blowing Cliff away. She felt sorry for him, but that didn't cloud her judgment. She ran everything about her meetings with Adam through her head, as well as what she'd heard about him. Nothing triggered that jittery feeling in her stomach.

Sadie had a huge collection of life-size snowwomen, made of all kinds of white fluffy materials, in her beauty shop window. Each snowwoman, clad in a thrift shop dress and tacky wig, was undergoing beautification. Hair, colored or permed, nails and toenails polished in outlandish colors, eyes highlighted by bristly lashes, purple and gold mascara and pouty lips accented by bright red lipstick. "Would you look at this?" Angie said. "Sadie went for the outrageous."

"She's a character all right," George said.

She was a character, but Sadie's hostile remarks about Cliff troubled Angie. Angie didn't want to believe Sadie was one of his love interests, but she might be. Did Sadie have a bone to pick with Cliff? One that embittered her enough to put a bullet through his heart? Was there no end to the list of people Cliff had pissed off?

As Angie and George walked down the sidewalk, she noticed an older woman sitting on a bench brushing snow off her boots. A clue to Cliff's murder tried to emerge but failed. Angie concentrated, even closing her eyes to block incoming static, but nothing materialized. That on-the-verge feeling faded away. Maybe this whole notion of a buried clue was all in her imagination.

***

"The snow sculptures are kind of sad," Angie said.

"Sad? I thought you liked them."

"I do, but so much work goes into them and they melt as soon as it gets warm," Angie replied.

George pulled her close to him as they walked and gave her a kiss on the side of her forehead. "Look at it this way," he said. "The sculptures are like *Frosty the Snowman*. He melts, but he comes back every year." Angie snuggled close to George. She felt sad again, but it had nothing to do with snowmen. In the few days she'd known him, George had burrowed into the core of her being. She was going to miss him desperately when she left to go home to North Carolina. A big, lonely empty space was all that would remain of this remarkable guy.

Chapter Seventeen

George pulled the pickup into a long tree-lined driveway on the outskirts of town. To the left, a rambling white farmhouse with a front porch wrapping around two sides nestled on a spacious snow-covered yard. "That's where my mother lives," George explained. He continued to the back of the property and pulled into an open bay of a four-car garage. Nev's Porsche was parked nearby.

"My goodness, George, does Nev ever get to drive the Porsche? I saw Scott in town with it today."

"What a question, Angie. Sure. Nev can drive it when he wants to. Now, Scotty--that's different. He doesn't have a car so Nev, Clarice and I share with him anytime he needs wheels. But if Nev wanted a Porsche, he'd go out and buy one. He wouldn't ask to borrow mine."

"Yours? The Porsche is yours?"

"Of course it is. Who did you think it belonged to? Nev? Where did you get an idea like that?"

"It was parked at Nev's greenhouse when you took me over there. I assumed it was his."

"No, my dear Angie. I drove *my* Porsche to Nev's greenhouse at five o'clock in the morning and parked it while I fixed *his* alarm and took *his* van packed with *his* flowers and delivered them. I took you to the greenhouse in *his* van, but we came back to town in *my* Porsche. Before you ask - no, I didn't break into a Porsche dealer and steal it."

"Oh," Angie mumbled.

George opened the pickup door for Angie. "Come on. I live above the garage in the chauffeur's quarters," he said, guiding her up the stairs. George unlocked the front door and they entered an open-style living space. Earth-toned walls, leather sofa and chair, walnut tables and bookcases. This was definitely a man's home.

Angie turned in the direction of meowing. A chubby black and white cat stood in the hallway stretching. "Hi, buddy," George said, greeting the cat and scooping him up. "Say hello to Angie."

Angie instinctively reached to pet the cat that responded with loud purring. "What's his name?" she asked.

George didn't reply. Angie continued to stroke the cat's head, looking expectantly at George for an answer.

"Uh--George."

"What did you say?" she asked.

"His name. You asked his name. It's George."

"You named your cat after yourself?"

"Of course not. Do I look that dumb?" Without waiting for an answer, he explained. "When Brigitte was about five, she wanted a kitten. After she and I got to the SPCA, she told me she wanted two kittens--a girl and a boy because she planned to name them Barbie and Ken. After she picked out Ken and Barbie, Ken's brother was left in the cage by himself. The last of the litter. The poor little thing meowed so pitifully, Brigitte and I felt sorry for him. We couldn't leave him in that cage, so we brought him home too. I thought Brigitte would name the extra kitten something like Skipper or after somebody else in Barbie's world, but she insisted on naming him George after me. And funny thing, George took to me from the beginning."

"You have a cat named George?" Angie said laughing. "That's priceless."

George whispered, "Don't make fun of his name. You'll hurt his feelings. Anyway, I was going to explain why George likes me. Brigitte dressed Barbie and Ken in her doll clothes when they were kittens. They didn't mind and snuggled up together and snoozed away in her doll crib. Brigitte loved those cats. Still does.

"George didn't like dressing up so he hung out with me. We're manly men. No dresses and bonnets for us." The more she learned about this man, the more she liked him.

Carrying Little George, Big George showed her the rest of the apartment. On the other side of a bar with stools was a well-equipped kitchen. The two Georges led the way to Brigitte's room. Unlike the rest of the apartment, this was a teenage girl's room done up in pale pink.

A collection of photos of George's daughter at different ages hung on one wall. A beautiful girl with fair skin and delicate features framed by long straight dark hair. In every photo, Brigitte's dark eyes sparkled like George's, and she smiled in the same teasing way. "My gosh, George, she looks like you!"

"That's the consensus. And in spite of it, she turned out pretty," he joked. George explained Brigitte's real bedroom was in his mother's house, but he fixed a room for her in his apartment so they could have nights alone sometimes. "She says it makes her feel like *Sabrina*."

"I can see why. Caroline and I love that movie. Brigitte's life channels Sabrina's too. They both live in the chauffeur's quarters with handsome fathers."

"And don't forget the Paris part."

"What do you mean?" Angie asked. George pointed to a photo of Brigitte at the Eiffel Tower. "Oh, yes. Sabrina went to cooking school in Paris. Did y'all go there on vacation?" she asked.

"Yeah, plus Brigitte goes to boarding school in Switzerland."

"Oh. I thought she went to a nearby school." Angie studied the photos of Brigitte from her childhood to the present. When she looked more closely, she recognized a lot of European backgrounds.

On the bedside table, Angie couldn't stop studying a photo of a young George, holding a baby in a christening dress, and standing beside an unusually thin and pale young woman who seemed to be wedged between him and a priest. George said, "That's Brigitte's mother. She... I want to tell you about her..."

The two of them returned to the living room. "Have a seat," George said motioning toward the sofa. Angie sat down and brushed her hand over real leather. George's mother must be the one with the money. That explained the leather sofa and the Porsche and Brigitte's school in Switzerland.

"I'll open a bottle of wine," George said. He returned with a bottle of Chardonnay and two glasses.

George sat on the sofa beside Angie. His teasing mood turned serious. She didn't like this side of him. She wanted his playful self to return. "You don't have to tell me anything."

George prefaced his story with a drawn-out sigh. "I know, but I want you to know about my marriage before we go further. What I've come to feel for you in the few days you've been here is real. Something special is happening between us." Angie fidgeted, fearful this was bad news for her. Something far more damning to their relationship than the distance that would separate them when she went back to North Carolina.

George poured wine for them. He took a sip and, looking directly at her, spoke. "After high school I went to MIT, and when I graduated I got an engineering job in Boston. One summer day, I met a beautiful girl in a park. Turned out she was from Switzerland and a student at Wellesley. I fell in love the day I met her, and as soon as she graduated, we were married in Geneva."

Listening to George speak about being in love and getting married made Angie uncomfortable, and she diverted her gaze from him to her wine glass. "Two years later, we had a baby daughter, and life couldn't have been brighter. Except my wife, Anne-Marie, didn't regain her energy and vitality after Brigitte was born." George's smile faded and his usual strong voice cracked. "Her doctor blamed her lack of energy on fatigue from the demands of taking care of a newborn. I didn't buy that though. She didn't have the strength to take care of Brigitte.

"I had someone staying with Anne-Marie all day taking care of the baby and doing most of the housework. When I got home from work, I cooked dinner, did the rest of the housework and looked after Brigitte. I even got up for her night bottles.

Instead of recovering, Anne-Marie became sicker. I knew it was more than fatigue."

George paused. He stared into the distance, his face revealing his anguish. In a tiny whisper, Angie asked, "What was wrong with her?"

"I had Anne-Marie's doctor refer her to someone else because she was losing precious strength daily. After a rush of tests, the new doctor diagnosed--cancer. It was too late for treatment." George choked up as if hearing the raw diagnosis again.

Angie tilted her head toward him to hear. "I arranged for a priest to come to the hospital chapel to christen Brigitte because Anne-Marie desperately wanted to attend. I knew she wouldn't live to see any of the other big moments in her daughter's life, but I could make sure she was present for the baby's baptism."

Angie cupped her hands over his.

"Anne-Marie wanted to dress up for the occasion and asked me to bring clothes to the hospital for her to wear. The nurses dressed her, did her hair and make-up and brought her to the chapel in a wheel chair. Anne-Marie was so weak, the only time she stood during the christening was a few seconds for the photo you saw in Brigitte's room. She didn't have enough strength to hold her baby.

"I didn't think I could get through the baptism, but I had to do it for Anne-Marie's sake. I wanted it to be a joyful occasion for her. When it was over, the nurses took Anne-Marie back to her room to bed, and I left the hospital with Brigitte."

Angie wiped away her tears with the back of her hand.

"I sat in my car in the hospital parking lot with my tiny little baby in my arms and--fell apart. I cried until I was numb."

George paused, his voice barely audible. "Anne-Marie died a week later. Brigitte was only four weeks old." George's tightly interlocked fingers turned white.

"Oh, George, I'm so, so sorry."

In a faint voice, George resumed. "I couldn't take care of a newborn baby and work too, so I quit my job in Boston and moved back to Whispering Pines. I was too brokenhearted to work anyway. I couldn't put two thoughts together much less deal with engineering calculations. If it hadn't been for Brigitte, I wouldn't have gotten out of bed ever again.

"When Brigitte and I moved back, I wanted a quiet life so I could be alone with my memories and my grief. Mother bought this place for us, and we moved here. I took care of Brigitte along with help from my mother and some nice ladies."

George nodded toward Brigitte's bedroom. "I took Brigitte to Geneva twice a year to visit Anne-Marie's family so they could be part of Brigitte's life and vice-versa. I had tutors who came to our house daily to speak French with Brigitte. I felt I owed it to her mother to make sure her daughter spoke her language and could converse freely with the Swiss side of her family." Angie was glad he moved to a less emotional topic.

"When it came time to choose a school, I felt comfortable with Brigitte being in Switzerland near family. She liked the idea of being able to spend time with them, and she loved living in Europe. No surprise there," he said, smiling.

He petted the cat lying with its head on his leg. "So George and I live up here. Barbie and Ken stay with Mother. That's home for them, and they still sleep in Brigitte's doll crib. They come visit George and me off and on all day, but they head home at bedtime." George sounded more like himself.

"Angie, I grieved for my wife for years. My mother worried that I would never get over Anne-Marie, and I often agreed with her. But as the years passed, I was ready to date, and I did go out once in a while. The problem was that I didn't meet anybody who appealed to me. I had a magical, passionate love with Anne-Marie, and I wasn't willing to settle for less.

"Believe me, everybody I've ever known tried to fix me up. I've been introduced to every single woman in a thirty-year age range in several states. But nothing happened until a woman with curly red hair came stampeding into the library Saturday night. You took my breath away. All I could think was please, don't let her be married. To make sure, I had Scotty ask you."

Angie confessed. "I was hoping you weren't married either." George took her hand in his and kissed it.

"I'd like to share something with you," Angie said. "At the café, I told you my husband walked out on me and took off when my children were babies. I got a divorce and hoped we'd never see him again. But he came back one time and almost got the children and me killed."

It took all of Angie's nerve to talk about the incident. She kept that day buried in a dark place in her mind and didn't allow it to emerge. Nor did she ever go to it.

A frown spread across George's face, and he sat up straight, as if to better hear.

"One Sunday morning ten years ago, the children and I were leaving our house to go on a picnic. As soon as I backed my car out of the driveway and put the car in gear to go forward, a series of deafening noises exploded."

"What on earth?" George asked.

"At the time I didn't know. My only thought was to get away. I accelerated, trying to speed away from whatever it was, until I saw neighbors rushing out onto their front porch to see what the commotion was. I careened into their driveway and told Caroline and Jonathan to unbuckle and get out. My neighbors shepherded the children into their house.

"When I got out to run into their house too, I saw holes in the front and rear doors on the driver's side of my car." Angie was trembling.

George pulled her close to him. "My God, Angie. What caused them?"

"Several hours later, the police visited my home and told me a man, sitting alone in a pickup, had been shot multiple times and pronounced dead at the scene. He was parked a few houses away on the opposite side of the street with a direct view of my house. They identified the deceased as Jack Stephens, my ex-husband."

"Your ex-husband was shooting at you?" George asked.

"No, he didn't do the shooting. He was the one being shot at. The bullets that hit my car were intended for him."

"How could that be? Why was somebody shooting at him? How could it happen in front of your house?"

"Complicated, isn't it? At the time, I was as confused as you are now. The following day, the police caught the three gunmen who'd done the shooting and pieced together a chain of events that explained it.

"Jack owed these three guys a substantial gambling debt which he couldn't pay, so he ran out on them. Unfortunately for Jack, he'd revealed bits of information when he was hanging out with them like how much he hated me, my name, where I lived and so on. The gambling buddies put the pieces together and came to my town looking for him. Using Jack's clues, they found him staked out in his pickup on my street with a loaded gun on the front seat.

"Highly pissed off at him for running away, they sneaked up while he was sitting in his pickup and ambushed him. Three angry men fired as fast as they could from close range. According to the police, bullets were flying all over the place. They hit Jack so fast that he didn't have time to reach for his gun.

"My bad luck was pulling out of my driveway just as their barrage began. That neither the children nor I was hit by stray shots was our good luck."

"So you think Jack intended to shoot you?"

"Yeah. A year before the shooting, Jack's mother, Myrtle, died and willed her farm, which turned out to be worth a lot of money, to Caroline and Jonathan, her only grandchildren. In addition, she appointed me to handle everything, as I saw fit, for them until they're twenty-one. It goes without saying that she trusted me to do the right thing. Sadly, she saw Jack for what he was and left him nothing.

"I knew nothing about his mother's will until after she died, but I'm sure Jack blamed me for her decision to leave everything to the children. It must've galled him to the core knowing I had complete control of money he believed belonged to him. In my opinion, he planned to get rid of me so he could get custody of the children and their money. I don't think any court would've granted him custody because he didn't support them at all. Plus, he hadn't seen them since the day he walked out on us when they were babies." George gathered her close as if to shield her from further danger. "Ironically, his gangster friends killed him before he could kill me."

He asked, "How did a smart girl like you get mixed up with somebody like Jack?"

"You know, he was fun and kind of reckless, and that appealed to me when I was young. He didn't go beyond six-packs and fast cars when we were dating. But after we married, he started running with a rough crowd. When he left us, I thought he was gone for good, and he probably would've been if he hadn't eventually heard about his mother's death. Being an only child, he hotfooted it back to cash in. Instead, the attorneys informed him that, not only had his mother left the farm to his children, but it had become a piece of property, and his ex-wife controlled it. He must've hated the children and me so much.

"The reason I'm telling you this is that our marriages were totally different. Yours was perfect, and mine was a disaster. But here's the similarity. After my divorce, I was emotionally drained and physically exhausted from being married to Jack. I'd lived on edge worrying what trouble he'd cause next.

"In time, I recovered from my hellish marriage, and I was ready to give dating a chance. I wanted a man, an interesting man, in my life especially as the children got older and began lives of their own. But my problem was the same as yours. I didn't know or meet anyone I liked. *My* mother thought I was soured on all men, but that wasn't true. I was soured on the one I married. I wanted a relationship, but having almost been killed by Jack's recklessness, I set my sights a whole lot higher. It had to be with someone super special or nobody at all."

Angie considered whether she should reveal her feelings to George and decided to go ahead. At this point in her life, she was too old to be coy. "Sunday night when we were sitting in my room in front of the fireplace, I knew that was the way I'd always envisioned romance. Just the two of us being close together, soft music in the background. We didn't need words, our feelings said it all."

George kissed Angie, a kiss different from his other kisses. More passionate and intense. Their relationship had changed and she intended to go where it took her. George stood and reached for her hand. She willingly placed her hand in his, and he led her into his bedroom.

It was no surprise to Angie that George was a romantic, passionate lover. He savored each moment of their discovery of each other. Without reservations, she responded to George's sensual lovemaking.

***

In the wee hours when Angie returned to her suite at the Lantern Inn, she put on her pajamas and settled on the fainting couch. An appropriate place to end her evening, she smiled. In the quiet, she replayed the entire evening in her mind. She knew one thing. She was crazy about George. Making love with him was a far cry from the clumsy, rushed sex she'd known during her brief marriage. She'd waited a long time for love, but it was worth it, even if the distance between them doomed it.

Love existed.

Chapter Eighteen

Just as Angie closed her door to go down to breakfast, her room phone rang. Hurrying back inside to answer it, she saw with surprise that the caller was Cliff's widow. "Hello, Polly, how are you doing?" Angie asked with concern.

In a monotone, Polly said, "To be truthful, I'd like to sleep for weeks, but I have to keep going and make arrangements for Cliff's funeral. Then comes settling legal and financial matters. The saddest part will be when all that busy work is finished, and I have to face the reality that Cliff is gone." Angie sympathized with her, and repeated consoling words that had been said to her when her father died. Although those sentiments hadn't lessened her heartache, they comforted her to know people cared.

"Angie, you were sweet to come with Roger and George Sunday morning to tell me about Cliff.

I appreciate your kindness, and it's selfish of me to impose on you again, but could you possibly do me a favor? I'm sorry to drag you into my troubles, but I can't find anyone else to help me."

"Of course. What can I do?"

Polly let out a sigh of relief. "Thank you. It'll only take a short time, and it could mean so much to Whispering Pines. Two out-of-town businessmen, looking for a site to expand their company, heard the old paper mill was for sale. They called here to talk to Cliff about showing it to them but he's..." Polly seemed unable to find a substitute for *dead* she could bring herself to say. "I've called several people to see if they would show these guys around the mill, but nobody's free to do it. Anyway, to make a long story short, I'll have to meet the men myself. The closer the time gets, the less I feel like doing it. Truth is, as much as I want to help Whispering Pines, I dread going into that building. I don't think I can face this alone. Will you please go with me?"

"Absolutely, Polly, but I don't have a car. Can you or someone pick me up?" Polly agreed, explaining she didn't have the energy or motivation to get dressed up and suggested picking Angie up at the back entrance of the Lantern Inn in half an hour.

"Don't mention the possibility of the mill being revived. I don't want people to get their hopes up. Plus, they'll call me night and day to find out what's happening. I can't deal with that," Polly added.

In spite of Polly's admonition, Angie dialed George anyway. She didn't worry about him blabbing. Besides if she could get in touch with him, he'd be a better choice to go with Polly and discuss the mill's so-called assets with prospective buyers.

Angie didn't get an answer on either his cell or home phones. Oh well, Polly surely knew enough about the mill to handle an initial tour. Angie wouldn't be expected to chime in or glorify the dilapidated buildings. Once the men saw the hideous site, they'd probably run for their car.

Just as Polly pulled up, Angie stepped out the back door of the inn. She got into Polly's four-wheel drive station wagon and tried to strike a balance between sounding cheerfully upbeat and respectfully subdued.

Polly wore jeans, a sweatshirt and a parka. With her hair pulled back into a straggly ponytail and no make-up, she looked nothing like the well-dressed woman Angie met Saturday night at the Lantern Inn or visited Sunday morning at her home dressed to go to church. Cliff's death had taken a visible toll on her attention to her appearance.

As she talked about the businessmen's interest in the mill, Polly began to sound a little more like herself, although lacking her appealing rah-rah enthusiasm.

Angie still thought Polly would've made a better mayor than Cliff. The town should consider electing her now that the position was vacant. "If these guys buy the mill and hire some of the local workers, it'll be great for the town. Most of them have no job prospects," Polly said. George had told Angie not all laid-off workers profited from the carnival's success and that many of them wouldn't leave their hometown and relocate even if offered a job. For sure, revitalizing the old mill property would be a boom for them.

Talking about the mill seemed to boost Polly's spirits so Angie, although she hated everything about it, sought to hold onto the topic by asking questions, "How did the buyers hear about the mill?"

"The one who called said they stayed at a hotel on the interstate last night, and in chatting with the desk clerk, they mentioned they'd been nearby looking at a building to house their new business. The clerk told them about our empty mill, and they decided to take a look while they were so close." For the town's sake, Angie hoped this out-of-the-blue stroke of luck panned out.

Polly pulled into the mill's driveway where a wide swath had been plowed from the cleared area where Angie and George had parked close to the entrance of the mill. Polly pulled in front of the main mill building in almost the same spot where Cliff's vehicle had been parked Sunday morning. Just being in the parking lot made Angie jittery. Going inside the building would require all the strength she could muster. Even that might not be enough to push her through the front door.

Polly checked her watch. "We're a few minutes early. We might as well open the doors and let the light in so these guys can see the inside of the building." Polly led the way and unlocked the front door.

Even before Angie walked through the door, the nauseating and frightening memories of finding Cliff's body hit her. As far as she was concerned, evil ruled in this building. Forcing aside her own anxiety, she focused on Polly's reaction to being in the building where her husband was murdered. Angie asked, "Do you feel okay about going inside?"

"No. Not really, but I'll try to keep my mind on why we're here. It won't take long for the guys to look around. If they're interested, they'll need to get in touch with the attorney who's handling it." Angie hoped there were no remaining signs of Cliff's murder, like big red blood stains on the floor that might upset Polly. Or herself.

Polly led the way into the building, stopping just inside the door, out of the wind. Angie knew it was absurd, but she couldn't shake the feeling that another body lurked in the shadows, hunkered down, waiting to trip her. While Polly concentrated on watching the parking lot for the businessmen, Angie used her time scanning the mill's cement floor for stray bodies. Making visual sweeps, she completed the area lit by the open door, her gaze coming to rest on her own boots before drifting to Polly's.

The elusive clue Angie had tried to recover popped into her brain fully resolved. It made sense why, the night she and George looked at festival decorations, the old woman sitting on a bench brushing snow off her boots chewed at her.

The clue. Boots. Polly's boots. The same two-toned tan suede boots Polly had been wearing Sunday morning when Roger, George and Angie arrived at her home to tell her about Cliff's death. Boots that were dark tan with a band of light tan at the top. The same boots Polly was wearing right now while they waited for the businessmen, except the boots were no longer two-toned. They were light tan from top to bottom. In spite of the color difference, Angie had no doubt these solid tan boots were the same two-toned boots Polly had worn Sunday morning. The boot designer's signature gold buckle and decorative straps left no doubt in Angie's mind.

While Polly stood in bright sunlight, her boots revealed her secret, a telltale wavy water line about two inches from the boots' tops clarified why Angie had mistaken the light color for trim. Polly's boots had been wet Sunday morning. Not just wet. But soaked. Soaked enough to turn light tan suede into dark tan suede.

In an attempt to deflect suspicion away from herself, Polly had made a point of telling Angie, George and Roger she'd stayed inside the house all morning waiting by the landline phone for Cliff to call, even emphasizing she hadn't gone outside to get the newspaper. So why was Polly wearing uncomfortable wet boots? So simple. She hadn't stayed in the house as she claimed. She'd been outside in the snow a long time for her boots to get soaked. Whether she forgot to change when she got home or whether she didn't think anyone would notice, she'd failed to hide a crucial clue in her husband's murder.

With this knowledge tumbling around in her head, panic threatened to obliterate Angie's capacity to reason. To counteract her mental processes shutting down, she focused her whole being on trying to remain casual and normal until the businessmen showed up. Please, hurry, she silently begged them. She stuck her shaking hands in her coat pockets so Polly wouldn't notice.

Where were those guys? Angie willed them to get to the mill. One way or another, she was leaving the mill with them. She didn't care where they were going--they had a new passenger. No way was she getting back in Polly's car.

***

Polly pointed a pistol at her. "What on earth, Polly?" Angie asked, resorting to a quickly improvised innocent expression.

249

"I'm sorry, Angie, but you know too much."

"Know too much? What are you talking about? I've only been in Whispering Pines a few days." Angie protested loudly. Her few minutes of mulling how Polly got her boots wet had earned her precious insight into what she faced. Even if it had come at the last minute, she knew what had happened to Cliff. Was there time to make use of her newfound truth?

In what she hoped sounded like a sincere, soothing voice, she said, "Oh, Polly, you don't know what you're doing. You've been through so much in the past few days. Put the gun away so we can talk. I lost my father, and I know how desperately it hurts. Let me help you." Polly showed no signs of relenting. Her usually vivacious eyes stared at Angie with the lackluster appearance of fake blue sapphires.

To her regret, she and George overlooked a suspect, the scorned wife. They put scorned mistresses on the list but neglected to consider the scorned wife who'd played the role of bereaved widow with stellar believability.

Sorting out the suspects was behind her. Her only concern now was how to save herself. With no plan in mind, her default strategy was to stall by slowing the pace and lowering Polly's boiling point.

Remembering the businessmen would come driving up any minute and her resolute plan to bail with them when they left, Angie brightened, but hope flowed out of Angie just as quickly. Polly had made up the businessmen. She wouldn't have arranged for witnesses while she dispatched Angie. Her spirits dropped with a thud.

No wonder Polly told her not to tell anyone they were going to the mill. It wasn't to stifle false hopes about selling the mill. It was to prevent anyone from knowing where they went. And Angie, cautious mother of two and tireless preacher of personal safety strategies, failed to follow one of her most basic rules, always let somebody know where you're going.

She violated that one by not leaving a message for George. Since she only planned to be gone a short time, she didn't bother to tell him she was going to the mill with Polly. His caller ID would show she called but not that she was in trouble or where he could find her. George wouldn't be coming to rescue her this time like he had when she had the nightmare about Cliff. This time, she really needed to be rescued.

Like all the other crises in her adult life, she was on her own.

Polly spoke, "Turn around and walk straight ahead." Moving in slow motion to gain time, Angie found herself facing the back of the building. That's when the rest of the missing clue hit her. Sunday morning after the police arrived at the mill, Officers Brendan and Andy pointed out tracks leading from the back of the mill to a service road behind the Stop'n'Shop Supermarket to the chief. While the officers examined and discussed how the tracks related to Cliff's murder, Angie noticed one set of tracks differed from the others. At first glance, the tracks appeared to have been made by a man wearing cowboy boots.

Instead, they were tracks made by a woman wearing boots with a chunky heel. Tracks made by Polly Schouten Sunday morning when she came to the mill to do away with Cliff. Tracks made by one of the few people in Whispering Pines not on the suspect list.

Polly shot Cliff, and now she intended to shoot Angie. Well, if Angie had a say in it, she wasn't going to die in this frigid, vile building. In the meantime, she'd keep Polly engaged until an idea formed. "Polly, Roger told you everything about Cliff's murder that we knew. Where did you get the idea that I knew more?"

"You and George have been playing detective, asking questions. I thought it was harmless until I saw you and Sadie going into her beauty shop yesterday morning. You see, Angie, only one person in the whole world could figure out that *I* was the one with the best reason to kill Cliff, and that was Sadie. When you started stirring her memory, she would remember things I told her ages ago. I couldn't wait around and let you two run to Roger, and tell him I killed Cliff.

"I've put way too much planning into this to let you and Sadie ruin it. All it would take is for one of you to run to Roger and convince him to turn his investigation toward me before I can get out of town. Yes, Angie, if you still have any doubts, I killed Cliff. And I would gladly do it again. I have to kill Sadie too, and I'm sorry about her. She's my friend and I'm terribly fond of her. And I'm sorry I have to shoot you. I would've liked being friends with you."

"Polly, you can't mean what you're saying!" Angie shouted at her. "You can't shoot Sadie!" Angie said, sincerely meaning it. "What could you possibly have told her that's so bad you think you have to kill her?"

"Several years ago I confided to Sadie I found proof that Cliff was screwing around on me. I'd heard rumors for a long time. One day, I had to borrow his SUV and found condoms in the glove compartment. He doesn't need to use them at home. Not only was it devastating to discover such indisputable evidence the rumors were true, but it hurt and insulted me that he'd gone for a younger woman. When I found out, I was so angry I began hatching up plots to get my revenge on him.

"I reported my latest diabolical plot to Sadie every week while she did my hair. At first the plots were fantastical, and the thrill served to preserve my sanity. Getting even with Cliff fueled my days. Then I thought, why not do it? The more I got used to the idea, the better I liked it. So I started planning the perfect murder. This time the plots were for real so I didn't talk to Sadie anymore. To my regret, I knew when I got ready to put my plan into action, I'd have to kill her. She knew I hated Cliff and wanted my revenge. Sadie would know I did it. Nobody else in Whispering Pines, but Sadie, thought simple-minded Polly could've found proof her bastard of a husband was running around on her and smart enough to conceive a plot to kill him."

"Polly, you're wrong. I'm sure Sadie didn't take you seriously. She didn't mention any of this to me."

"Regardless, I have to make sure neither of you talks. I put a lot of planning into my plot, along with a nice bit of help from Lady Luck. About six months ago, Cliff had chest pains during a town meeting and was rushed off to the local hospital and then transferred to the city for by-pass surgery. The nurses gave me his valuables including his coveted key ring, which never left his tight fist.

"While Cliff fought to save his miserable life, I was hoping the son of a bitch would die and save me the trouble of killing him. But I couldn't count on him co-operating. While I had the chance, I snagged his keys and had a duplicate set made and went through every inch of Cliff's office. I do mean every inch.

"I told Cliff's doctors I was too upset to make the trip to the hospital to visit him. That let me off the hook of playing the distraught wife. I spent my days going through Cliff's disgusting romper room."

Polly was proud of her discoveries and told Angie she found the videos early in her search and took them home to make copies. "I have them packed, addressed to the husbands involved and ready to drop in the mail on my way to the airport. Wouldn't you like to be a fly on the wall when those husbands pop their little surprise gifts in the DVD player? I addressed Prissy's video to her because I don't hold a grudge against her. I always felt sorry for her. I do want her to know what a foolish mistake she made trusting Cliff and how evil he was. Maybe she'll learn something. She hasn't had much of a life. I certainly didn't want to give that sister of hers any ammunition."

"How did you get Cliff to come to the mill Sunday morning?" Angie asked.

Angie flinched at the sound of Polly's metallic laugh. "The same way I did you. I called him at Ben's Diner Sunday morning and told him he just had a call from two businessmen who wanted to look at the old mill. The dumb ass fell for it as easily as you did." Angie didn't like being compared to Cliff, especially when it came to their dumbassed-ness. "I parked behind the Stop'n'Shop so Cliff wouldn't see my station wagon and walked over. I used my set of duplicate keys to let myself in and waited for my quarry. Clever, huh?"

Angie grunted a response. Diabolically clever.

"I had every little detail planned for Cliff's murder. I experimented with different routes from my house to here so that I could make the trip without being seen. I parked behind the Stop'n'Shop a number of times and tromped through the snow to make a path. I learned to get around in the mill in complete darkness. Sometimes I brought lunch and sat on an upside-down bucket while I plotted how I wanted the whole thing to play out." It made Angie queasy to think of Polly sitting in this dark building munching on a Big Mac while plotting the most lethal way to blast Cliff.

"So Cliff came here expecting to show the mill to some prospective buyers?"

"That's right. When he got here, he unlocked the front door and stood inside the building out of the wind watching for the buyers to drive up. I waited in the shadows. Cliff didn't know I was here until I spoke. You should have seen him jump!" Chilly bumps broke out on Angie's arms. She wanted to rub them away, but she didn't dare startle Polly. "Then he saw the pistol... and he knew I had caught him. Caught and trapped. I told him to walk toward the back of the building, and he went along with it. I expected him to lunge at the gun or do something heroic to save himself. I was ready and would've pulled the trigger if he'd even thought about coming at me."

"Did you talk to him during this?" Angie asked.

"Oh, yes, indeed. I made sure he knew I uncovered all his filthy secrets. I told him about having duplicate keys made and searching his office while he was in the hospital. I described in detail who and what I saw on his videos. I told him copies of his videos were ready to go into the mail to the husbands of his lady friends. How I found the cash in his safe and records of how much money each woman paid him in blackmail. While I was in his office, I took out handfuls of cash. Since nobody had access to his safe but him, I figured he didn't bother to count it. I'll tell you what's funny, Angie. I went back to that safe in Cliff's office every time he went to the city to see his doctor, and I took all the cash I could stuff in my purse. Then I went out and bought extravagant clothes and shoes with it. I have plenty money of my own, but spending Cliff's made me feel a whole lot better.

"What gave me the most pleasure was the look on Cliff's face when I told him I transferred all the funds from his embezzling account into an international bank account of my own. That cut deep. He looked like he just might have another heart attack on the spot. That would've been his least painful outcome.

"I reminded him that I had him sign Power of Attorney documents when he was in the hospital and thought he might die. I used that handy little document to obtain maximum loans on all our properties. I put those funds in my account too.

Then I asked him, 'Which of us is the dumb one now?'

"Didn't he try to get away?"

"As cold as it was in this frigid building, he was sweating like crazy and his eyes were wild, darting all over the place. I knew he was going to make a move. When he lunged at me, I shot him right in his lying heart."

Cliff might have been sweating, but Angie was having chills. Who would've guessed so much calculating hatred lurked behind Polly's cheerful, sweet-looking face?

Angie wanted to cover her ears to shut out Polly's shrill cackle. "Of course, in all my planning I never dreamed that anyone would show up out here at the mill on that Sunday morning. Here came you and George muddling into my plans. Lucky for me, I heard you coming and hid in the back of the building. I didn't figure you'd stay long, especially when you found Cliff with a bullet hole in him. I saw you run out the door, but I had to fire a shot at George to get him moving. I didn't intend to hit him or else he'd have been lying dead beside Cliff. After I got rid of both of you, I turned Cliff over and went through his wallet."

"Why take the time? You said you already went through his office."

"He had a little piece of paper in his wallet with the account numbers and passwords where he'd stashed all the money he embezzled from the Winter Carnival Committee. I wrote them down when he was in the hospital, but I needed to destroy his copy so the police couldn't find out where he deposited the money. I didn't want them tracing the money until I got out of the country.

"It's good timing I chose that Sunday. Cliff's passport and airline ticket were in his SUV. He was leaving that night for South America. But even if he'd got away, he wouldn't have had any money except what he blackmailed from those stupid women. I transferred the rest of it out of the country, and in my name and mine alone.

"After I got the scrap of paper with the account numbers from Cliff's wallet, I left by the mill's back door. I figured the police would be on their way soon so I hustled home and put on my worried wife look and practiced playing the grief-stricken widow.

"As soon as I'm finished with you and Sadie, *poor simple-minded Polly* will have completed the perfect murder and disappeared forever," she said.

"You wasted precious time bringing me out here. Sadie doesn't remember what you told her. She thinks you're still her friend, and she feels compassion for you."

Angie planned her move while Polly prattled about how she beat Cliff in their death duel. Cliff's ill-advised lunging at Polly was etched on Angie's brain. It didn't work for him, so she mentally erased that from her short list of options.

Angie played up to Polly. "I should have figured this out, but you were so convincing as

Whispering Pines' cheerleader and sweet, trusting wife. As a grieving widow, you've given an outstanding performance." Polly looked pleased. "I give you full credit, Polly. Nobody thought you knew about Cliff's infidelity. Nobody suspected you of having a motive for killing him."

Angie shifted her weight from one foot to the other, moving a few inches to the left. She hoped it looked natural, not a threatening move. She needed Polly to have to readjust her aim, ever so slightly though. "Everybody thought of you as the wronged wife who didn't have any idea her husband was a philanderer." Polly didn't react to Angie's slight shift so she made another tiny shuffle. One more baby step, and she'd be set. She better get it right. This would be her only opportunity to save herself.

Angie moved again. She was about to find out how good a teacher Martin Vanderwelde was. Her timing had to be perfect or Polly would shoot her on the spot and she'd be as dead as Cliff. Keeping the conversation on Polly's exceptional husband-killing skills, Angie complimented her on her ingenious use of Cliff's illness to set up her plans. Polly volunteered the flawless ploys she used to pull it off. While Polly relished relating Cliff's last moments, Angie saw the barrel of the pistol wobble slightly downward toward the floor. In mock admiration of Polly's coup, Angie laughed with Polly.

At that moment, Angie squirted pepper spray directly at Polly's head. Polly dropped her pistol, clutching her face with both hands.

Angie snatched up the pistol and ran toward the door, frighteningly aware this was the second time in three days she'd run out of this building. Polly's scream kept coming from the same spot. She hadn't moved. Yet.

Angie ran until she was outside and leaned against Polly's car for a moment to catch her breath. She had no illusions that Polly's key would be in the ignition, waiting to whisk her to safety. When they'd arrived at the mill, Polly took her key ring with her to unlock the mill door. She'd then dropped the keys in her coat pocket.

"As she gasped for breath, Angie spotted Polly's cell phone lying on the console. She opened the unlocked door, snatched up the phone and started running toward the clearing. Angie didn't know how quickly Polly might recover from the pepper spray. Martin only taught her to spray, not going into details of how long the victim would remain out of commission.

At least Angie had a cell phone and a pistol. She didn't know anything about using the gun, but she'd try if she had to. She wished she could stop for a minute and see if she could find the safety catch. Or did pistols have safety catches? Instead of stopping, she kept running, stopping only long enough to dial George's cell phone. "Please pick up," she begged.

George answered on the first ring. "Who is this?" he asked abruptly.

On the run again, she replied, "George, it's me, Angie. I came to the old mill with Polly. She was going to shoot me, but I got away. I'm running toward town on that road that leads from the old mill. My--lungs--are--going--to—burst...

"Where's Polly? Does she still have the gun?" George yelled.

Angie was so winded, she could barely speak. "In the mill. No, no. I have her gun. Tell me how to use it. Where's the safety catch?"

"Angie, don't mess with the gun," George commanded. "We're nearly to the mill. Stop running. We'll be there in a minute." Panting, Angie flopped down on a snowy stump. She kept her eyes on the road leading from the mill, alert for any sign Polly was coming after her. If Polly's car moved, Angie planned to jump into the woods. Polly couldn't drive through trees.

Angie examined the pistol clutched in her hand. Aha, she found a safety catch, but she couldn't tell if it was on or off. She wanted to test it, but approaching sirens signaled arriving police. She stood up when Roger's car, followed by Andy and Brendan in a second car, came into view. She waved them on as they raced past her toward the mill.

In the third car, her knight-hero skidded to a stop. No white horse but a silver Porsche convertible was close enough. Angie waved her hands to him. George ran toward her. "Put the gun down, Angie!" he yelled. Without thinking, she realized she was waving it in the air. She held her arms straight out to her sides. George took the gun from her and checked it. "Loaded and the safety's off. Good lord, Angie, you could've wiped out a good chunk of Whispering Pines' police force and its favorite son waving that thing around." He put the safety on and placed the pistol in a cubby in his car.

He pulled Angie close to him and she melted into his arms. He held her, murmuring, "I was so scared Polly had hurt you." Oh, how she like being consoled by this guy!

***

Angie and George sat in his car in the clearing waiting for instructions from Roger. George held Angie close, telling her over and over how glad he was that she was safe.

"Why was Polly going to kill you?" he asked.

"Some time back when Polly was getting her hair done, she confided to Sadie she knew Cliff was running around and shared fantasy plots to get even with him. When Polly saw Sadie and me go into the shop alone Monday, she was afraid Sadie would remember the plots and reveal Polly likely was Cliff's killer before she could make her getaway. In Polly's warped logic, she determined she had to get rid of both of Sadie and me so we couldn't spoil her plans. Polly's fears were groundless, because Sadie didn't tell me about Polly's plots. Sadie must've passed them off as idle threats. You and I were focused on the girlfriends, their husbands, the blackmail and the embezzling. I tried to tell Polly that Sadie didn't connect her to the murder."

"Maybe not yesterday, but she did today."

"What do you mean?" Angie asked.

"Sadie left a voice mail for you at the Lantern Inn, but she got worried you wouldn't get it so she called me. It seems after the two of you talked at her shop, she remembered Polly's threats about getting even with Cliff and that, for no apparent reason, Polly stopped mentioning them."

"That was when she started weaving real plots."

"Sadie wanted to warn you. She had a terrible feeling that Polly put her plan to get even with Cliff into action and shot him. When I called the Lantern trying to find you, Scotty told me Polly had called your room earlier. He knew because he answered the phone and recognized her voice. He and Clarice both worked in reception all morning and didn't see you leave, so they dashed all over the inn trying to find out where you were. One of the kitchen workers was on a smoke break behind the inn and saw you go out the back and get into a station wagon with Polly."

"Oh, I'm so grateful."

"Ben helped you out, too, although he didn't know you were with Polly and in danger. He'd heard several versions about Polly's phone calls to the diner. Some of the rumors weren't true, and Ben wanted to make sure that part of the record was correct. He contacted Roger and made an official statement.

"According to Ben, Polly called Cliff at the diner yesterday morning and talked to him for a few minutes. Ben heard Cliff's end of the conversation which went something like, 'Okay, I'll meet them out there at ten o'clock. What's their names?' Polly didn't mention anything to us about that call. What she actually said in her statement was that she called Ben when Cliff was late coming home to see if Ben knew where he was. Ben swears she didn't make that call. Ben always answers the phone. He's had problems with his staff getting too many personal calls.

"Cliff turns his cell phone off when he's at the diner, so Polly had to call the diner's number to reach him. Ben said she only called once when she talked to Cliff about meeting businessmen at the mill. Imaginary businessmen as we now know."

"Ben's right. Polly told me she called Cliff at the diner about the businessmen. That's how she got him to go out to the mill."

"After we knew Polly lied about her phone calls, we were in a panic to find you. The police and half the town were looking for Polly's station wagon. Word spread fast that you were in trouble. When Prissy heard the police were looking for Polly's car, she called Roger right away reporting she'd seen it about fifteen minutes earlier heading in the direction of the old mill."

"Polly's station wagon's pretty generic looking. How did she know?"

"Easy. Polly has a big smiley-face bumper sticker."

Chapter Nineteen

Roger and another officer led Polly outside to a waiting police car. Instead of the self-assured, contemptuous woman who'd held a gun on Angie with every intention of pulling the trigger, Polly walked hunched over, her body sagging, her head bowed low. Her plan, so painstakingly hatched, had failed. She got her revenge on Cliff but at a terrible price to herself.

Angie buried her face in George's shoulder, not looking toward Polly as the police car drove past them.

***

Roger greeted Angie and George at the police station. "Sorry to have to drag you through this before you've had a chance to calm down, but I need to get your story while it's fresh in your mind."

"It's okay," she told him. "Talking about it's not nearly as bad as living through it. And besides, it's over. Polly killed Cliff; nobody else was involved." Roger allowed George to stay with her during the questioning. Angie carefully explained everything that happened beginning with Polly's phony telephone plea to her for help. "I thought I was doing a grieving widow a favor," Angie told them. "I didn't know how wrong I was until we got inside the mill and I saw Polly's boots--"

"What's Polly's boots got to do with this?" the chief asked.

"They're the clue I've been trying to remember for two days. It would've been a lot better if I figured it out earlier."

"Are you saying Polly's boots were a clue to Cliff's murder?" Roger asked.

"Her boots were *the* clue. What I struggled so hard to remember was that Polly's boots were soaked when you, George and I went to her house Sunday morning to tell her Cliff was dead. Yet, she told us she was so worried about Cliff that she hadn't been out of the house all morning, even to get the newspaper. Wet boots proved she walked or stood in deep snow for an extended period of time. And then it clicked that her boots must have made the set of tracks behind the mill, the ones I thought were cowboy boots." Angie paused, expecting a question from Roger.

"Just keep talking. You're doing fine."

"After I was already in the mill with Polly, I noticed she was wearing those same boots, except they were dry. At that moment, I knew she killed Cliff and planned the same for me. My only chance of getting out of that mill alive was that remembering Polly's wet boots gave me a few minutes warning. And it was only a few minutes between the time I knew she killed Cliff and when she pulled a gun on me. I didn't have a plan but, at least, I knew I needed one."

"How did you get loose?" George asked.

"Polly thought she was home free and ready to celebrate getting rid of Cliff. She recounted how she caught Cliff in his web of deceit, bragged about putting his assets into her name, luring him to the mill to do him in and getting even with Cliff's girlfriends by mailing their telltale videos to their husbands on her way out of the country.

"While Polly was on her euphoric ego trip, I was careful not to interrupt her glorious mood and grasped for a scheme, however half-assed, to get away from her. Cliff's dead, bloody body had proved Polly could shoot faster than a person could run so splitting for the door wasn't an option.

"To carry out my hasty, fuzzy plan, I took baby steps to maneuver myself into position for what would likely be my only chance to escape. When I thought I had my best chance, I squirted pepper spray at Polly's face."

"You what?" Roger boomed. George beamed admiringly at Angie, keeping his arm around her.

"Pepper spray. I bought it yesterday at Vanderwelde's drug store. Martin gave me lessons and insisted I go out back for a couple of minutes to practice. He went with me to make sure I could open and aim it without squirting myself in the face. I give Martin an A plus as a teacher and another A plus for rejecting my claim that I could do it without instruction or supervised shots."

"I'll be damned," Roger said. "What happened next?"

"When Polly grabbed her face, she dropped the gun, and I scooped it off the floor and ran like hell. I grabbed her phone out of her car and used it to call George when I got out on the main road. End of story." Angie was surprised how matter of fact she sounded. All in all, the outcome was all that mattered.

"You saved yourself and got the whole story out of Polly," Roger told her.

"Congrats on quick thinking. If she'd got away..." In turn, Angie thanked him for rushing to her aid.

George beamed with pride as he listened to Angie's story.

Roger turned the recorder off. "Did you two already know about these videos Polly planned to mail?" George and Angie nodded. "Who else knows about them?" Angie let George answer. This was his town, his people.

"We've discussed them with Clarice, Nev, Scott and my mother. Anybody else, Angie?" Angie added Sadie to the list.

"Okay, next question. Who's involved in this video business?" Again Angie was silent as George listed Jenny, Karen and others. "Karen?" Roger asked incredulously. George explained the videos didn't leave any doubt. "I'll be damned," declared Roger.

"There's at least one other woman who's probably going to be on the tapes, Prissy Wilken. Sadie told me she was seeing Cliff," Angie added.

They both stared at her. "Prissy got herself a boyfriend?" Roger asked.

"According to Sadie."

Roger closed his eyes for a minute, letting it sink in. "So, a set of these videos showing these three women and probably more, are locked up in Cliff's office, and Polly made another set to send to the husbands? What about Prissy? She doesn't have a husband."

"Polly said she was sending it directly to Prissy as a warning to be more careful in her choice of boyfriends. She didn't want Prissy's sister to get her hands on it. Polly had sympathy for Prissy but not Cliff's other loves."

"Figures. It was past time for Prissy to find herself a boyfriend. Too bad it was Cliff," Roger said. "One more question. Where's Polly's set of the videos now?"

"She said she planned to mail them on her way to the airport. My guess is they're at her house or in her station wagon."

Roger told his desk clerk to call Gordon for a search warrant for Polly's station wagon. A few minutes later, the clerk reported Gordon wasn't in his office. "Hell, George, call your mother and find out where the judge is. I've got to put those videos in safekeeping."

George dialed several numbers on his cell phone before tracking Francesca and Gordon down at the Lantern Inn and handing the phone to Roger. After a brief conversation with the judge, Roger said to Angie and George, "Let's get over to Cliff's office. George, since we don't have a locksmith in town, I need your help." Angie wondered how Roger knew about George's lock picking. Of course, everybody in Whispering Pines knew everything about everybody so why not? It wouldn't be easy to keep a secret in this town.

Roger told them, "I already have search warrants for Cliff's office and house. Gordon's going to issue one for Polly's car and send it to me shortly."

Roger in his police car and Angie and George in his car pulled into the little parking lot behind Cliff's office. Angie couldn't believe she was going back inside Cliff's office. At least this time, George's lock picking was sanctioned by the police chief with a search warrant in his possession.

George led the way to the room marked Inventory.

"So this is where Cliff conducted his after-hours business, huh?" Roger asked, walking around the secret bedroom. George showed him Cliff's secret video camera hook-up. "I see all this, and I don't believe it."

"Creepy, huh? Here are the videos," George told him, deftly unlocking the cabinet with his knife.

"Let's see how incriminating these things are and who's involved. It's private here. I don't want to look at them at the station or at home."

George said in a loud whisper to Roger, "Don't act like you're enjoying this. Angie'll accuse you of being kinky." Angie glared at him. George ignored her and pulled the first video from the cabinet and inserted it in the player. Angie didn't recognize the woman. It wasn't Jenny or Karen or Prissy. The scene was quite erotic and when Cliff shifted position so that his companion's face was clearly visible, Roger stared at the woman on the screen. "Hell, George, I didn't expect anything like this! No wonder Polly shot Cliff. Just between us, she might've been justified." Roger told George to stop the video. George played short bits of the others, and Roger jotted down names. Roger flopped down on a chair and said, "Nothing in my college courses covered this. I'll never get used to what stupid things people get themselves into, but I'd hate to see these videos made public."

"Well, we know the videos didn't have anything directly to do with Polly's decision to pump a bullet into her husband," Angie advanced. "Finding condoms in Cliff's glove compartment was the catalyst that led to her plot for revenge. Finding the videos fueled her obsession to get even with him. She pulled the trigger to settle her score with Cliff for cheating on her. She planned to finish the job by ruining the women's lives and their marriages with the videos. *Hell hath no fury like a woman scorned.* And Polly was the most scorned woman I know."

"Well put, my dear," George said. "And the videos didn't have any bearing on Polly thinking she had to kill Sadie to keep her from remembering Polly had the strongest motive for killing Cliff," he stared at a window, "or attempting to kill Angie. Like Angie said, it all goes back to Polly's first evidence that Cliff was fooling around. You think Cliff would've had better sense than to leave anything incriminating where his wife could find it."

"And, if he went to the trouble to buy condoms, he should've used them and had enough sense not to get Jenny pregnant," Angie said.

"This is a mess all right," Roger said. I'll keep the videos under lock and key in the evidence room. I hope they aren't needed in the trial and never see the light of day."

"None of the people who know about the videos will talk unless it's Polly, and I can't see her bringing them up. It would be humiliating for her to have all that dragged out. She has to save some of her dignity in spite of what's happened," George said. "You know, I need to give Maggie a quick call and see if she's heard from the auditors. Okay if I do it now?" Roger told him to go ahead and asked Angie to put the videos in a bag. Angie could barely stand to touch them. She wiped her fingers on her coat when she finished.

"You won't believe what the auditors already found," he said to Angie and Roger while still talking on the phone. "Cliff diverted nearly a million dollars of the committee's funds to his own accounts. He thought big. I thought maybe he skimmed off a hundred thousand dollars max." When he finished the call, George said, "I bet you Maggie would pay big bucks for those fire ants and a chance to get at Cliff."

Roger asked about the fire ants. Angie explained. "Kate said Maggie wouldn't have shot Cliff over the embezzling because she would've wanted him to suffer excruciatingly, hence, staking him over a colony of fire ants." Roger grinned and said that sounded like Maggie.

"Is there any chance of recovering the money? That's what I want to know," Roger said.

"Maggie's auditors are working on it," George said. "They'll try to trace the funds from Cliff's accounts to wherever Polly transferred them."

"That sounds like a lot of tracing," the chief replied. "I've got two murders, an attempted murder, a murder threat and a big-time embezzling case. Tell those auditors to hustle."

"At least, you can forget blackmail since I don't think any of Cliff's girlfriends will push that, plus Cliff's dead anyway," George said. His cell phone rang, and he relayed a message to Angie and Roger. "Some friends have gathered at the Lantern to see Angie after her ordeal. Clarice is serving coffee and snacks. She said for you to come too, Roger."

"Sounds good. I haven't had lunch. What I need is a cold shower after watching those videos," Roger joked, "and a stiff drink. Tell you what, I'm going to pick up that search warrant and retrieve Polly's videos. I'll meet you at the Lantern shortly."

***

"Before we go to the Lantern, let's stop at the diner for a minute," George said.

"Why? You said Clarice was serving food."

"Nothing to do with food. This is last piece of the puzzle, my dear."

George parked the Porsche in front of the diner. It was relatively empty when Angie and George entered. When Ben saw them, his face drooped from sad to crushed. Ben was a man in pain. George led Angie to the farthest booth from other customers. Ben brought over three cups of coffee without taking an order and sat down on the other side of the booth. He said to George, "So you found out about me, huh? I knew it was just a matter of time." Angie had no idea what he was talking about.

George took a drink of his coffee and said in a soft voice, "I'm not here to try to pin anything on you. Tell me what happened."

Ben looked at the floor, then raised his head to face George. "When I was eighteen, I was out with a couple of guys I met at my job. We stopped at a convenience store for them to buy cigarettes. While the guys were in the store, they decided to take a drawer full of cash along with the cigarettes. I didn't know they pulled the robbery until later that night. A few days later, we were all arrested. Two of the guys insisted I didn't know what was going on, but the third one wouldn't back it up. The police charged me with accessory.

"This thing nearly killed my mother. I'd never been in trouble. I was the quiet, shy kid who stayed home and did my homework. I was working full-time and taking a couple of classes at community college. My dream was to have a little restaurant someday.

"Due to good behavior, I was released after serving eight months of my sentence and went back to live with my mother. I saved every penny I could from my salary to get a new start in life. I happened upon Whispering Pines by accident, liked it and invested my savings in buying this diner. My mother moved here with me and we made a go of it. That's the truth, George, every word of it."

"I believe you, Ben. I remember how hard you and your mother worked back in the early days. How did Cliff find out about your run-in with the law?"

"I don't know. When Cliff was eating here, he asked questions now and then about my background, where I was from, that sort of thing. He had a way of being able to tell if somebody had a flaw, the way a lion or tiger can pick out the weakest animal in a herd. Once he got suspicious, he must've searched my hometown records."

"When Cliff found out about your past, what did he do?"

"He told me what he knew and asked if Susie and the kids knew about my prison record. Of course, he already knew the answer to that. Susie would never have gone out with anybody who got in trouble with the law. I might as well have told her I came from outer space."

"Did Cliff want money from you?"

"No, he wanted a favor. He needed a place where some women could drop off envelopes for him every week. In return, he'd keep quiet about my past. All I had to do was pass the envelopes on to him. The diner was a perfect drop-off. The women came in here all the time anyway so there was nothing about the arrangement to arouse suspicion. Cliff didn't want anything going through the mail. He was paranoid it might end up in the wrong hands, like Polly's.

Angie asked a question for the first time. "Do you know what was in the envelopes?"

"Usually the flaps were sealed but occasionally one was loose, and I eased it open to take a look. It was always sixty dollars. Twelve women paying him sixty dollars a week. That's over $30,000 a year. Tax-free. I knew it had to be blackmail, and I figured it had something to do with sex. No other reason these women would fork over that kind of money."

George asked Ben to identify the women, and he checked them against the list he made at Cliff's office. George didn't know two women. Ben said they were from nearby towns, patients of Cliff's. George asked if Cliff coerced Ben to do any other dirty jobs for him.

"Just one," he said, hanging his head. "I searched your room at the Lantern, Miss," he said to Angie. "I'm sorry."

"How did you get in? There was no damage to the lock."

"It's an old lock. Not very sturdy," he told her.

"Why was Cliff interested in me? He didn't have any reason to suspect me of anything, did he?"

"Frankly, I think Cliff got so deep in so many dirty dealings, he started looking over his shoulder all the time. He had more going on than he could keep up with. Plus, it was all coming unraveled. Maggie confronted him about money disappearing from the Carnival Committee funds, and Jenny hounded him about taking care of her and the baby."

"You knew Cliff was the father of Jenny's baby?"

"Yeah. Cliff didn't tell me, and he didn't know I knew, but I read some notes Jenny put in her money envelopes. She was pressuring Cliff to leave Polly and marry her. Jenny wanted the baby, but Cliff didn't want anything to do with it. He warned her to get rid of it. I'm not surprised he killed her."

"But what does any of this have to do with me and searching my room?" Angie asked.

"Cliff thought you were some kind of investigator or FBI or something. In my opinion, Cliff was losing it. Half the time, he didn't pay attention to what people said to him. When he answered, it didn't usually make sense. He realized it too because he started speaking carefully and talking a lot less. He knew it was time to hit the trail and made plans to leave, but he didn't tell me when or where. Soon though."

"Polly said he was leaving for South America this past Sunday night," Angie told him.

"Thank God this is over. I'll get your recorder, Miss. It's in the back. I don't know why I went through with the search knowing Cliff was dead, except I was still scared of him. Sounds foolish but he was an evil SOB."

While Ben was gone, Angie asked George, "How did you know Cliff found out about Ben's past?"

"When I was going through Cliff's manila envelope this morning, I came across copies of Ben's prison records. I had a feeling Ben was your burglar. He was in the Lantern about the time your room was burgled.

"Ben and Clarice buy meat from the same distributor, and their orders got mixed up. It was supposed to be all straightened out, but Ben came back again, supposedly to return something else to Clarice's freezer. The staff didn't think anything about it because they knew about the mix-up. I knew about Ben being there because Clarice told me to call the meat distributor and tell them to be more careful so we could avoid the inconvenience of having to swap stuff."

"Aren't you clever? We could never have figured out who broke into my room without copies of Ben's prison records."

"You're the clever one who found the manila envelope," George said, upping the compliment.

Ben returned and handed Angie the recorder, apologizing again. "What are you going to do about me, George? The police will come across my records when they go through Cliff's stuff."

"I can guarantee you they won't find them," George said, pulling the documents out of his pocket and handing them to Ben. "Your name won't come up."

Visibly moved by George's gesture, Ben's hand trembled as he took them. "I don't know how to thank you. Do you think I should tell Susie? If I do, I'm afraid she'll take the kids and leave me."

"Sorry, I can't help you on that one, buddy. But if you decide to tell her, let me know first, and I'll find somebody who can give you professional advice on the best way to handle it. We'll do our best to get you through it and save your marriage. Fair?"

"More than fair," Ben replied, shaking hands with George.

George invited Ben to come to the Lantern. Angie joined in, asking him to please come since he helped solve the case. Ben didn't answer.

Chapter Twenty

George and Angie entered the Lantern together. Scott, who was coming out of the elevator, gave Angie a bone-crushing bear hug. "Thank goodness you're okay. Everybody's in the library. They're antsy and giggly because they're so relieved you're in one piece."

Angie saw Prissy first and embraced her warmly. "Thank you, thank you, Prissy, for reporting Polly's car heading toward the old mill. I didn't think anybody knew I was in danger or would come to help me. Without you, nobody would've known where I was. I would've had to run all the way from the mill to town."

"I'm just glad I happened to see Polly's station wagon. I knew somebody was with her, but I had no idea it was you until town starting buzzing with the news that Polly sort of kidnapped you. I called Roger ASAP." For a change, Angie was grateful news travelled fast through Whispering Pines.

Sadie rushed into the library breathlessly telling Angie she couldn't stay. "I got a customer under the dryer. I just wanted to see for myself that you're okay. I was so afraid George and Roger wouldn't find you in time. Way to go with that pepper spray, girl! I'm going to get some of that stuff."

Angie thanked Sadie for remembering Polly's threats. "It was your visit to the shop yesterday and our talk that got me to remembering. Out of the blue, it hit me about all the painful, nasty stuff Polly said she wanted to do to Cliff. In her make-believe revenge plots, shooting Cliff was her favorite way of doing him in. He dished out more than Polly could take, and her fantasy planning turned real.

"I still can't believe Polly intended to kill me though," Sadie said. "We've been friends since we were kids. Maybe I could've helped her some way." Sadie dabbed at her eyes with a tissue. She whispered, "But I'm not sorry she killed Cliff. I didn't tell you this, Angie, but I hated Cliff. I was afraid if I told you, you'd add me to your list of suspects, and I knew I didn't kill him. You see, I had a run-in with Cliff when I was a teenager. He was supposed to be checking my eyes, but he wanted me to check some parts of his body. I could've killed him then, for sure," she said defiantly wiping away tears.

"Oops! Look at the time. I gotta get back to the shop before I singe what little bit of hair poor old Mrs. Marcum has left. I'll talk to you tomorrow." With that, Sadie gave Angie a quick hug and shot out the door. So Sadie was George's friend accosted by Cliff during her eye exam. No wonder she hated him. Angie was glad Sadie didn't tell her earlier. Her motive was powerful enough to add her to the list of suspects.

Roger was already at the inn, drinking coffee and looking expectantly for the promised food that hadn't yet been served. Angie and George went straight to him. "Roger, let's step out in hall for a minute. I have something to give you," Angie told him.

"I hope it's a pack of crackers and cheese. I'm starving," he said.

Angie took the recorder out of her purse and handed it to Roger. "What's this?" he asked. "Is this what you were talking about in my voice mail?"

"Yes. It's a few minutes of the quarrel between the man and woman in the linen room. When I heard them, I remembered I had my new recorder in my purse and held it against the door. I should've given it to you Saturday night, but I was embarrassed to admit I recorded a private conversation. Anyway, when I played it, I discovered the man's voice is recognizable and understandable. It should help your case. I'll write up or sign a statement or whatever you need about how I recorded it." She didn't mention playing it for Scott or George or Ben taking it from her room. The right person had it now.

Roger, George and Angie moved into a small alcove off reception and hovered together while Roger listened to the recorder with the volume on low. "Damn, there's no mistaking Cliff's voice. He got mad at me one time because an officer ticketed his car, and he yelled at me like that. He was on the verge of threatening to get me fired when I told him to shut up, or I'd throw his mayoral ass in jail.

"Angie, this recording is going to be a key piece of evidence in our case. You're a whiz of a journalist." Angie beamed at the compliment.

"Now for my news," Roger told them. "I found the video packages in Polly's station wagon and locked them in the evidence room along with the originals. I'll have an officer take the recorder to the lab and see if they can enhance the woman's voice. Technology can do wonders these days."

The three returned to the party and to Roger's satisfaction, the food was on the table.

Nev and George brought a tray of coffee for the group. "Polly and Cliff come here often for dinner. They always seemed so normal," Nev remarked.

"I know," Francesca said. "I see Polly several times a week around town. She acted exactly like she always did. It's hard to believe she carried on as usual while she plotted Cliff's murder."

George said, "Polly killed Cliff instantly or close to it with just one bullet. I'm surprised she was such an accurate shot."

Francesca spoke up. "Oh, she was an expert. This happened when you were little, but Polly's father had her shooting at targets from the time she could hold a gun. He excelled at marksmanship and so did she. They traveled all over the place to competitions. They even won some international tournaments." Angie's knees started to lose strength. She hadn't known she was up against Annie Oakley. She tightened her grip on George's arm.

Clarice said, "I remember all the publicity about the championships Polly and her father won. Articles in the newspaper about the tournaments. Photos of them with their trophies."

The judge, silver-haired and judicial looking, said, "You know, Polly was an only child and inherited everything her parents had including her father's extensive gun collection. I bet she's kept up her shooting proficiency. Easy enough for her to go out to the shooting range and stay in practice. Kept herself sharp enough to take Cliff out with a single shot."

"Didn't Cliff know she was handy with guns?" George asked.

"He should have. He grew up here with her," remarked Clarice. "He should've thought twice about provoking her."

Angie saw Ben enter the Lantern. He looked nervous and stood aside from the gathering, so she made her way over to him. "I feel so bad about what happened, Miss," he told her. "I wanted to tell you again how sorry I am."

"No harm done," she told him and meant it. "I turned the recorder over to Roger without any mention of you." Poor Ben faced the agony of possibly losing his wife and children because of Cliff. Cliff was a bastard and a force of doom hovering over Whispering Pines, claiming victims even after he was gone.

"I sure didn't think Polly killed Cliff though. I thought it was one of those blackmailed women or their husbands," Ben said.

Ben acted as if he wanted to say something else. Angie waited. "Would you tell George I've decided to take him up on his offer to help? It would've been awful if my wife found out about me from Cliff. It's weighing on my mind."

"Well, let's tell George now, and he can start working on it," she volunteered. Angie shook hands with him. "Good luck, Ben." Angie added social worker to George's lengthy resume.

When Angie and Ben located George, he was in an animated conversation with a diminutive but animated woman. She seemed angry with him the way she flung her arms around to make her point. "Hi, Ben. Glad you came," George said. "Angie, this is Maggie Thurston." Angie shook her hand and recognized her as the woman at the dessert in the library who told the let's-lynch-Nev-mob to shut up. This little white-haired, fired-up woman was Maggie. Ben asked to speak to George privately, and they stepped aside.

Maggie got right to the point. "George Junior was telling me about your awful run-in with Polly." Oh, no, somebody else called him George Junior. "Who on earth thought simple-minded Polly ran that deep and bitter? Hell's bells! Talk about fooling the world or at least this little piece of it.

"I'm so glad you're safe, my dear. You did some quick thinking and acting. I owe you a real debt of gratitude for your help in locating the information we needed to prove Cliff embezzled our funds and what he did with our money." She whispered, "George told me how you did it." Angie explained George deserved the credit, but Maggie wouldn't hear of it.

Francesca and the judge joined Angie and Maggie. The judge said, "Angie, the part of this story I haven't heard is how you got away from Polly. Please tell us."

Everybody got quiet and Angie told the pepper spray story again. She thought of a few details she forgot when she talked to Roger and added them to this version. They made the story better. After all, storytelling was her profession.

"You had pepper spray in your purse?" Scott asked with humor and admiration written all over his face. Angie couldn't keep from beaming. "Awesome," he replied, giving her a thumbs-up.

"George, you're going to have to watch it!" Clarice said. "You've met your match."

"I'm grateful to Martin Vanderwelde for showing me how to use it and making me practice behind the drugstore. I certainly didn't have time to read the directions when Polly pulled a gun on me. When I bought it, I didn't know how soon I'd need to use it."

The judge excused himself to talk to Roger. Angie turned to Clarice and Francesca, "It's sad that Cliff hurt so many people."

Clarice spoke first. "It doesn't take much for a lonely woman to respond to a man who pays attention to her. I expect Cliff could be doting and charming when it was in his interest."

"He certainly tried," interjected Francesca. "After my husband died, Cliff made all kinds of overtures that he'd like to be my special friend in my period of loneliness. I had a pretty good idea how he intended to cheer me up."

Clarice laughed out loud. "You never told me about that." Francesca replied it was too embarrassing to tell anybody.

The group that had gathered spontaneously to wait for news their new friend was safe began to trickle out the door. Angie made it a point to hug Prissy again. She thanked Ben again.

She thanked Roger multiple times for coming to her rescue, but one more time seemed in order. "Roger, I've never been so glad to see a police car."

Not to mention a certain silver Porsche convertible belonging to the man standing beside her and holding her hand.

She owed these people so much. They barely knew her, but they rallied together to save her. Thank goodness Polly had that smiley face bumper sticker. Talk about an unlikely symbol for an embittered, vengeful, murderous woman.

***

After a delicious dinner at *Me Gusta* and an even more delicious love making session in the chauffeur's quarters, Angie and George lay cuddled in his bed.

"George," Angie said dreamily, "you said you'd tell me about that exchange between you and Clarice Sunday night before she left my room."

"You mean when she whispered something to me? Clarice said, 'George Junior, you're a pain in the ass, but I love you.'

And I said, 'I love you too, Sis.'"

"Sis?"

"Yeah, you didn't know Clarice is my sister? Big sister, and she's not likely to ever let me forget it. The George Junior stuff goes back to when I was little, and everybody in town called me that. Clarice only uses it now when she's pissed at me."

"I didn't know Clarice is your sister. Why didn't y'all tell me these things?"

"I figured Clarice told you my life story. She never passes up a chance to tell everything she knows about me."

"Actually I haven't had a chance to talk to Clarice much. I've been too busy running around with you, getting into trouble and almost getting myself shot. If she's your sister, is that the reason you never pay for anything you eat or drink at the Lantern?"

"N-o-o. The reason I don't pay for anything at the Lantern is because I own half of it. I don't need to pay for what is already mine."

"I'm guessing Clarice owns the other half. Right?"

"You're absolutely right."

"Wait a minute. How can Clarice be your sister? Francesca's too young to be Clarice's mother."

"Let me start at the beginning... My father was married to Clarice's mother who was killed in a car accident when Clarice was five years old. Clarice's mother lost control of her car on an icy road and hit a tree. Clarice was in the back seat and unharmed.

"After a few years, my father, being a good-looking dude, found himself a second wife, the beautiful daughter of the town's one and only Italian tailor. And they produced me. Mother and Clarice hit it off from the beginning. They've always been extremely close. I guess my mother was a combination mother and older sister to Clarice. Clarice was mother and sister to me. I was never sure if I had two mothers or two older sisters.

"Our family home was the Lantern, and it was a great place to grow up. My father adored my mother as, I've been told, he did Clarice's mother. He indulged Clarice and me until it's a wonder we amounted to anything.

"My father died shortly after I graduated from college, and he left the house to Clarice, Mother and me. Mother continued to live with Clarice and Nev until I returned home with Brigitte, and she bought our place. When Clarice came up with the idea of converting the house into an inn, the two of us bought out Mother's share because she didn't want to be in the inn-keeping business. Clarice and I got busy buying adjacent properties, joining them and converting them into an inn. Clarice runs the business, and I handle the finances, as well as toil in the kitchen, mop floors and any other grungy jobs that she needs done."

"So that's why you were working in the kitchen the night I met you in the library?"

"Yeah. We were short-staffed so, as usual, Clarice drafted me to work. She thinks I'm eight years old and she's the boss."

"I thought you were very genial about being ordered around."

"I am as long as it's to my benefit. I'm not so willing, otherwise."

"So you're not a trolley driver or kitchen helper. Do you work for Nev?"

"No, no and no. I don't work anywhere, period. I help Nev because when he expanded his greenhouse operation, I designed and installed his computerized watering and heating and cooling systems. Remember I told you I was an engineer? Nev gave me a percentage of the business for my services, so I help him when he needs it because it saves us money and increases our profits. Again, it's to my benefit to help out."

"You're something else. I thought you had about a dozen part-time jobs. I considered giving you career counseling with the recommendation you get one full-time job. So, what do you do for a living, aside from your income from the Lantern and Nev's greenhouses?"

"An-gie. We've already been through this. Remember what I said about asking a gentleman about his finances?" he asked.

"New subject," Angie said to George. "Where is Brigitte now?"

"On her way to Paris."

"Paris?"

"Yeah. I told you she goes to school in Switzerland. Geneva, to be specific. That's what her frantic phone calls were all about. She just found out she can leave school tomorrow, a day early, for a mid-term break and wants to stop in

Paris for a night with a girlfriend. She needed money for a hotel and a little shopping. She has a reservation to fly to the US from Brussels in a few days, but she wanted to stop in Paris on the way.

"Why fly from Brussels?"

"Colin made airline reservations for all of them to fly home together for a short visit. He has meetings in DC."

"Start at the beginning, George. Who is Colin?"

"Colin is Clarice and Nev's son. He works with the US State Department in Brussels, Belgium."

"Colin is Scott's dad?"

"Right. Sophia, Scott's sister, and Brigitte are the same age and best friends so they enjoy flying back and forth from home together. Gives them a chance to catch up on their teenage gossip."

"So, the reason your mother offered to put money in Brigitte's account was because she's her granddaughter. And Clarice was supervising the operation because she's Brigitte's aunt. Right?"

"Congratulations. You've mastered the Satterfield-Winston family tree. We're all related."

"A missing branch on that tree--if Colin is Clarice and Nev's son, that makes Scott their grandson. Yet he calls Clarice and Nev by their first names."

"Yeah. Clarice's idea. She couldn't abide any of that *Granny* stuff, so her grandchildren call her and Nev by their names."

"The way Scott talks about Clarice, she sounds like a slave driver."

"Scotty's right. She is a slave driver. But, in all fairness, she drives herself just as hard."

"One more thing. I thought Clarice and Nev were recently married, but if Colin's their son, I guess not."

"Well, they act like they're on their honeymoon." George said they'd been married forever, but they never got past the honeymoon phase. "Actually, we're a pretty romantic lot. When we fall, we fall hard," he told her.

"Another new subject," she told him. "Was my room your mother's room at the Lantern? Is that why it's your favorite?"

George confirmed it was part of his parents' bedroom suite when he was growing up. "I spent a lot of happy hours with my mother and father and Clarice there. Perfect childhood."

Angie stopped asking questions. She put the bizarre events of the day out of her mind and concentrated on the sheer pleasure of being with this delightful man.

***

At George's invitation, Angie extended her trip to Whispering Pines and moved from the Lantern to the chauffeur's quarters. The arrangement was so out of character for her. At first she felt uncomfortable living openly with George.

Spending the last nineteen years raising Caroline and Jonathan hadn't left much time for romance.

Although she wasn't a prude or even close to it, she had a strict Puritan sense of how she behaved in front of her children. That meant no overnight male guests at her house. Her few romantic trysts took place at her boyfriends' places with her being home in her own bed at a respectable hour.

George assured her their living arrangement was nobody's business. "We're adults who've waited a long time to fall in love again, and we can and will do whatever we want."

"I know, but I'm not used to this. I'm glad your family and the town accept me as your girlfriend."

"Actually I think they like you better than they do me," he told her joking.

Angie appreciated that the town gave her and George their collective blessing. Clarice and Francesca acted like Angie and George had been together forever rather than a few days.

***

Angie adored her new life as a journalist-in-love. While George conducted his business on his laptop, she sat close to him writing her magazine article on her laptop. In the evening, they explored *Me Gusta's* menu and returned to the chauffeur's quarters for another night of sensual passion.

***

On her last night in Whispering Pines, George said, "Put on your warmest clothes. I have a surprise. Snowflakes fell as they drove to the surprise. George pulled his pickup into a parking lot behind a barn. "Where are we?" she asked. Without comment, George led her to the front of the barn.

"Oh, George, I've always wanted to go for a ride in a sleigh," Angie said, hugging him.

"Hop in, and let's go," he told her. The driver spread a warm blanket over their legs and climbed to his seat.

"Perfect. Fresh snow just for us." George put his arm around her, and she cuddled close to him as the horse pulled the sleigh through the countryside.

Chapter Twenty-One

Angie walked out of the Asheville, NC, Regional Airport past snow hills, unceremoniously mounded by plows. While she'd been immersed in the events of solving murders, researching her magazine article, falling for George and generally not paying attention to the rest of the world, a major storm had dumped a big snow on her North Carolina mountains. Was she destined to be greeted by snowstorms everywhere she went?

She walked straight to her entombed Honda CRV, which she'd wisely parked beside a pole marker. Without that guide, her vehicle looked like any other pile of snow with pieces of car parts sticking out.

"Damn," she said, pushing enough snow away from her license plate to be certain it was her car. She looked around, hopeful that obliging maintenance workers with shovels and ice scrapers waited to rush to her aid. However, her only fellow humans were like Angie, dazed airline passengers staring at their own snow piles.

Accustomed to dealing with crises on her own, Angie got to work, swore loudly, partially dug out the driver's door with her hands, forced it open, squeezed into the front seat and started the car. She turned the heater on full-blast. The cold air blowing out the vents gave her another round of goose bumps. Not to worry, it would be plenty warm by the time she got the car cleared and ready to drive away. She brushed snow, chiseled and scraped ice until her mittens froze stiff, and her arms ached from brushing and pushing snow off the top, windows and hood of her car. A half hour later she climbed into the driver's seat, relishing the mega-blast of hot air the heater was throwing out.

Using the full power of her car's four-wheel drive, she forced the Honda backwards over a snow bank. An hour and a half after her plane landed, Angie pulled out of the airport parking lot on her way home. With the heater on max, Angie settled wearily in the driver's seat, grateful the sky was clear and the road was dry.

She wondered if her gift had been delivered to George. In an art gallery in Whispering Pines, she found a whimsical block print of a cat whose coloring matched Little George as she called his cat. The work of a local artist, Angie thought the print was a perfect present for Big George. She knew he wouldn't be expecting a gift from her and would be totally surprised when it was delivered to his home. She loved her secret purchase and wished she could be there to see George's face when he opened it.

Angie had another secret. She didn't tell George, but she found out what he did for a living. Her buddy, Scott, came through with the scuttlebutt. George's father, a well-to-do entrepreneur, left Francesca, Clarice and George wealthy. After George returned to Whispering Pines with newborn Brigitte, he studied finance and invested his inheritance. "He had a real knack for it," Scott told Angie. "He advised Francesca and Clarice too. George made some serious money for all of them. Investing was good for George because it took his mind off the death of his wife plus he could work at home and take care of Brigitte."

Angie was relieved George had an easier way of making a living than holding down a bunch of part-time jobs. That was a crazy life style.

***

Driving down her street, she noticed every light in her house was burning. She wondered if her neighbor, Grace, had turned on the lights to welcome her home. No. Grace was too frugal to use that much electricity.

Angie knew only two people who'd turn on all the lights--Caroline or Jonathan. She left her bags in the car and ran up the front steps. Her darling Chaucer sat in the window, silhouetted by lights. Angie waved to him, and he promptly jumped down. By the time she got the front door unlocked, Chaucer met her, weaving himself around her legs.

"Hello, my sweet Master," she said, picking him up and giving him a squeeze. She rubbed noses, getting kisses in return. Angie yelled, "I'm home. Who's here? Caroline? Jonathan?"

Caroline and Jonathan tumbled from the kitchen. "You're both here! Wonderful!" she said. "I didn't expect you home," she told them. Squashed in the middle of a three-way hug, Chaucer head-butted arms and shoulders of his reunited family.

Caroline and Jonathan and Angie tried to talk at the same time. "Hold on a minute," interrupted Caroline. "Dinner's ready. Homemade soup. French bread from Ingles' bakery. Let's eat, Mom, and you can tell us all about your trip."

"I'm starved. Lead the way, my chefs."

Her kids pushed her to the front of the line to fill a bowl from the pot on the stove. She tore off a chunk of bread and sat down at the kitchen island. When Jonathan and Caroline joined her, Angie asked, "What are you doing home? It isn't time for Spring Break."

Jonathan answered first. "My interview for the summer internship in Chicago was moved up two days because of a change in the interviewer's schedule. I'm officially excused from classes for a couple of days more, so I did the only sensible thing and came home. And guess what! The internship--a paid internship, by the way--was offered to me, and I accepted. It's a done deal."

Angie reached over and hugged Jonathan. "I'm so thrilled for you." On the inside, she didn't feel thrilled though. That meant Jonathan wouldn't be coming home for the summer. The first summer in his life he wouldn't be with her and Caroline for part or all of it. "Tell us what you'll be doing," Angie said, forcing herself to sound upbeat.

When Jonathan finished the details of his internship, Angie turned to Caroline and asked why she was home early.

"When I found out Jonathan was coming home, I wanted to see him and my mommy too. I got the last seat on a plane, and here I am." Angie listened, loving their chatter about tests, homework, internships and the struggling life of college students.

As always, Angie was eternally grateful to Jonathan and Caroline's grandmother for the inheritance she left them. Each day she took a moment to say thank you to her deceased mother-in-law. Without the money from the sale of her farm, Jonathan and Caroline wouldn't be attending Princeton and Georgetown unless they'd gone into massive debt.

In addition to putting money aside for their college tuition and expenses, Angie had traveled with her children, showing them the great and small wonders of the world, taking them to places she never expected to go. The three of them had set foot on all seven continents by the time the kids finished high school. Caroline and Jonathan were well-travelled, knowledgeable and understanding of people, customs and places far beyond their North Carolina home and the shores of their own country. Angie nearly exploded with pride.

What a marvelous gift Grandmother Myrtle Stephens had given them. And what a worthy use for the proceeds from the life's work of a decent, hard-working farm woman. Education and enlightenment for her only two grandchildren was a million times better than leaving it to wasteful Jack, who would've gambled it away. Myrtle would be proud of the young adults Jonathan and Caroline had become.

Myrtle's will, unexpected as it was, went further, stipulating an annual management fee paid to Angie. Accustomed to scrimping to make ends meet, Angie saved her fee in case hard times returned.

As her investments grew, Angie relaxed. After she paid off her house, she started treating herself to small luxuries she'd never been able to afford. "It's about time, Mom," Jonathan told her. "Grandma meant for you to spend that money on yourself." Without a doubt, Myrtle included the fee as a way of forcing Angie to accept it, a sweet and thoughtful act to make up for her son's lack of responsibility toward his wife and children.

***

When Caroline asked Angie about Whispering Pines, she stuck to the fun stuff. She carefully skirted around events she didn't want to share now or ever. She didn't want her children to know about her involvement in two murders.

They'd drive her crazy about putting herself in danger for a career in journalism. But she wasn't backing away from her twenty-year longing to become a journalist. The children were already away at school most of the year, and Jonathan would be away for the coming summer too. In only a few years, both would be gone from home for good. Angie was determined to have her new life up and running before that day came.

When dinner was done and the dishwasher loaded, Angie announced she was pooped and going to bed.

"Oh, by the way, Mom, you've got voice mails from some newspapers and cable news," Caroline said before she and Jonathan headed to their media room to watch a movie.

Uh-oh, Angie thought. Newspapers? Cable news? Why? They couldn't possibly know about Jenny and Cliff. Could they? She picked up the phone and listened to the messages. In one message after another, editors identified themselves and asked her to call them. One specifically mentioned her role in solving two murders in Whispering Pines. So much for the story not leaking out of Whispering Pines. She hadn't dreamed two small town murders would be of interest to the national press. Like Scarlett O'Hara, she'd deal with it tomorrow.

***

Angie put on old, warm pajamas and crawled into bed. Chaucer, who'd followed her since she got home, hopped in bed beside her, snuggled close and gave her cheek a few loving goodnight licks. Sleepily, she rubbed his velvety ears. "I missed you too, Chaucer Cat."

The phone on Angie's nightstand rang, causing her eyes to pop open. "Gosh, it's late for a phone call," she told Chaucer. Back to talking to her cat. Back to doing old lady stuff.

"Hey, Angie," Ted's voice boomed. Music and noise in the background sounded like a party in progress. "You sure made headlines on your first assignment. Way to go!"

Reluctantly, Angie asked what he meant although she had a pretty good idea. "What am I talking about? You solved two murders, that's what. Everybody's running the story. The mention of Whispering Pines caught my attention. Then I heard your name and about you finding those bodies. Awesome.

"Good timing too. A permanent job just opened up, the perfect spot for you. You can get started by writing about those murders and, of course, finishing the winter carnival article."

"I'm so ready," she told him. He promised to tell her about the new job when he came to North Carolina in two weeks for a family wedding.

Angie lay down and closed her eyes. She was almost asleep when the phone rang again. "Who now?" she asked Chaucer.

"Hi, Angie, how was your trip home?"

Her voice softened. "Hi, George, how sweet of you to call. The trip was fine. How are you?"

"To tell you the truth--lonesome. I miss having a certain lady journalist for company."

"She misses having you for company too." He didn't know how much she missed him.

"I received a surprise package today. The cat in the print looks just like George. He could've posed for it. It's already on the living room wall. We both thank you."

"I'm glad you both like it. Has Whispering Pines recovered from the murders? Do you think they'll hurt the carnival business?"

"You won't believe this, Angie, but we're inundated with the media, not just local stuff but the networks and cable news. You probably haven't had a chance to see the news today, but Roger and Maggie and Sadie have been interviewed on national TV. I'm not returning any calls. I want to stay out of this. I wouldn't be surprised if the TV people try to get in touch with you though."

"Oh, hell, they already have. I didn't want the children to hear about the murders, but it seems inevitable. I have a bunch of messages from news outlets. Ted's already heard about it too. Oh! Big news! Ted offered me a real job with the magazine. He'll be coming home to Asheville soon, and we'll discuss the details."

"Congratulations. You've waited a long time for that job offer."

"Thanks. I have waited a long time, and I'm ready to get going." Angie paused. "I miss you already."

"After Brigitte goes back to school, I'll be down to visit you if the invitation still stands."

"You better believe it."

"Good night, Angie. I love you."

"I love you too." When she hung up, she whispered in Chaucer's ear, "That was my boyfriend. He's coming to visit us. He's a cat person. He has three cats at his house--Barbie, Ken and Little George."

Pat Meece Davis

Although I am a seventh generation native of North Carolina's Blue Ridge Mountains, I've spent most of my adult life in State College, Pennsylvania, except for stints living in the Netherlands and Australia.

Upon graduating from Western Carolina University, I was employed as a social worker in North Carolina Department of Social Services. Following a move to Pennsylvania, I attended graduate school at Penn State University, earning a Master's in Public Administration and a Ph.D. in Instructional Systems. In addition to caring for my six children, I ran a small business producing children's travel books. The most popular, *My Washington DC Activity Book*, was sold in major gift shops throughout our nation's capital. It is now out of production.

Because of my lifelong love of words, I turned to fiction writing a few years ago. *The Night the Dancing Stopped*, the debut novel in *The Nosy Chicks Mysteries* Series, was published in 2014. *Stumbling On Wet Grass*, the debut novel in *Stumbling Into Murder Mystery Series Book 1* came out in 2015, and *Stumbling Through An Unlocked Door, Stumbling Into Mystery Series Book 2* was published in 2016. *Deadly Delivery to Amsterdam*, a romantic mystery, is partially completed and is my first book to combine my love of writing with my love of international travel.

With my six children as adventurous traveling companions, we've visited approximately fifty countries on six of the seven continents – Antarctica remains to be decided. I truly love experiencing the natural, exotic, manmade, tacky, breathtaking, bizarre, ancient and mindboggling wonders of this diverse planet we inhabit. I used to be concerned I'd run out of destinations, but the more I travel, the more places I discover to go. I follow the advice of fellow wanderer, Mark Twain: "The world is a book and those who do not travel read only a page."

I am a member of the North Carolina Writers' Network (NCWN), Net-West division-NCWN, and the Writers' Guild of Western North Carolina (WGWNC).

To learn when new books will be available or to leave comments:

Email her at patmeecedavis.author@gmail.com

Visit her website at http://patmeecedavis.com